Dear

Dahlia & Carys

I hope you enjoy reading my debut novel.

Thanks

[illegible]

Dahlia & Carys

Published by The Conrad Press Ltd. in the United Kingdom 2022

Tel: +44(0)1227 472 874
www.theconradpress.com
info@theconradpress.com

ISBN 978-1-915494-31-3

Printed and bound in Great Britain by Clays Ltd, Elcograf S.p.A

Typesetting and cover design by The Book Typesetters
www.thebooktypesetters.com

The Conrad Press logo was designed by Maria Priestley.

Dahlia & Carys

Hastie Salih

For my daughter Lana

1

She and Yasmine had been inseparable school friends. That is, until ISIS came to ravage not only the countryside, but also the girls living in it, and life changed forever.

The memory kept coming back to haunt Dahlia, dissolving as quickly as it appeared: a fog-cloaked mountain, two girls, one of them perched safely on top of the hill and the other, a lamb awaiting slaughter in a valley, a look of reproach lurking beneath the wilted smile. *How confining to be separated by politics and religion,* she thought. *Only love prevails.*

Dahlia's neck felt tight. She quickly loosened her cashmere scarf, the one she wore when she needed to soothe herself. Damn it! She felt like an uprooted mulberry tree in the middle of the rumbling London traffic. The musky scent of the river had already started to unearth memories. How she missed watering her garden in Sinjar where vegetables like aubergines, courgettes and potatoes flourished! A mulberry tree stood tall and proud, protecting the legumes and herself when she played hide and seek with her younger brother, Elias. She used to be taller than him but now he towered over her. She felt her stomach churn and massaged herself lightly.

Dahlia tried to catch her reflection in the mud-spattered Thames. It was splintered and hazy, pale like a small silver-birch tree. Her dark raincoat was recognisable, but the small shape of her head was blurred, just like the whirling thoughts that were trapped inside it. She was a different woman now, had a job with the BBC, lived in a flat with two messy bedrooms and was a free woman, right?

She took a deep breath and set off on her walk towards Lambeth Bridge, hoping she wouldn't arrive late for the interview in St Thomas Hospital. A formation of cormorants flew overhead like a family defying borders, transcending man-made boundaries. Her pet partridge, Coco, would have envied them. *The liberty these birds enjoyed! If only she had wings.* She chuckled.

The tufts of dark, curly hair brushed against her eyelids which felt heavier than usual. She felt like retreating underneath them. If only she could! The dominating February cold stung her eyes as she scanned her surroundings. She felt like a deer in lost territory. Dahlia was tall enough but felt she had to make herself smaller when she met anyone new.

She looked up to London's undulating skyline, the pointed Shard, glistening with hope, the chubby Gherkin and the perceptive London Eye, that constantly watched over her unpredictable movements. These buildings were innocuous, and she had that rare feeling of being able to stretch out fully whilst walking past them.

The tower blocks climbed up to meet the sky seamlessly. Fluidly, non-binary. Her brother, Elias, said they were intimidating, but she coveted their freedom. They were her protectors. They let her hide beneath them.

I'm twenty-five now, she mused, *it's about time I found a more human source of comfort, other than a mulberry tree and a pet partridge!* Dahlia stepped over broken glass lying on the asphalt. It glinted at her as she did so. She looked away. Once an enticing product, it was fragmented and discarded now. It had lost its consumerist appeal, tossed away, no longer useful. Where was Yasmine? Was she a ghost? Better not think about her whilst going to her interview. She pulled up the lapels of her raincoat.

She couldn't wait for the magnolia flowers to herald spring. For a moment, she envisaged herself walking to the market in Sinjar to buy okra for her family. On her way, she would watch the rattling trucks on gravel paths and wave at her neighbours, Yasmine's family. Hens would scuttle up and down the paths, butterflies flitted past her on a nonchalant path. Time was a languid thing, one hour slipping into the next.

A faint smile passed her lips. The trees back home were thick with fruit, orange and mango trees, bending down, just enough for Dahlia to pick and eat. The juice would burst into her mouth and give way to a river of orange.

She suddenly felt her aching forearms. Last night, she had fiercely dug her nails into them. It was less painful than engaging in an argument with her brother. She pressed her wrists briskly inside her coat.

Dahlia slowed down as she reached the Houses of Parliament, recalling from school that they had been built to blend in with Westminster Abbey. The towering height of this neighbouring cathedral and the intricacies of its Gothic architecture made her look up in respect. They promised sanctuary to its visitors, protection she would have loved to enjoy in another part of the world.

She slowed down as she heard some chanting. It came from a nearby crowd of Brexit protesters. She stopped to watch a hunched old man draped in the Union Jack and a bowler hat. He stood opposite a taller, younger man in frayed jeans holding up a placard: 'EU – OUR FAMILY'. Dahlia could make out their words now as the younger man shouted, 'Why didn't you demonstrate after Grenfell burned down? Where were you then?'

Dahlia shuddered when she remembered the fire that had broken out in a block of flats in Kensington a few years before. Seventy-Two people had died from cheap, combustible cladding of the walls. Life and Death lay close together like a sprawling ocean which meets an inflamed sky. *Was Yasmine like the spreading ocean or the intense sky, alive or dead?* It was easier to turn her gaze towards the two opponents rather than confront herself with the imposing thoughts about her school friend and what she could have done for her in 2014, in another part of the world.

The old Brexiteer glared at the Remainer, and with screwed-up eyes, barked, 'We need to take back control of our country. Onwards and upwards.' Dahlia stepped away from the Brexiteer, acutely aware of her dark hair and olive skin. She felt like she was on the run again, like she needed to hide.

A middle-aged woman with silver hair standing next to the Remainer laughed and eying Dahlia, she shouted, 'Ignore them love. Ikea has better cabinets.' The men disregarded her and swung closer together till their noses touched. *Do they too crave connection despite the separation they're envisioning,* she asked herself. She couldn't hear what they were shouting as she moved away, but she felt the tension reverberating far beyond their bodies.

Out of the corner of her eye, she noticed a rainbow forming above the two men and stopped once more. Dahlia tried to remember where she had seen a rainbow flag recently. It had been outside the Admiral Duncan gay pub in Old Compton Street, Soho. She had grimaced when her friend

Jennifer had mentioned a nail-bomb explosion by a Neo-Nazi there twenty years before. The three bombings in London were aimed at Black, Bengali and LGBT communities in Brixton and Brick Lane. The perpetrator had not deemed these communities worthy of a safe haven in London. Dahlia felt the rage rise in her.

She pressed on to the interview she was due to attend with a doctor in St Thomas Hospital. She was determined to hand in an article to the BBC on 'working conditions within the NHS' in one week's time. This was her last chance to keep her job as a reporter with the Broadcasting Company, who had not been happy about her frequent sick notes; gastritis, anxiety – the list seemed to be endless. Her GP had been very understanding despite time constraints. The limbs of Dahlia's body, her torso and head had all seemed to be going in different directions! She straightened her posture. *It's time to find a thread to bring them all together again like a marionette on a string,* she thought and peered at her watch. A few more minutes to reach the hospital for her interview.

Dahlia hoped she wouldn't be kept waiting for too long and that this doctor wouldn't just rattle out statistics like the one she interviewed last week.

Big Ben towered above her. Its clock face was only illuminated at night. If only she could have Big Ben as a brother, spoon him, feel his energy and warmth! She stopped briefly to glance at the Houses of Parliament again before crossing Lambeth Bridge. The Union Jack was flying which meant that Parliament was sitting. Number ten Downing Street, the official residency of Britain's Prime Minister, was less than a mile away.

No torture. No kidnapping.

Dahlia stopped walking as she tried remembering the data

which she had retrieved from the internet the previous night whilst preparing for today's interview. Her heroine Florence Nightingale undertook training at the school of nursing in St Thomas hospital and there was a museum within one of its compounds. Soon they would be celebrating the two-hundredth anniversary of her birth. Florence's 'Notes on Nursing' had been released to show people how to care for their sick relatives. She had sent nurses into workhouses to treat the underprivileged.

The disadvantaged, Dahlia mused, *am I one of them?* She brushed the thought aside. Even her pet partridge Coco had been disadvantaged in Iraq. He had been kidnapped during the night and taken to Erbil for bird-fighting! She conjured up the image of her red-legged and beaked Coco, the chin and throat snow white, surrounded by a black streak. Dahlia loved its plump, reddish-chestnut plumage. Coco would wake her up in the mornings, perched on her window-ledge, with a short, scratchy call sounding like *chuk-chuk-chuk*. For a moment, she savoured the melody.

She hurried towards the postgraduate centre and entered the building, grateful for the warmth it offered her. Four chequered ambulances were parked outside the A&E building, constantly awaiting the next emergency. How reassuring it was to know that danger could be preempted. But not always, and this had certainly not been the case in Iraq.

Dahlia strode past the ambulances and entered the huge hall of St Thomas Hospital. The warm air soothed her cold face. She yearned for the heat as much as a human print of kindness, even if it was in a hospital.

2

Carys had to quicken her pace. She didn't want to be late for her shift in St Thomas's Hospital. The argument with her husband had slowed her down. He had told her that he needed to fly to Düsseldorf in Germany the following weekend, forgetting that it was their wedding anniversary weekend. Surely one of his registrars would be able to give the lecture on new guidelines in chronic obstructive pulmonary disease!

Last month, he had flown to Amsterdam and two months ago, he had spent the weekend in Davos. When Carys had asked him whether he was taking Sarah, his new registrar, with him, he had laughed, saying that she had a vivid imagination. All attempts at engaging her husband in a discussion had failed. She took a deep breath and smiled – she had flung his new white shirt into their washing machine and mixed it with her red T-shirt. *Ha! His shirt had turned pink!*

Carys stopped at the zebra crossing, tucked her fringe behind her ear and scrutinised the silhouette of the hospital she had worked in for more than a decade. It had appeared huge when she had started work there as a young senior house officer. She had been proud to be part of the NHS, where everyone was entitled to medical help, no matter their background.

Lately, however, she had felt burdened by overwhelming bureaucracy; learning new NICE guidelines and being reminded of updated Blue Stream academy modules on fire-safety, dementia and chaperoning weren't exciting any more. Was there any way of expanding her horizon, breaking out of the quagmire of tick-boxing medical modules and submitting yearly appraisals?

Carys peered at the sun, suddenly appearing behind the silhouette of St Thomas Hospital. The mist had settled. She felt restless, wondering how sunrise would appear in another part of the world. How she would love to travel to the Middle East or Africa, taste the delicacies there, smell the blooming flowers and set eyes on bold sunrays, instead of chasing hidden ones, stealthily coming out of hiding from behind high-rises and nebulous fog. She felt herself being nudged to step onto the zebra crossing and clutched her brown leather bag before being propelled onto the black-and-white crossing, suddenly aware of how colourless her life was. She yearned to see the world in vivid red or cool blue or any shades in between. There was no need for Phil to accompany her.

3

Dahlia couldn't help coughing. Was it the sudden gush of warm air, her anxiety or her asthma? She looked up and spotted two receptionists behind the bare desk of the Postgraduate Centre. One of them looked up wearily. She had cropped, whitening hair. Dahlia's gaze fell on her arthritic fingers as the receptionist moved her mouse away from the computer. *The poor woman!* She heard her groan.

The receptionist looked at Dahlia with a mixed expression of irritation and fatigue. Was she underpaid or just fed up with people losing their way in the big building? It reminded her of a maze she had entered near Heslington Hall in York where she had been studying English. Damn it! Mazes everywhere.

'If you're looking to see a doctor, Madam, you're in the wrong building. Please turn left out of the front door and –'

Dahlia took a deep breath. Surely the receptionist didn't view her as a fraught patient! She straightened her posture, hoping it would make her look more confident. She had made sure to wear a long-sleeved, dark blouse underneath her blue trouser suit. Dahlia preferred her high waist Mom jeans, but this was an official meeting and she had to look professional even if she didn't feel that way.

'I'm not a patient, I work for the BBC.' She noticed the

receptionist's head tilt in acknowledgement of her job and enjoyed her own pleasurable reaction to this. She raised her voice to match the receptionist's. *Why did she always have a low voice?*

'I have an interview with Doctor Carys Williams scheduled for this morning. Where would I be able to find her?' Dahlia cleared her throat. She was not going to show the receptionist how anxious she was. She could hide parts of herself very well.

The pale-faced receptionist looked at her dubiously, then checked the appointment time. She pointed towards the conference room at the end of the hallway.

Entering it cautiously, Dahlia noted how bare it was. Stacked chairs and a long table stood in the middle of the room. On a flipchart at the front of the room, the words 'Medical Emergencies' were written in bold blue. Underneath, she read the subtitles – heart attack, stroke, breathing difficulties... She looked away at that point to open the nearest window and pace her erratic breathing.

She took her raincoat off, draped it on a chair and looked out of the window. Then, she inhaled the air slowly as she watched the taxis struggling to get through the rumbling London traffic. Despite the hectic tube-trains, crowded streets and busy people, she loved the city. She welcomed the distraction it provided her from her racing thoughts about her former life and Yasmine's past. Dahlia decided it was time to take a puff of her asthma device. After inhaling, she held her breath for a few seconds.

At that moment, a slender lady opened the door, holding some journals and unopened mail in her left hand. Her shoulder-length, curly, light brown hair looked ungroomed as if she had not had enough time to comb it. She smiled as she caught sight of Dahlia releasing the asthma pump from her lips. The woman slipped into the room with enviable ease.

She must be used to walking a lot because of her job, Dahlia thought. She appeared to be in her mid-thirties to early forties. Her light blue NHS uniform hung loosely on her. Her tranquil eyes, slightly darker than her uniform, held a hint of curiosity. *Was there an inkling of admiration too?*

'I hope I didn't frighten you?' She watched Dahlia teasingly, whilst pushing back some strands of hair which had dropped into her eyes.

Dahlia held her gaze. 'Sorry, I've had to use my inhaler several times today.' She forced a smile. How ironic it would be if this doctor had to admit her instead of participating in an interview. 'I've been assigned to interview you...'

'Well, what a treat this interview is, eh! I can sit back and relax for now instead of taking down a patient's medical history in A&E. Is it bright enough for you here or shall I put the light on?'

Dahlia thought she detected a slight roll to the word *bright* that the doctor had used and wondered if she was of Welsh heritage.

'No need for more light. Glad to hear you're ready for our interview, then. It's Dr Carys Williams, right?'

Dahlia smiled weakly and tried to sound more self-assured. She was sorry she had had to mention her asthma at the first meeting. Why was she thinking of a next get-together when she had only just met this woman? Anyway, she was a doctor and should be able to deal with any physical ailments. Were doctors able to deal with emotional flaws when not at work? How awful to be saturated by the density of human suffering when they got back home. She waited for Carys to answer her.

'Call me Carys. Don't worry. I might be wearing my scrubs but I'm off duty for now! We'll see how long it takes for them to figure out that I'm here before they call me back in for something or other.'

Dahlia felt her lips curve into a smile and her neck muscles relax as she held Carys' gaze for a split second. It was like looking into calm, blue-green waters. *The depth is mesmerising,* she thought. It was as though she looked down from a high rock, not knowing how the landing would be if she leapt into the beautiful water! She forced herself to focus on her notebook. This was no time for reverie. 'Hi Carys. Let's start with the basics then. My name is Dahlia Aziz, but my friends call me Dee. I'll be interviewing you on the working conditions in the NHS.'

Carys moved towards her in quick strides. Dahlia stifled a smile as she watched Carys briskly push away a chair that stood in her way. She enjoyed observing women more resolute than herself. Dahlia wanted to experience more of her determination and vigour. She waited for Carys' next move.

'A pleasure to meet you, but I'd prefer calling you Dahlia, not Dee. It sounds more natural.'

Dahlia smiled. How she yearned to reconnect with nature – Mulberry trees, water in the sea, flowers and Coco her partridge.

Would you like a drink first, by the way?'

Carys watched her curiously and offered her own water bottle as they sat down on uncomfortable wooden chairs.

Dahlia took a few polite sips from a plastic cup before Carys gulped down the rest. She appeared unperturbed about the noisy way she drank the water. Unlike Dahlia, she didn't care about how she came across to anyone. She swiftly wiped her full lips with her hand. Carys wore no make-up. She didn't need any eyeshadow to accentuate her large, blue eyes. They appeared immeasurable. *What a beautiful face.*

Dahlia's musing was interrupted when Carys put up one of her long fingers and said, 'Do excuse me. I was thirsty and haven't had a break since we started this morning. A&E's been heaving. Even with no breaks, we're struggling to meet the target of seeing patients within four hours.'

Dahlia tried to empathise with her as she put pen to paper. There seemed to be increasing pressure on the doctors and nurses. For all her joviality, Dahlia could still pick up on Carys' fatigue. How much longer Carys would have to continue with these responsibilities? Another two decades at least. Unless there was an alternative, she wasn't yet aware of. Dahlia's eyes flitted towards the door. She fidgeted for a few seconds, thinking that she had heard scraping outside the door. She held her breath. *Please God, don't let my brother follow me here!*

Carys noticed her diverted stare and said, 'You're not going to go already? I expect you think I look more like a vet with all these scrubs, but I really am a doctor. My thermometer isn't tucked behind my ear because it got lost on the way here.'

Her playful tone brought Dahlia's mind back into the room. She crossed her arms as she looked at the door. What was she trying to run from? Sometimes she didn't know whether she was sprinting away from people or running towards them, especially when dealing with her younger brother Elias and her mother Hannah. 'I'm sorry. You're a very busy person and have a heap of tasks you need to sort out today.'

Carys brushed aside her apology. 'Don't say sorry for being here,' then added,

'Or for being anywhere, in fact.'

Dahlia felt embarrassed about apologising for being present and keeping Carys away from her work. *Will I ever stop being sorry for events that have happened or are going to happen,* she mused. Whatever would she regret next? Hopefully, Carys wouldn't pick up on her anxieties or vulnerabilities. On the other hand, maybe this was what she was hoping for.

Dahlia's cheeks reddened faintly as she took out her notebook.

She turned the pages clumsily. She straightened the blue trouser suit and said, 'Thank you for agreeing to do this interview. These are difficult times for the NHS I'm sure, especially with Brexit and flu or other possible viral pandemics looming.'

Carys looked more serious at the mention of pandemics. *Had she already experienced these in her working career?*

'I'm here on my own because the photographer was held up with a terrible bout of migraine this morning.' She looked at Carys shyly. 'So, it's looking like it'll just be me and you today.' Dahlia shifted in her wooden chair. She didn't want Carys to be disappointed.

'Well then, we'll have to do some selfies instead.' Carys chuckled, the wrinkles around the eyes deepening. She made Dahlia let out a chortle, even though she was trying to appear serious.

'Would you tell me a bit about your perceptions of the NHS before we approach the working conditions?' Dahlia had never wanted to work as a nurse or a doctor. *It's difficult enough dealing with my own fragility,* she thought.

Carys said, 'Most people know that the NHS was founded in post-war Britain, 1948 I believe, and that its services are largely free and funded by our taxes. I'm proud of that.' She smiled and continued, 'It employs over a million people which makes it one of the largest employers in Europe. We're always on the lookout for employees if you ever want to change your job.' *Surely she's joking.* Dahlia jotted her words down and paused for a moment to think about her next question.

'What about the present employees? Are they frightened about being afflicted by the superbug MRSA or other viral epidemics?'

Dahlia knew that MRSA wasn't a problem in some poorer countries as antibiotics for infections were not readily available because doctors had to be seen privately, which proved expensive. Her GP was getting stricter on prescribing antibiotics. She had informed Dahlia that the Chief Medical Officer for England had warned against becoming resistant to them. Dahlia had been given anti-inflammatories for her sore throat the previous week instead of antibiotics. It had helped her, Dahlia acknowledged thankfully, swallowing once more to check. But what did this doctor think about antibiotics?

Carys had a worried expression on her face. 'In Britain, we're hoping to eradicate MRSA by simple measures like washing hands and using fewer antibiotics. Viruses can't be tackled by antibiotics though. In 2003 we were endangered by the SARS disease – the severe acute respiratory syndrome. The SARS coronavirus which originated in bats spread to humans either directly or through animals held in Chinese markets... Viruses don't respect boundaries. They can spread through our world rapidly which just goes to show how interconnected our countries are.' She winked at Dahlia whilst straightening her scrubs.

'Humans are good hosts for viruses. I remember having to

wear a mask when the first patient was admitted with SARS. God knows when the next pandemic will occur and how the NHS will be able to cope with it.' She frowned. 'Crazy to think that was more than a decade ago. Do you remember where you were then?'

Dahlia winced. She didn't want to remember the years following that episode. They were worse than the SARS epidemic. Protective clothing wouldn't have helped her then. She waited for Carys to start talking again and ignored her question.

Carys continued, 'I didn't want to frighten you but who knows what casualties the next viral pandemic will cause? Antibiotics aren't the remedy for all ailments. Broad-spectrum antibiotics target a wide range of bacteria. As a result, they can negatively disrupt the balance of the gut microbes.' She looked at Dahlia's notebook with interest and added,

'If we don't prescribe fewer antibiotics, our children will die of simple infections. Anyway, we managed to eradicate smallpox in the 1970s and the plague a few centuries ago. Let's not be too pessimistic!'

The shrill tenor of a phone interrupted the conversation. Dahlia looked up from her notebook. Carys fumbled for her bleeper in the pocket of her tunic and frowned as she listened.

'Okay. I'll be there in five minutes.'

She turned to look at Dahlia who locked eyes with her. 'Listen Dahlia. I have to go to the Emergency department to sort out patients injured in a road traffic accident. We're short on staff.'

Dahlia put her notebook away as Carys stood up to leave.

She started coughing again and felt her eyes fill up with tears. Carys touched her arm lightly.

'What else are you taking for these coughing bouts?'

'Just... the blue... inhaler.' Dahlia wheezed.

'You should be taking the brown inhaler too – the preventer inhaler. Asthma sufferers need both.'

Dahlia leaned forward, arms on her lap. It eased her breathing. Carys held her arm as they walked towards a window and opened it wide. Dahlia took in the fresh air outside. She felt Carys' presence beside her and turned to her smiling.

The full lips were chapped slightly. She detected a small scar underneath them. It was a thin line, hardly visible. Dahlia averted her stare. *She shouldn't be watching Carys' lips.*

'Come with me and I'll give you a preventative inhaler. You reporters are so busy that you don't even have time to go to a doctor! I promise I won't send you down to radiology!'

Dahlia nodded her head. 'Thank you.' *How would she tolerate the acrid smell of chemicals in the emergency department?* She shuddered.

'Remember, whatever you see in the A & E department is off the record. But you will learn more about working conditions there than through whatever I say.'

Dahlia thought she could feel the cool breeze of Carys' flickering eyelids. The network of wrinkles around her eyes spread joyfully to her temples. Dahlia felt an unexpected wave of gentleness. She had to resist the impulse to smooth the creases. Suddenly, Carys grabbed Dahlia's raincoat and chucked it towards her. Then she seized her hand and led her outside into the winter cold. Maybe the experience in A&E would distract her from being so self-absorbed! She felt a tingling in her fingers. The quick pace was making her feel dizzy, like speeding ahead on a train. It was a pleasant disorientation, contrary to the ones she felt when with other people or her own family.

4

Nurses and one of her colleagues were running in the direction of the patients coming in from a road traffic accident. Carys raced towards one of the trolleys, almost knocking down some contorted tubes of a breathing mask. *How calm it had been with Dahlia.* She would have loved to savour the encounter for longer, especially the meaningful glances.

But now it was back to chaos and noisiness! She was intercepted by a large man with a ruddy face. He ran his fingers through his dishevelled hair and shouted, 'I've been here for three hours and still haven't had an X-ray of my foot!'

Carys recoiled and, trying to sound authoritative, said 'We've had a road traffic accident and are very busy, sir. The triage nurse hasn't classified your foot as an emergency.'

Shit! She hated being polite with aggressive patients but didn't feel like responding to a malicious letter of complaint. She tried moving to the side of the patient. He raised his voice and flung the X-ray form in his hand at Carys. It fell to the ground. She left it there, biting her lip. She was a professional and had to keep calm.

'You bitch! I pay your wages. I'm a taxpayer and it's my right to be seen. I'm supposed to be dealt with within four hours.' His nostrils flared up. 'You'll be hearing from me, mark my words and remember my name, Thornton.'

Carys smelt the patient's stale breath, which was almost as toxic as his words.

She had dealt with spinal injuries, heart attacks, collapsed lungs and asthma attacks that morning. The patients had been grateful until now. Mr Thornton's attention turned towards the male nurse who came to Carys' aid and tried to intervene.

'If you hadn't been drinking tea and eating biscuits with your Filipino nurses, I would have been seen by now!'

She felt the colour rise to her cheeks as she took a second, deep breath. There was so much to be worried about, like global warming and artificial intelligence and yet people were preoccupied with immigration and Brexit! When would this end?

Carys looked Mr Thornton in the eye. He was waiting for an answer. 'Mr Thornton, there's no need to be rude. We're all doing our best.' She raised her voice to match his. 'I read your notes. You bumped your foot three days ago. You could have consulted your GP and got the X-ray form there.'

His neck appeared to expand with every word she uttered. *It wouldn't be easy to strangle him,* she thought wistfully. But no, every medical student was taught to be level headed and professional. First, do no harm. That's what she kept telling herself. The patient glared at her.

'Bloody GPs. You can never get an appointment with them. The phone lines are always engaged and the receptionists are downright rude!'

Mr Thornton raised his arm to hit her. She backed away, almost stumbling.

Dahlia, who had been following Carys, stepped forward to shield her. The patient ended up hitting her right arm which elicited a sharp cry from Dahlia.

Carys drew Dahlia backwards. 'Security!' she shouted, and glanced at Dahlia who looked distraught. She should never have allowed this journalist into A&E. Dahlia reminded her of a slender silver birch tree that would snap if a hurricane pushed it. Dahlia would most probably not write anything favourable about the department! Furthermore, Carys had not asked her consultant if he would agree to a journalist setting foot in their department. Why had she made such a rash decision? She shuddered and hoped her actions wouldn't be followed by drastic repercussions from the hospital managers. *She needed a break!*

Mr Thornton shook himself free from the Security Officer and hobbled towards the door, hissing. 'You'll hear from my local councillor. I'm lodging a complaint. Lazy bitches like you don't deserve to be registered with the NHS.'

He turned to look at Dahlia who had tears running down her ashen face whilst she was stroking her wrist. 'And who's this side-kick of yours? I only want to be served by an English doctor or nurse.'

He shuffled away, enraged and triumphant at the same time.

Carys frowned and turned her attention to Dahlia who was squeezing her upper arm, trying to alleviate her pain.

'Are you okay? Let me have a look at your arm.'

She gave her a tissue to wipe her tears.

Dahlia looked up at her anxiously, 'Don't look at my arm please. I'll be fine.'

Carys looked at her mystified, 'You're clearly in pain. Wait a minute.' She shouldn't have brought this vulnerable reporter here. And yet, she felt elated that someone she had just met had instinctively sacrificed her well-being by joining in the fight with Mr Thornton. Dahlia's head was bowed.

Carys needed to focus on her professional duties, or what was left of them.

She sighed. 'I need to file a report on this incident. It may be used in court.'

She put her arm around Dahlia and moved to a more secluded area where a computer could be used to implement this and recorded the details of the altercation with Mr Thornton. Dahlia touched Carys' hand lightly, 'You work so hard, I can't believe people can be so ungrateful.'

The warmth in Dahlia's hand! Carys held it for a few seconds. It felt light and strengthening at the same time. She shook her head, 'We're ridiculously short-staffed. I don't know how we can make this job more appealing for future students to join us. We also need more places in Medical colleges.'

She jotted down some more lines in Mr Thornton's file and apologised to Gabriel, the young Filipino nurse who had run towards her during the argument. He had been working extra shifts to raise money for his family in the Philippines. It was financial necessity and loyalty to his family which kept him in London. *Loyalty, what a lovely word!* Carys frowned.

'Don't these patients get punished for their abusive behaviour?' Dahlia asked cautiously.

'We do have a zero-tolerance approach to verbal and physical abuse. But even when our security guard escorts them out, they come back after a while!'

Carys watched Mr Thornton hobbling away towards the exit with the security guard. Her husband Phil would have lost his temper by now. His work on the geriatric ward was easier as his patients were more docile. *Lucky Phil!* She had often discussed their frustrations about NHS money spent on the epidemic of compensation claims by patients. This was even though medicine had advanced in the last few decades. How paradoxical, she thought angrily.

'Why is there such a shortage of doctors and nurses? Where have they gone?' she heard Dahlia ask.

'Australia, Abu Dhabi, Canada.' Carys sighed and continued in a lighter tone, 'Where the weather is sunny, and they can go surfing.'

Then she extended her arm to Dahlia and added 'Now, let me look at your arm.'

Dahlia put her arms behind her back. Carys put her arm down quickly. Why was she thinking of the squirrels she had been feeding in St James's park recently? She looked into Dahlia's dark brown eyes. *As dense as a woodland!* Dahlia was hiding something and it wasn't just her arms. She couldn't help shaking her head. She wasn't Dahlia's doctor and Dahlia was not her patient. Whatever their relationship was, precarious or not, she couldn't help reaching out to her.

Carys said, 'Okay. I won't hurt you. But I do owe you an inhaler.' Dahlia nodded her head and moved closer.

'When did you start suffering from asthma?'

'I was a teenager when ISIS fighters stormed a village near Sinjar, in Northern Iraq… I was one of the Peshmerga, the Kurdish freedom fighters, based near that area to protect the Yazidi people there.'

Dahlia's voice trailed off and she focussed on a cup of coffee on one of the nearby trolleys.

Carys tried to remember where she had heard the name of that city.

'Oh yes… The Yazidi women… Hmm… I'm so sorry. I didn't want to remind you of anything unpleasant.'

An expression of puzzlement crossed Dahlia's face as she struggled to restore her composure. *It was time to perk up the corrosive mood which had descended upon them!*

'I remember seeing Amal Clooney with a Yazidi girl on TV last year. Her name was Nadya Murad, wasn't it?'

Dahlia nodded her head silently.

Carys didn't expect her to elaborate on Nadya's experiences or her own. Some people carried their secrets to the grave. Carys wanted her to look up again. Her dark, unruly hair gave her a raw, juvenile look. Maybe her eyes would slowly reveal more of her soul. She had to stop thinking about her in this way! They should be shifting back to their roles of interviewer and interviewee.

That would be appropriate and less emotional, after all, she was a doctor and needed to stay ethical, whatever that meant! If morals had a colour, they would not be purely white. Shades of hopeful green and raging red would creep in. It all depended from which angle you were looking at these standards. Carys chuckled at her own interpretation. Could it be that Dahlia was making her feel more floral? She changed her tone of voice to a jovial one.

'Intelligent and beautiful woman, Amal... Would you be able to arrange a meeting?'

Dahlia smiled briefly, blushed and said, 'Amal means 'hope' in Arabic and Kurdish. Maybe we can anticipate a happy gathering.'

Thank goodness Dahlia's mood had changed to a more light-hearted one! *What natural beauty, like a cautious antelope.* Carys took Dahlia's soft hand and observed her with mixed feelings of concern and wonder.

'I think I owe you dinner after your experiences in our department today.' Carys hesitated as she peered into the younger woman's anxious eyes. 'Would you like to join me Friday evening? In front of the London Eye at seven-thirty?

You can see all London from there.'

Dahlia hesitated. Carys continued quickly, 'Of-course, if you prefer, we could try and climb the backs of the bronze lions that surround Nelson's Column at Trafalgar Square.' Dahlia smiled shyly.

'We could also walk to Leicester Square and wait for a celebrity like George Clooney and swoon! We may even be lucky to meet his wife, Amal!'

Dahlia's eyes sparkled as she replied, 'Oh! I'll opt for South Bank. It's one of my favourite places, full of literary events and street artists.'

Carys smiled. She wouldn't need to put that in her diary.

She gave Dahlia a quick kiss on her cheek and took in the smell of sweat mingled with a sweet scent she could not label. Carys didn't want to identify any of her feelings for this interviewer who had breezed into her department. She watched her walk out through the doors. She would remember her doe-like eyes and timid warmth. *Hmm, I wonder, Miss Dahlia Aziz, if you're always so emotionally uptight?*

The meeting had been a welcome change to the mundane life she led with her husband Phil. There never seemed to be enough time. One of them was always on call in the hospital. He always thought he knew what was best for them. He knew what car was the best bargain and what needed fixing in the house they shared. They were no longer emotionally connected.

Anyhow, Carys didn't have time to think about that just now. She needed to get back to work. It was like that in A&E, one was dealing with calamities all the time. Patching up patients was her role with no time left for fixing the broken pieces of her own relationship.

5

Dahlia arrived first. She strained her neck to look up at the London Eye. This time of evening always offered the best view of the sky: a celestial palette of colours, mellow and blushing, hopeful. She took out her gloves from the brown duffle coat she was wearing and watched two Pomeranians with fluffy orange fur being led away from the crowds by a lady whose auburn hair looked just as velvety.

'Hi Dahlia!'

She swirled around to face Carys and took note of her black trench coat. A green scarf hung loosely from her neck. *How lovely it would feel to tighten it!*

'I thought you wouldn't come,' Carys laughed. 'Don't worry. I haven't got a scalpel with me today.'

Dahlia couldn't help but smile at Carys' buoyancy. How could she stay so cheerful with a job like hers? Maybe she was happy in her personal life, with a husband showering her with his love and affection. *What an irritating thought.* She tried hard to stop herself from scowling.

Dahlia watched Carys look up at the London Eye, standing erect and proud. Her scarf was swept into her eyes by a gust of wind. Dahlia peered into her blue-green eyes, mischievous, but caring at the same time. Carys pushed the scarf away. She didn't seem to let anything get in the way of her vision.

Dahlia smiled inwardly. This was a woman who walked her path and didn't let obstacles disturb her. *What was the secret that prompted her steadfast regard?* Dahlia couldn't help feeling somewhat inadequate. She put her hands in her pockets as she felt the cool air brush her cheeks.

'Isn't it amazing how the Wheel doesn't stop to take on passengers?' Carys said, eying the high wheel. 'It's like our world… Turning and churning…' Carys trailed off and turned to face her.

'So, when did you join us in London?'

Dahlia pondered on the ambiguity of the sudden question. Deep-set eyes expressed more than just curiosity. Would it be wise to open up a bit to her? It would be better to know from the beginning whether Carys would jolt at the mention of a struggle.

Dahlia took a deep breath. 'My mother escaped to Europe when I was a teenager. Post-war Iraq was dangerous and my Kurdish parents were political opponents of the establishment. Also…' she lowered her voice. 'There was a girl I used to know… She was Yazidi and ISIS branded Yazidis in Iraq as devil worshippers…' She looked around her.

Carys didn't look shocked, but rather more nonchalant as she said, 'Witches belong to the dark ages and superstitious religions. I think of God as a Spiritual Being.'

Dahlia hesitated; maybe Carys wanted her to explain more about Yasmine's religion. She took a deep breath, averted her eyes and continued, 'The Yazidi follow an ancient religion which derives from Zoroastrianism, Christianity and Islam.'

Carys nodded, willing her to continue. Dahlia felt encouraged to explain everything in one go. *It would be cathartic!*

'The Yazidi are ethnically Kurdish and live in Northern Iraq. There are at least half a million of them in our homeland

and in the diaspora. The Yazidis think they are the world's oldest people.'

She explained that they believed that God was the creator of the world and that seven spirits emanated from him. Malek Taus, the Peacock Angel, was the greatest one to whom Most Yazidis prayed five times a day while turning towards the sun. *Didn't all religions address God? Why did they not find common ground instead of fighting?* Dahlia explained that God elevated the Peacock Angel to serve as the intermediary between himself and humanity.

There was no need to elaborate on the Yazidi religion any longer. She didn't belong to it, Yasmine did. She hoped Carys realised that she didn't belong to any Pagan identity, but then again, was that important? Yasmine and herself had played together and thrown snowballs at each other despite their different religions. Yasmine was Yazidi and Dahlia's parents were Muslim. Arabs had conquered most Kurdish regions and gradually converted most Kurds to Islam. There had been no options; convert to Islam or die.

She looked at the enormous Ferris wheel and for a moment, wished she could see the symbol and pride of Iraq – date trees! She took a deep breath, savouring the memory of the smell of dried mulberries in spring. No wonder, Carys had a perplexed expression on her face! She had started talking again.

'Hmm, in early Christianity, the peacock symbolised the Resurrection and immortality because it was believed its flesh didn't decay.' Carys looked intrigued and added, 'I've never met a Yazidi or a Kurd before… except on TV when Nadya Murad won the Nobel Peace Prize a few years ago.'

How much had this human rights activist suffered at the hands of ISIS? Dahlia felt her heart beating quickly. She reminded herself that the world had at least validated Nadya's resilience by giving her the Nobel Peace Prize. This was admirable. She felt the urge to explain more about the Peacock Angel because Carys had most probably never heard about him. 'The Yazidi, including my school friend Yasmine, are persecuted because people think they only worship the fallen Peacock angel, Malek Taus.'

An absorbed expression appeared on Carys' face. 'This life knows many angels. Winged or not.'

Dahlia opened her mouth in disbelief. She tucked a tuft of hair behind her ear and looked away. Carys didn't seem to understand the restrictive regime of terror that religions could impose on their communities. Her flippant remarks were beginning to annoy her.

'I'm not a pious person and can't stand religious zealots,' Carys said as if reading her thoughts, 'But I've read about most religions and believe they have a few things in common, kindness being one of them. Unfortunately, a lot of people don't enact their religion.'

Dahlia was quiet. Carys had a steady rhythm to her voice whilst talking about religions. She was obviously not worried about it, not till now, Dahlia thought relieved. Faith and the expectations of strict communities constituted only some of Dahlia's problems. *It would be better to move slowly with the other ones.* Carys stepped closer as if she wanted to explain some sensitive issues.

'My father's Welsh. My mother is Jewish, and her parents were killed in Auschwitz. So, I know about persecution.'

Dahlia's eyes opened wide. This woman did understand about discrimination. Carys touched Dahlia's forearm lightly.

Dahlia leaned in awkwardly with her hands in her pockets, wondering if Carys still belonged to a tight-knit community.

Small societies could cultivate safety, but also wear you down with their oppressive shackles!

Carys pointed at the wheel and said brusquely. 'Do you know how high it is?'

'A hundred metres?'

Dahlia guessed, sidestepping some tourists.

'Almost. 135 metres. Takes about half an hour to go around once. Have you ever been on it?'

'I'm scared of heights.'

Carys chuckled, 'Falling off a building? Falling for a person? How many fears have you got? This is the equivalent of the Eiffel Tower in Paris! Okay, let's go to the Tate Modern instead. There's a Frida Kahlo exhibition. I reckon you'll like this one. Do you like art?'

'Yes, I do, preferably expressionism.' Grateful for the change of topic, Dahlia thought of the Mexican artist's self-portraits and wondered how they would look compared to her own. Her self-portraits were characterised by bold colours and expressive brushwork, much like Van Gogh's.

She needed to break out of her reverie and said, 'Look how Van Gogh suffered from depression and psychotic episodes. His friendship with his fellow artist Gauguin ended with him cutting off part of his ear in a rage.' Was it possible that artists and writers became creative to shake off their own demons?

Carys was watching her. Dahlia took her hands out of her pockets. It would take time to come out into the open about her experiences with ISIS and her brother. *It might not be a good idea for Carys to meet her brother so quickly.* Something about the way Carys listened made Dahlia hope that she would be strong enough to cope if and when she revealed more of her past.

They strolled past the Royal Festival Hall taking in the twilight which was scintillating quietly on the ripples in the river. Water could be pure, and it could be sullied. Its permutations and possibilities fascinated her. Flowing freely like feelings of love, defying restricting forms and compartments. Water was non-binary, neither here nor there, past or present, male or female, gay or straight.

6

There was a long queue for the Frida Kahlo exhibition at the Tate Modern. 'Never mind,' Carys said, 'It's worth the wait; a bit of art therapy might help us both with our anxieties.' She grinned. They stood waiting in comfortable silence; their minds busy. On two of the gallery floors, modern art was displayed.

Carys took a deep breath to calm herself as she thought of the young drug addict who had screamed at her as she tried to put in a drip. The veins in his elbow and lower arm were bruised, and it was difficult to find a healthy one. The patient was in pain and pushed her violently against the nearby trolley. By the time she called the security guard, the young man had already escaped!

She sighed. At least in A&E they had diagnostics such as CT and ultrasound scans readily available. They could be sure of results, whereas the GPs were vilified by the media if cancers weren't picked up quickly even though they didn't have such quick access to these diagnostics; that was one of the reasons she hadn't converted to the GP training offered more than a decade ago.

The other was that, after university, she thought work in an A&E department would be more intriguing. But her deep-seated hope was that it would be a stepping-stone to working abroad with *Médecins sans Frontières* elsewhere in the world, and therefore fulfil her dream of travelling.

Working abroad had never materialised. Her husband Phil had not been interested in going to another country. He was more interested in other women! Their son Brynn was born, and he was their priority. It was amazing that Brynn had managed to get through school relatively unscathed despite his dyslexia. His secondary school had assisted him a lot, giving him more time during exams. *If only she had given him more attention as a child and teenager.* Her son's late diagnosis of dyslexia had made her feel guilty about being too preoccupied with work. How could a female doctor balance family life with full time work? Brynn's anxiety levels had been high with nail biting and bedwetting both regular features till his teens. Carys regretted constraints on her time with him due to her challenging work in the hospital. She was lucky that her parents in North Wales had been willing to look after Brynn during summer and midterm holidays.

She believed firmly in the restorative powers of artistic recreation and storytelling, be it in art or literature. Her flat was stacked with books. She thought fondly of Virginia Woolf, the troubled writer, and her artistic sister Vanessa Bell. There was a period of time when the emotional power of Virginia's books had kept her sane. Dahlia had already told her that she loved painting self-portraits and Carys longed to see them one day. *Would she ever succeed in catching the essence of Dahlia?*

She glanced at her and said teasingly, 'Don't forget this is work for you and I can be quizzed on the NHS after the exhibition.'

Dahlia let out a light groan and said, 'Oh, I think I've seen and heard enough on that subject already.' Then, shaking her head, she added, 'I don't know how you manage to work in that atmosphere all the time.'

Carys looked at Dahlia and rubbed her chin. 'It's not that tough all the time. But when I'm ill, I hesitate to take sick-leave, worrying about who's going to cover my shift. Unless one goes to Australia or America, is there any other alternative?'

Dahlia looked at her thoughtfully and crossed her arms as she answered, 'Of course you have a choice. I'll think of one. It may not be the easiest preference though.'

Carys waited for an elaboration of this thought but Dahlia smiled and kept quiet. Her cheeks had reddened from the fresh air giving her a more feminine look. Despite Dahlia's complicated background, there was a kindness emanating from her that Carys found appealing. She wondered if she was the only person to recognise this warm-heartedness. 'Is anyone waiting for you at home? How much time have you got?'

Dahlia raised her eyebrows and smiled, 'My mother may be wondering where I am. She lives in a flat near me in Stratford.'

'You need her permission to be out and about?'

She waited for Dahlia to answer but Dahlia's glance darted around the hall and she ignored the question. Instead she asked, 'Do you come here often?'

Carys replied slowly, 'As often as I can. It's how I relax from work. There's always a different exhibition on.'

Dahlia, glanced at the gold wedding ring Carys was wearing and asked 'What about you? Don't you have anyone waiting for you at home?'

Carys laughed at Dahlia's sudden curiosity. 'I'm married. Not sure where the marriage is going though as we hardly see each other… .' She hesitated, then winked at Dahlia adding, 'Never date a doctor.' Dahlia blushed and let out a subtle laugh.

'My son Brynn has just started studying sociology in Bath…' She let out a sigh. 'I wish I could see Brynn more often, but work commitments make this difficult. She shrugged 'Luckily, my parents and relatives live in the village of Llanberis at the foot of Mount Snowdon and the Snowdon Mountain Railway. I used to send Brynn to them for his summer holidays. He loved it there.' *Was it a tear she detected in Dahlia's eyes?*

'I miss the towering mountains of North Wales reaching up like the giants of Welsh folklore. Do you miss the mountains in your country?'

Dahlia turned away abruptly. She appeared overwhelmed with the thought of the mountains in her country. Did they signify danger or were they saviours?

'I love the mountains in my country. But there's a saying – 'The Kurds have no friends but the mountains.'

Carys tried to suppress the quizzical expression spreading on her face but Dahlia noticed it and added, 'After World War I and the defeat of the Ottoman Empire, the victorious Western allies, the United Kingdom and France, formed a Kurdish state in the 1920 Treaty of Sevres. But that promise, creating artificial borders like 'lines in the sand', was broken three years later when they were left with minority status in Turkey, Iran, Iraq and Syria.'

She looked at the floor, then added, 'We are about 30-45 million people but we don't have a country.'

Carys felt inept. She had always hated listening to stories of colonial gains in history lessons at school. She watched the queue move on and so she quickly said,

'Look, it's our turn to buy tickets.' She was relieved that Dahlia moved towards the exhibition hall. Carys followed her and opened a book lying on a nearby desk.

'It says here that Frida's father Wilhelm was born in Baden-Baden, Germany as the son of the jeweller and goldsmith Jakob Heinrich Kahlo and his wife Henriette. Both were Hungarian Jews who had immigrated to Germany. It was after the death of his mother, that Wilhelm Kahlo sailed for Mexico.'

Carys mind returned to Dahlia's mother. How far did she have to travel to get to safety? *Her homeland was probably not a beacon of peace.* But Dahlia was not volunteering more information at present.

'It must be difficult with such a background of immigration,' Carys heard herself say. 'My mother Helga didn't talk about her journey to Britain, you know. I learnt that she had been sent to Liverpool Street Station as a child in order to escape the Nazism which was moving across Germany.' She made a sweeping movement as if to pull out weeds.

Carys was finding herself captivated about Dahlia's escape from Iraq and ISIS. She needed to find out what made her want to see Dahlia again. It didn't feel as if it was just an interest in her origins! But she frowned as she thought about the intricate situation. Dahlia was her interviewer and yet she had let Carys glimpse some details of her family background and cultural heritage.

'Poor Frida didn't only have an experience of migration, did she?' Dahlia said begrudgingly. 'I don't know how she painted so wonderfully when she was in continuous pain after her accident which led to such serious injuries to her back and hips.'

Dahlia flinched as she mentioned this agony. Was she

thinking of her own pain whilst painting? Carys noticed that Dahlia always seemed to absorb the pain of others. She felt a surge of something that she couldn't identify – a protective impulse? She was a doctor, after all, trying to make sense of it. But Dahlia wasn't her patient. That would make matters complicated if their relationship became more complex and emotional. She was aware that she had to be careful. There was a thin line between professionalism and intimacy!

Dr Carl Jung, whose pantheism Carys admired, had entered a relationship with Sabina Spielrein when she was an in-patient, before she studied medicine and became his colleague. Carys sighed. Sabina had described their encounters as 'poetry' in her diaries. *Poetry is never dangerous,* Carys told herself as she watched Dahlia eying one of Frida's canvases shyly.

Carys thought that if she focussed on Frida's suffering, it would distract Dahlia from her own tortuous feelings, wherever they stemmed from.

'Frida suffered because she couldn't bear any children after the accident.'

Dahlia frowned and said, 'I'd love to have children.'

She tucked some strands of hair behind her ear.

'So why not?' Carys asked.

'I haven't found a man yet.'

Dahlia swept her hand in a gesture to take in *a man.*

'Surely there's one out there,' Carys said, waving her hand towards some young men nearby.

'My mother has a few in mind.'

'What's the problem?'

'I thought I was the one who was supposed to interview you?'

Dahlia replied with a wry smile.

Carys hauled at Dahlia's sleeve. 'Sorry Dahlia. Ask me any question you like. You don't have to talk about yourself.'

As if to show that she intended to do just that, Dahlia headed towards the canvas opposite them. There was a quiet intensity to her but also threads of impulsive actions. Carys scrutinised the self-portrait. Frida's tight-knit eyebrows almost formed a straight line above her big melancholic eyes. Carys turned to look at Dahlia's thick, groomed eyebrows. One was raised upwards; Immaculate eyebrows. *What were they struggling with?*

'Frida's eyebrows look like a lonely bird's wings,' Carys probed, watching Dahlia's reaction. She added, 'Always ready to take flight.'

Dahlia chuckled but stopped herself after a split second. *For heaven's sake, had she ever been frivolous?* Carys felt like teasing her. But this would have to wait till they knew each other better.

'She must have felt very isolated... Her works portray herself against barren landscapes or cold, empty rooms.'

Dahlia didn't respond and moved brusquely towards a canvas of warm, earthy brown and green colours. It was called *Two nudes in the Forest.* Carys followed her slowly. The picture portrayed a naked woman laying her head on the lap of another, darker, naked woman who held her head protect-ively.

Dahlia leaned in closer to read the explanatory note next to the painting. Carys watched her quietly absorb the expressive flow of colours and shapes of the painting.

'This picture was a gift from Frida to her friend, the film star Dolores del Rio.'

Carys nudged Dahlia as she said, 'They look lovely lying in each other's arms, don't they?' She leaned in towards Dahlia as if to examine the painting closer. Carys breathed in her perfume. It smelt like Lancôme, mixed with a spice she could not quite place. Maybe incense or some Middle Eastern spice.

Dahlia blushed, knitted her eyebrows closer together and remonstrated, 'They might look serene. But see the tangled branches above them. They look menacing.' She shivered.

Carys groaned. *Why did Dahlia see signs of danger quicker than other people?* Better to skip the painting of Kahlo's flesh punctured with nails, thorns and arrows. Even in beautiful paintings, Dahlia's view was restricted by fear. Carys decided to pursue her own view of life.

She said, 'The two women look content and even happy in their little cosmos. The colour of their bodies almost mingles with the colour of the ground they're lying on.' The women were united not only with themselves but also with nature! *Surely, this would enlighten and strengthen them.* Dahlia and herself should venture out into the countryside, instead of confining themselves to the big city of London.

She said levelly, 'The painting has two other titles, '*The Earth itself*' or '*My nurse and I*.''

Dahlia picked at the skin on her hand but stopped abruptly as Carys' scrutiny fell on it. She was not Dahlia's nurse or doctor, but the thought kept imposing itself on her.

She glanced at Dahlia's hair and observed that Dahlia had made no effort to detangle her dishevelled hairstyle. *It wasn't only her hair that needed disentangling!* Dahlia had a layered personality, the core of which hidden away like the pearl of an oyster. She leaned in towards her again and said, 'There's a leaf taking refuge in your hair.' Dahlia trembled as she brushed her hand against her ear to take the leaf out.

'Am I so frightening?' Carys asked, letting out a mellow chuckle.

She enjoyed the reaction she had induced in Dahlia.

'No. I just felt a bit cold.'

Carys smiled and moved towards the end of the exhibition hall where the next painting hung, *The Mask*. A paper mask of a woman was propped up by her own slender fingers. Fear and anxiety marked her face.

Carys said, 'I like this portrait the best. You can see Frida's real feelings behind the mask of her other self-portraits.'

How she would love to tear down the constraints Dahlia had built up for herself. She sought out Dahlia's eyes to gauge her reaction.

Dahlia was looking down at her black boots as she said, 'I don't believe in bearing your emotions so openly. It makes you vulnerable and open to criticism.'

She laughed nervously.

Carys grasped Dahlia's hands and squeezed them. There was something endearing about the way she averted her eyes when emotions got too strong for her. She found her vulnerability appealing. She leaned towards Dahlia and said, 'The top level has a good cafe-restaurant with a stunning view of the City. Let's grab something to eat there?' After a split second, she added 'That's if you want to continue your interview?'

Dahlia rolled her eyes. 'I wouldn't mind some dinner.'

'Let's go then,' Carys said quickly as she grabbed hold of Dahlia's hand.

7

A few minutes later, they were leaning across the banister in the cafe, looking at the pedestrian-only Millennium Bridge and the Baroque styled St Paul's Cathedral with its delicate spires. Carys turned her observation towards one of her favourite landmarks, Shakespeare's Globe. She admired the thatched roof. *Surely there was nothing wrong in feeling proud of her culture?*

'Dahlia, have you ever been to see a play in Shakespeare's Globe?'

Dahlia shook her head which gave Carys the opportunity to explain that the Globe was a replica of an Elizabethan playhouse for which Shakespeare wrote some plays. She felt like telling Dahlia about some of his plays then decided to do this another time. The art exhibition was enough for today. She hoped the exhibition had offered Dahlia solace and a sanctuary. But from what exactly? Carys pointed at the Globe and said,

'You must go there one day. The original theatre was destroyed by fire and closed during the plague…'

Dahlia suddenly turned to leave the hall. 'Oh God! Sorry. I have to go.'

Carys took a deep breath. Dahlia always seemed to be moving, on the go, away from something… Away from what?

'I just remembered I'm supposed to be meeting my brother

this evening after the exhibition.'

Carys hesitated. Dahlia seemed gripped with an emotion she couldn't quite put her finger on. *Unease and fear, yet still tender.*

'You look terrified.'

Dahlia turned to scrutinise her as if she were about to explain her fear, then decided not to.

'And what about the alternative job for me that you mentioned earlier on?'

What kind of a job would a BBC journalist have to offer her? She needed to distract Dahlia from what appeared to be a distressing meeting with her brother. She couldn't help holding on to Dahlia's sleeve.

'I won't forget my offer. But I need to talk to my brother Elias first.'

Dahlia was looking more and more like an Egyptian Sphinx, a mixture of strength and weakness. Carys raised her eyebrows, 'I may be in court soon about Mr Thornton… Will I see you again?' She hoped she didn't sound desperate or clingy. Dahlia might loosen up with a bit of teasing but just now her eyes were searching the hall. She explained she was looking for her brother Elias who had intended to meet her after the exhibition. However, he didn't know that she would be attending the exhibition with Carys. Not that he was interested in art. Dahlia explained that he worked as a postman and although single and lacking many interests, rarely had time to meet his sister.

There was a tap on Dahlia's shoulder. She swerved backwards and locked eyes with a younger man. He appeared haggard and yet defiant.

'Who is this woman, Dahlia?'

Carys felt uncomfortable with Elias staring at her. He was

slightly taller than Dahlia and had a goatee beard. His blue jeans were ripped, and he wore a black T-shirt and cardigan. His eyes looked glazed, not soft like Dahlia's. Was he stoned?

'I interviewed her last week, Elias. She's my friend.'

Carys turned towards Elias to see if he was happy with this explanation.

'Interview finished. How quickly she became *friends* with you!'

Carys felt Elias take in her slender figure, half scornfully, half with desire. He spat out his next words,

'She's a *kafir*.'

Carys felt her shoulder muscles tighten. This expression was pejorative and used for non-believers of Islam. She glanced at Dahlia who was frowning but didn't appear to distance herself from her brother.

Elias waited for a reaction from Carys. There was none so he continued, 'Capitalist and greedy.'

Carys stepped forward to face him. *No need to restrain herself any longer.* She looked around her. No other visitors were about to witness what she said next. She replied in a low voice, 'Then why are you living in this country?'

Elias' face took on a contorted expression, mixed with rage.

'You spoiled everything in our country. Raqqa and Mosul will be our capitals again.' He took a step towards Carys. 'Abu Bakr al-Baghdadi isn't dead. He's our father.'

Elias was almost panting. He looked past her, maybe reminiscing of his time with ISIS. Carys frowned. The Hitler Youth membership after 1936 was compulsory. Joining ISIS was not. She kept quiet. She knew that in early 2014, the leader of ISIS, Baghdadi, had urged Muslims all over the world to join the caliphate.

Carys was used to violent patients at her workplace and

knew how to defuse dangerous situations. But, Elias had already turned his contempt to Dahlia and said,

'We may be melting. But our caliphate will reform again, even stronger.'

Dahlia looked at the ground. Carys watched Elias raise his hands and say, 'La illah u illllah.'

Dahlia clenched her hands, then tried to grab hold of Elias' raised one. Dahlia's scream tapered into silence. She winced as he held her wrist, the one that had been hurt a week ago.

Carys heard her rasp of pain. She scanned their surroundings. Luckily, there were still no bystanders as it was a Monday. With a mixture of embarrassment and fear, she placed herself in front of Dahlia to face Elias and said, 'Are you living in the twenty-first century mate? Back off or I'll call security. I know the guard here.' *Oh, God, please let him believe her threat.* Elias looked around him warily. His beady eyes darkened.

'We're the lion cubs of the Caliphate. The Abbasid Caliphate was at its peak in Iraq and overthrew the Umayyad Caliphate.' He glared at Carys. 'We will reform and renew ourselves, whatever you do to our leaders. You can't stop us.'

Dahlia was still looking at the floor. Carys held Elias' fierce gaze. He appeared unaware of the Kafkaesque world he had entered with ISIS.

Elias tried to look past Carys as he spoke to Dahlia, lowering his voice.

'*Khuske gyan*, my dear sister, you're our flesh and blood. Our bond is thicker than water. Without your family, you'd be an orphan.'

He spat at the floor in front of Carys saying, 'This is the first but not the last time you'll be hearing from me.'

Carys bit her lip. Mr Thornton, the patient she had treated

a few days ago for his sore foot, had said the same. She thought she could feel Dahlia trembling behind her. Suddenly, Elias stormed off pushing past Carys. She heaved a sigh of relief. Then she turned around to face Dahlia who was swaying like a silver birch in stormy weather. She steadied her by giving her a quick embrace.

As Dahlia's breathing became more regular, she let go of her and said, 'Fucking hell. Next thing your brother will be saying is that he's the bloody Lion King!'

She tried to sound light-hearted, but Dahlia had a reproachful look in her eyes.

'No need to curse.'

'That should be the least of your problems now, Dahlia. I can do French expletives if you prefer.'

Dahlia gave her a stern look. Then she looked past Carys fearfully.

Carys decided to steer her to a sofa in a quieter area of the hall. She waited for Dahlia to speak. They were quiet for a few minutes as Dahlia tried to compose herself. Carys put her hand on Dahlia's hand and they leaned back on the sofa.

'Carys, I know this was difficult for you and I appreciate your support.'

Carys waited a few seconds, then said, 'It was nothing compared to how terrible it must have been for you. I hope this is the only brother you have.' She tried smiling at Dahlia who nodded slowly.

Carys continued, 'Elias bragged about belonging to the lion's cubs. Well, I belonged to the Brownies.'

Dahlia's mouth formed half a smile. She looked into Carys' sincere eyes as she tried to explain her brother's behaviour.

'Elias was nine years old when he was sent to a training camp by his ISIS kidnappers. He told me that ISIS captains would punish them with more than a hundred lashes if they didn't do as they were told.'

Carys kept quiet for a few seconds, then said, 'He's not in the training camp now. Unless he's training to be the Hulk.'

Dahlia moved closer to Carys. She gave her a faint smile and asked, 'Have you heard of Captagon?'

Carys frowned as she tried to remember where she had heard that word before.

'Yeah. It's an addictive Amphetamine which isn't prescribed anymore, right?'

Dahlia nodded. 'Elias and other child warriors were given this pill before being sent to plant bombs in villages. It made them euphoric. Some died because the bombs detonated before being planted.' Her voice was almost a whisper.

Carys was silent. Had propaganda not been enough for ISIS? Was force feeding children Captagon pills needed to keep their ideology alive? Dahlia had told her that Elias had run away from ISIS and joined Dahlia and her mother when they escaped to Europe. Carys frowned as the ideology he had just propagated did not convey this at all. Had he really left ISIS? What were his plans? She shuddered.

Dahlia rubbed her temples and winced. Carys motioned her to lay her head on her shoulder. Dahlia's preoccupation with her troubled family contrasted strongly with Carys and her unperturbed parents who lived in North Wales. She stroked Dahlia's curly hair, wishing she could disentangle a knot at the side. Carys had never met anyone like her, so defenceless and yet so strong to have endured all this aggression. She reminded her of an uprooted tree. *How would she be able to cope with Dahlia's troubled past and belligerent family?* At the moment, she could only feel the softness of Dahlia's curls, drawing her into a vortex of mixed emotions.

8

Pain, physical and emotional pain, was something that could be endured stoically, Elias had believed. But that was before he had met Farid in Raqqa. Farid, his older friend, mentor and ISIS colleague, had told him about Abu Ghraib prison and how it had shaped him. Shape was the wrong word, Elias thought. *It had destroyed him.*

He had heard that the prison had been a jumble of top-security houses built in the 1960's by British contractors and that it was situated between Baghdad and Fallujah. The British might just as well have named it 'House of Horrors'. What had happened to Farid was all their fault. They would pay for it.

He sat on a bench opposite the Thames, waiting for Farid to join him for a walk along the South Bank and watched the muddy ripples lifting and spreading dirty plastic bottles and paper further away. Elias wished he could distance himself from the murky thoughts in his head. They overcame him, even in his sleep. His eyes welled up with tears just as someone tapped him on his shoulder. He turned around quickly. It was Farid, with hunched shoulders and gaunt looking.

'Salaam u Alaikum.'

'Alaikum u Salaam.' Elias answered obediently.

Farid sat down next to Elias. They kept quiet for a few moments. Then Farid turned to look at Elias.

'I need to get something off my chest, Elias. You need to understand why ISIS was necessary.'

Elias noticed that Farid was shivering although he had a coat on, and it was mild that day.

'Abu Ghraib prison had walls that were two-and-a half metres high. It was impossible to escape.'

Elias nodded, dreading what Farid was about to elaborate.

'I don't know why the prison warden, Mustafa, singled me out,' Farid began. 'I was always on good behaviour and even tried smiling at him whenever we crossed paths.'

Farid gulped a few times, then continued, 'Once he offered me a sandwich. I almost took it, but an insect crawled out of it. So, I politely refused. That was all I did! Honestly! But Mustafa was enraged. He took me to a cell I had never seen before. Then…'

He buried his face in his hands and whispered through the gaps in his fingers.

'He applied electric shocks to my genitals.'

Elias felt his jaw muscles tightening. He wanted to put his arms around Farid. However, he knew that this was not only frowned upon, but also dangerous in ISIS.

'We were 15,000 prisoners,' Farid went on, 'and each cell contained thirty to forty prisoners. At times 100 prisoners would be put into one small cell giving them standing room only. But the cell we were in was empty.'

Elias clenched his fist. He focussed his gaze on a limping pigeon with one leg. It was stuck on the muddy shore nearby, waiting for death. If he were a bit closer to it, he would throw a rock on it, putting an end to its pain.

'Sometimes Saddam's sons came to the prison to order

mass executions of thousands of prisoners to ease overcrowding. Saddam was known to have pulled the trigger himself when he was in a good mood.'

Elias felt like covering his ears, but he was compelled to continue listening to Farid.

'I lost consciousness but regained it after Mustafa, the prison guard, threw water at me. He told me it was nothing compared to the beatings he had received from his brother as a child.'

Elias felt his face burning with anger and shame on behalf of his friend Farid.

'I was incarcerated for criticising the Iraqi president where I was surrounded by petty thieves. My cell was about one-and-a-half metres square. I could only sleep curled up in the foetal position or standing upright.'

Elias' fists were clenched. Farid told him in a low voice that Mustafa had told him he would make him feel better. Elias looked puzzled.

'Mustafa smelt of Tiriac, you know, like drug addicts smoke. He got another guard to help him tie my feet together and they hoisted me upside-down to a hook in the ceiling. I refused his offer to smoke his cigarette and he stubbed it out on my thigh.'

He hesitated a few seconds. 'My memory is a bit blurred after that, but I remember the guard's shirt was white, with missing buttons, and the sky outside was a beautiful blue. They did the 'deed' after that, flattened me against a wall and dropped my trousers to my ankles.'

Elias clenched his teeth.

'It was… Elias, I felt… it was like a hot rod with a contorted blue vein sticking out. Mustafa parted my legs. I felt the rod brush against my thigh… and then… oh, the piercing pain! It felt as though it reached all the nerve endings in my body.'

Elias was speechless. Farid started sobbing. Elias pressed him closer to himself.

'I will avenge you Farid. All this wouldn't have happened if the West hadn't allowed Saddam to stay in power for so long.'

Elias felt nauseous. He scanned the horizon for a possible way to retaliate, in any way, even if it meant terror to the country he was living in. His eyes narrowed as he caught sight of London Bridge and he felt a sense of satisfaction and relief. Let the capitalists suffer.

By taking part in the war, Britain had ridiculed and vilified Muslims. In America they had been paraded in orange jumpsuits. Together, the Western powers continually belittled his brothers. Elias felt himself biting his lips. He tasted a drop of blood. This did not hurt him as much as the rage he felt in his chest.

Elias remembered how he had looked up to his sister. She had been aloof at times and he had tried to gain her attention by making jokes to make her laugh. He had watched curiously as her breasts had started to grow and he remembered the exact moment she had started to wear a bra. It was when their mother had taken them to a nearby village to visit an uncle.

Their mother had been so good to them. She had given Dahlia a golden chain on her thirteenth birthday and Elias had beamed at her as she had put it around her slender neck. Elias bit his lip again. The flesh felt real. His sister was ungrateful! She did not appreciate family values. All these broken relationships wouldn't have happened if the West hadn't interfered with the Caliphate. This was his family and he would avenge them. The prophet Muhammad had been chased from Medina. Elias did not intend to be hounded anywhere! He glanced at the London Bridge and started singing,

'London Bridge is falling down, falling down…'

He strolled down the embankment, raising his voice. Passers-by looked at him, frightened. He stroked his beard and felt happy. Let them be scared. He would make his plans soon. His sister would find out who was in control!

9

Dahlia had chosen to meet up with her mother Hannah in Spitalfields Market in the East End, knowing that it was her mother's favourite market. It was time to talk to her mother more clearly about how she identified herself. *Will I be strong enough to stop talking in riddles and explain more clearly?* She looked at her hands and unfurled her tense fingers. She knew her mother had enough love to give as she gave it abundantly to Elias!

Today, her mother would have already visited the British Museum to see her curator friend Jonathan, and Dahlia had proposed that they have lunch together.

It had taken ten minutes on the tube from her flat in Stratford to Liverpool Street Station. The loud screeching of the Central Line train on the tracks had irritated her. She hoped that the meeting with her mother would be more peaceful.

Dahlia felt nervous since the previous terrorist attacks on tubes. Cycling was hardly a safer alternative amid London's ruthless, pulsating traffic and the air was often polluted. Dahlia left the tube station in Liverpool Street and walked down to the covered market which stood halfway up Commercial Street. Fridays there were always lively.

She caught a glimpse of the Gherkin towering over the buildings like a diamond, both modern and ancient at the same time, just like the Gilgamesh Epic she had been reading. She intended to tell her mother about this Epic. *Were there parallels in her own life?*

As she approached the market, familiar spices awakened her memories of her homeland, Iraq. London was her home for the time being. Dahlia pushed her way through crowds of people, passing stalls that offered international meals, snacks, jewellery, keepsakes...

Vivid images of a much younger Dahlia chasing her brother Elias near Mount Sinjar overcame her. That was before ISIS had entered the village and lives had been turned upside-down. She decided not to tell her mother about the confrontation between Elias, Carys and herself. Her mother would most probably take her son's side. Anyone who didn't belong to the family was a stranger to her mother.

She caught sight of a Jamaican stall and strolled towards it. A yellow, oval shaped lampshade caught her gaze. It looked like a golden cage with a trapped lightbulb in it. It made Dahlia feel uncomfortable and imprisoned. She turned away and felt for her inhaler. It was soothing to know that it was in her pocket and hidden from the overpowering lampshade and other overwhelming entities. *Why did she feel she was waiting in the shadows, not able to bask in sunlight?*

'Dahlia *gyan*, darling, I know yellow used to be your favourite colour as a child. But don't you think that lamp-shade is kitsch now?'

Dahlia swung around to face her mother. She had put on some weight since the last time she had seen her a few months ago. Her eyes looked hurt. *What had she experienced to be hurt?* Compared to what Dahlia had been through with ISIS looming and on the lookout for prey, like Yasmine, her mother was almost unscathed. Indignant eyelids hovered beneath her mother's well-groomed eyebrows and translucent skin. Red Henna complemented her dark, short hair. She looked younger than fifty-five years of age.

Dahlia laughed at her mother's use of the word kitsch. She had used the Kurdish word for darling, *gyan*. Her English was getting better since she started working with Jonathan. She wondered how close they were. It would be lovely to meet him, Dahlia thought. He had been to Iraq to visit the museum in Baghdad. Her mother never talked about having a second relationship after her husband Amir had died of a heart attack. She deserved another life, even though it would be frowned upon by some people in her conservative community.

'I could use the gaudy lampshade as a hat, *Daya*.' Dahlia occasionally used the Kurdish word for Mother.

Dahlia put her head under it as Hannah rolled her eyes. The stall holder edged nearer to them watchfully. Dahlia nudged her mother towards another stall with Kashmiri shawls and scarves.

'Isn't it colourful here? All these different cultures in London, living peacefully side by side… without torture…!'

Would Brexit hamper this? Few people from European cultures would dare to enter the country. Some of her friends on the continent had already said they didn't want to risk coming to England to study or work due to the uncertainty of Brexit.

Her mother raised her eyebrows, 'Might be peaceful here now, but don't forget the knife crime, Dahlia. Be careful when you're out late.'

Dahlia looked at her mother warily. Here she was at twenty five years of age and she still warranted protection from her.

Hannah quickly changed the subject, 'Arts and crafts,

organic fruit and vegetables, flowers, housewares. I like it more than Brick Lane Market.' She feigned a smile as they walked past vintage records, picture frames, hats of various forms and colours.

They wandered past an artisan chocolatier's stall and Dahlia seized the chance to delay further serious talk. 'Here, let's get some chocolate, my treat.'

'You're in a good mood today, aren't you?' Her mother said, readily accepting the chocolates wrapped individually in silver foil.

'Why shouldn't I be? The sun's finally out for us to enjoy together.'

Her mother eyed her suspiciously. Dahlia proceeded to ask, 'Did you know this area was originally inhabited by silk weavers?'

She massaged her temples.

Her mother stopped walking. 'Dahlia, are you alright?'

Dahlia turned her head abruptly trying to hide the nervous blinking of her eyes. They were out in the open, time to be honest about her feelings.

'Let's go to the Tandoori Hut. I'm starving.'

She led her mother to the middle of the market. They waited for a few minutes until a table was free. Dahlia went to buy the Tandoori chicken and returned to the seat that Hannah had kept for her.

She tilted her head to the side and studied her mother as she was putting down the hot chicken. *Was this the moment she should explain her tortuous feelings?* She took a deep breath.

'Daya, it's not just water that is fluid.' She hesitated. 'Gender is too.'

Her mother cut her short as she snarled, 'It's fixed. You were born a girl. You have become a woman.' She folded her napkin quickly.

Dahlia tried to be patient. This was her chance to express herself for the first time.

'Gender roles are learned and not innate. Girls can be brave, and boys can be cowards. Society creates our roles. Who decides why girls should play with dolls and boys should play with toy cars or trains? Elias and I both played with toy cars we built ourselves.' She stopped to gauge her mother's expression. It was vacant. Dahlia continued to question her, 'Why aren't boys supposed to cry?'

Her mother rolled her eyes. 'Traditions decide this, Dahlia. Conventional values give us a basis without which we would be lost.'

Her mother had a semi-triumphant look in her eyes. Dahlia felt frustrated but tried to keep calm as she said, 'Moving towards gender fluidity may be frightening for you but it opens up exciting possibilities for everyone else.'

Her mother put her finger up and said, 'Stop it. You're tired. Tell me about your work instead.'

Dahlia tried to decipher her mother's expression. Her eyes looked weary. But behind that lay frailty and fear. She would need to tread more carefully and slowly. Her mother was not ready for quick changes to her mentality, morals or prejudices.

'Daya, I've been looking into some ancient poetry recently. The BBC bosses would like to focus on some stories from Babylon. Gilgamesh and Enkidu came to my mind. I don't suppose you've read any of the collections, have you?'

She took note of her mother's quizzical expression and pressed on.

'The poems were written around a thousand years before the Iliad. Now, two millennia later, they're still full of passion for the present.'

'We studied some of Gilgamesh in school,' her mother said. 'That was a long time ago. You have that excited look in your eyes now, Dahlia. Go on then, tell me about the poems.'

'The Babylonian myth starts with Gilgamesh, who was both divine and human. He sent the priestess of Ishtar, Shamhat, to seduce and tame Enkidu, the wild creature. She's not seen as someone dangerous like Eve in the Garden of Eden but rather more as a tender woman who shows Enkidu how liberating lovemaking can be.'

'When did you start speaking so openly like this? Where's this going?'

Dahlia fell silent for a moment. It had been difficult enough for her to acknowledge sexuality and conveying this to her mother was even more daunting. She continued but she averted her eyes, 'Enkidu's words about Gilgamesh say, '*Deep in his heart, he felt something stir, a longing he had never known before, the longing for a true friend.*"

'What are you implying?' Her mother said in a low-pitched voice, putting down her plastic fork.

'*Daya*, I've been thinking about it a lot. *Gilgamesh* shows intimacy to be a civilising act, a beautiful way of expressing yourself, whether it is with a man or with a woman. Why is it taken to be such a threat today? Why should it be shameful in some cultures?'

She observed her mother's eyes darken, as they always did whenever Dahlia approached her with thoughts on femininity or masculinity. More softly than before, she said, 'Gilgamesh bonded with Enkidu, but they also had a fight, a wild fight, with crashing into walls and making houses tremble.'

She noticed her mother's hand shaking and felt emboldened to continue. *Let her mother tremble just as she had before their meeting.*

'Before the fight, Gilgamesh dreams of Enkidu. A boulder falls from the sky and becomes his beloved Enkidu in his arms.'

Her mother leaned into their table and said, 'Keep your voice down. There's no need for others to listen to this nonsense. You've been influenced by your Western friends.'

'No, *Daya*. Let me speak. A boulder representing Enkidu fell from the sky. It was too heavy to move. Gilgamesh's mother interpreted the dream saying that the boulder stood for a dear friend, a mighty hero.'

Dahlia clasped her mother's hands as tears began to roll down her pale face. She watched her mother's face take on a disgusted expression, but she cleared her throat and went on, 'In all cultures, these loveable friendships exist. Just think of Achilles and Patroclus or David and Jonathan. Don't you remember when I told you I read about them in school?'

Dahlia felt faint as she tried to hold on to her mother's hand. 'You used to love reading ghazals by Abu Nawaz. Did you know he loved men as much as he loved wine?' She hesitated for a moment, 'Shakespeare also wrote some exquisite gay love sonnets.'

Her mother snatched her hand away and said in a subdued voice, 'I don't want to hear your interpretations anymore.'

Dahlia wiped her tears away with her sleeve and said, 'Gilgamesh's mother had a lot of understanding for her son.' *Did her mother not want to reach out to her?*

Her mother flung the paper plate in her hand on the floor as she thumped the table with her other hand and said, 'Enough is enough. What has gotten into you, Dahlia? I won't tolerate your…' She hesitated, 'Your unnatural implications.'

Dahlia felt her heart pounding as she asked, 'What is it that bothers you exactly?'

Her mother had a mixed expression of bewilderment and anxiety. She felt urged to go on pressuring her mother. *Why should she keep all the tension to herself?*

'Surely an ancient Mesopotamian poem doesn't bother you that much? Or is it my interpretation of love?'

Dahlia hated how helpless she sounded. Mother and daughter glared at each other.

Dahlia shivered, then almost subconsciously, she pressed the edge of her plastic knife into a scab wound in her left arm and felt the blood slowly ooze out. Her breathing slowed down. The blood was pure and innocent. Her feelings were transformed into a physical form. She could punish herself and feel in control at the same time. Dahlia hated her feelings. There was her way out, puncturing her body. It was just a piercing, she told herself. Many people had piercings and tattoos. It was no big deal. It made her feel real and alive. Her piercing silenced the chaos in her heart and in her soul and eased this damning communication with her mother.

Dahlia felt her soiled body purified and toxins released when she freed her blood. Surely, this was a good thing. She felt euphoric. She looked up at her mother once more and felt her rage rise. Her mother had been admiring the overpowering lampshade they had passed a few minutes ago. She had not heard Dahlia's painful sigh as she stabbed her arm.

She walked towards the direction of the nearest tube station where she would be meeting Carys. Did Carys already sense her need for change?

10

Dahlia was shivering when she arrived at Tower Bridge. The few minutes' walk from Spitalfields Market had not calmed her down. Her mother wasn't interested in any of her outlooks on life or how her daughter was trying to cope with her anguish after the Sinjar massacre in Iraq. She hadn't even had time to talk about Yasmine's disappearance. Her mother was only engrossed by the respect she thought she deserved as a mother. She felt rage rise up and clasped her hands, trying to quell it.

Was she losing her mother, her beliefs and her motherland? Had she ever been given the chance to be close to them? Even her mother tongue was slipping away from her like a ghost slipping away into the background. Suddenly, her eyes shone at the memory of Carys standing next to her, gripping her waist gently when they stood side by side, taking in the stimulating paintings of Frida Kahlo.

Dahlia frowned. She had been supportive when her mother had chosen Jonathan as her new partner even though he was not of her religion. She doubted her mother would accept any of her relationships, not that she had anyone she intended to introduce to her as yet.

She shuffled her feet and looked around, hoping to spot Carys. She was pleased to know Carys had not withdrawn her friendship after the argument with her brother. Hopefully, Carys was dealing with enough worries to distract her from thinking about him!

Dahlia beamed every time she thought of Carys. She always seemed so light-hearted, in a job which was difficult at best, and often hostile. She felt confused by the way Carys would talk about matters in riddles, making it sound ambiguous and more exciting, such as the narratives in Frida Kahlo's paintings.

Dahlia suddenly felt a longing to paint a self-portrait of herself snarling at her audience. She loved the freedom her paintings gave her, breaking down boundaries between art and life.

Dahlia watched as the ripples of the mucky Thames spread slowly towards the sand on her side of the bank. She breathed in the cool air as she walked to Tower Bridge and then stood observing the Thames. Water in all forms, rivers, pools and oceans fascinated her. It could be dirty; it could be pure. It was the fluidity that reassured her, calmed her down.

A little girl of about ten years of age threw a pebble and laughed out loud as it splashed twice and then disappeared into the deep muddy water. Dahlia watched wistfully as the child's mother laughed and cuddled her daughter. The little girl was obviously trying to get the pebble to skim the water a few times before sinking into the dark river. She squealed when her mother clasped her and ruffled her hair.

When had her mother last tousled her hair? How she longed for an embrace! She coughed into her handkerchief. Then she laid her wrists on the railing to cool them in the cold air. She dabbed at the fine, horizontal lines on her wrists. The lines were perfect, in order and under control. She was proud of these demarcations. Everyone should be able to do these fine lines, expand on their emotions. It didn't hurt too much. Anyway, if it was painful, it would be less painful than the memories she buried in her soul.

Boats passing on the Thames left effervescent waves which spread out towards her, only to re-join like cumulus clouds. The river was the amniotic fluid of the city. Dahlia smiled as she thought of how the fluid served as a cushion for a growing unborn baby. Nutrients and water were exchanged between mother and foetus.

She had asked her mother whether she would have had an amniotic fluid test during her pregnancy if she had been pregnant with her in London. Her mother had laughed, saying that she had been young when she had Dahlia, so it was not needed. Dahlia had probed further, wanting to know what else one could find out by using this procedure.

Her mother had looked at her exasperated but Dahlia persisted, saying that she could have found out if she was going to have a boy or a girl.

Hannah had tried to conclude the short conversation. In her opinion it was early enough for a mother at birth to find out whether she was having a boy or a girl.

Dahlia had not let her mother dissuade her so quickly and replied that the chromosomes were not the only thing that defined a boy or a girl. Her mother had wrung her hands nervously and implied that Dahlia must be feverish to be thinking such odd possibilities.

A shaft of sunlight settled on Dahlia's face. She turned to look towards the sky. The dark clouds had parted to let the sun shine on her. She smiled. The sparkling blue- green shades behind the dark clouds reminded her of Carys. *I'm the shade. Carys is the light, the tunnel to a better place,* she mused.

'What's your favourite season?'

Dahlia recognised the playful voice and swung around to face Carys whose dimples deepened as she smiled. 'Am I supposed to be happy about every season?' Dahlia asked, matching her teasing smile.

Carys answered, 'If you didn't know how winter feels, you wouldn't appreciate the spring.'

Dahlia stifled a giggle. Her eyes shone when Carys tilted her head. Sincere blue-green eyes reflecting recognition and acceptance. *Beautiful as always.*

'Who knows what's up with this weather, it could rain any minute. Let's find a café to chat about the trip you mentioned, Dahlia. I know where we can get some good coffee. Follow me. You can change your mind later on if you don't like it there.'

Dahlia hesitated. She always seemed to be following someone in her life, her mother, her brother Elias. Carys felt different though. She gave her options and the opportunity to say no.

Carys led her to an independent coffee house tucked away in St Katherine's Docks. Dahlia's pace quickened along the way until she was almost running into the café. Carys followed her slowly and touched her arm lightly,

'Slow down Dahlia.'

'I'm sorry. I can't take this any longer.'

She leaned in towards Carys, wanting to mould herself into her body, feel the muscles, the strength, the gentle pressure. *How does one articulate a feeling?* Was this a seed of something developing? She couldn't allow that, not just yet. Physical pain was better than this!

Carys held her in an encompassing embrace, her palm against her back, steadying her, cradling her.

'Is it your mother?'

Dahlia was silent. She couldn't see the expression on Carys' face. Dahlia heard her sigh slowly. She savoured the moment for a few seconds more, then pulled away. She shouldn't have gravitated towards Carys so readily, scared now by her own eagerness to feel Carys and her warmth.

They sat down opposite each other as a waitress cleaned their table and took their orders. Carys took her moss green rain mac off quickly. She readjusted her seat and Dahlia noticed a Star of David amulet dangling from her long neck. Carys seemed unapologetic about her mother's religion. Was she unrepentant about any other aspects of her life? Where was her husband and what was he doing right now?

Dahlia took off her new North Face Parka. She loved the down insulation because it kept her warm in winter. Dahlia pulled the sleeves further down and peered at Carys. *Oh, to be enveloped by those long arms, strong but delicate at the same time.*

'Why can't my mother accept me just the way I am?' She blurted out.

'What is the way you are, Dahlia?' Carys said quietly, taking a loose thread out of her sleeve.

Dahlia fidgeted with the ring on her thumb and kept quiet. She peered out of the window, feeling as drab as the slate-grey sky.

'If you can't first fully accept yourself, how can you expect her to embrace who you are?'

Dahlia pushed away her cup of tea. Carys wouldn't know what it felt like to crave and fear affection at the same time. She was privileged, no baggage, unharmed, ready for living life to the full. She glared at her.

'You don't know anything about me!' Dahlia felt stinging tears well up inside her eyes.

'But I'm willing to find out, whenever you let me.'

Carys' tone was more unobtrusive than usual. Her tone revealed something else – *was it compassion or even tenderness?* Dahlia slowly moved her hand towards Carys' elbow. Then briskly redirected it to her cup of tea. Carys watched her with an unwavering gaze. She decided to change the conversation to a more neutral, safer topic.

'How was your day?' She hoped she didn't sound too evasive or cold.

Carys frowned. 'I had a letter from the General Medical Council this morning.'

Dahlia put her cup down and waited for the explanation. Carys sipped her cappuccino quickly and winced as she felt the hot drink burn the roof of her mouth. Dahlia watched her closely. It was odd that Carys had not foreseen the burn as the hot drink was steaming when the waitress had bought it over. Carys appeared more preoccupied with the contents of her letter.

Dahlia looked up at one of the small windows opposite her. The clear glass was stained with smatterings of coffee. She suppressed the urge to get up and clean the splashes. This would be better than looking at her own blurred reflection. She touched Carys' sleeve lightly. Dahlia was afraid that Carys' professional work would be dented by a GMC investigation. The enquiry would probably devastate her belief in herself.

'Was the letter about Mr Thornton and his foot, the angry patient who verbally attacked you in A&E?'

'No. I wish it were about him.' Carys hesitated. 'It's about a man in his forties who came in after tripping in the garden. I remember him well – tall, gaunt. Anyway, his ankle was painful, so we sent him for an x-ray.'

Dahlia nodded her head, leaning closer to Carys who had lowered her voice. She smelt her Penhaligon perfume, the melange of cardamom, cloves and rose reminded her of her home in Iraq. She suppressed a smile but felt warm inside, sensed the familiarity of this woman, although they were from different countries and dissimilar backgrounds.

'The x-ray revealed a fracture and the patient had an air-cast boot put on.' Carys said, looking past Dahlia.

'That sounds okay to me.' Dahlia tried to sound sympathetic. *Stop being distracted by her long fingers,* she mused as Carys put down her cup.

'Hmm. But you see, I asked for blood tests to be done because he had been feeling dizzy for a few weeks.'

'Sounds nice and thorough, Carys.' Dahlia tried not to show how confused she was about this patient. Carys obviously felt responsible for whatever happened to this man.

'By the time the blood results came back, the patient had self-discharged himself. I wrote to his GP to call the patient in for further tests as his Haemoglobin was very low.'

'What does that mean?' Dahlia couldn't help asking with some trepidation.

Carys sighed, 'Exactly. That there must have been a reason, and it needed to be explored.'

Dahlia searched her face for an answer. She wasn't a doctor, but this case sounded ominous.

'How is the patient now?' Dahlia asked carefully.

'He is undergoing chemotherapy!'

Carys covered her face with the long fingers. *Healing hands that may have been less curative in this case.* Dahlia had never seen her stay quiet for so long.

She broke the silence, 'You mean he had cancer?' She shuffled in her wooden chair.

'Progressive lung cancer!' Carys peered at her with red-rimmed eyes as if she was struggling to keep back her tears.

Dahlia touched Carys' wrist as she wrung her hands tightly.

'Did the GP not do any further tests?' Dahlia tried to sound remedial, hopeful.

'Yes. He asked for a chest x-ray as the patient was a smoker.' Carys seemed happy to get this case off her chest, and discuss it with a caring friend. Or were they more than that now? Dahlia brought her thoughts back to the dreadful incident.

'So, where's the problem?'

'The patient didn't go for the x-ray as he had to fly abroad on a business trip.' Carys said flatly.

Dahlia looked puzzled.

'So, how was the cancer detected?'

'The patient started coughing up blood in Dubai. When he came back after three weeks, he went for his chest x-ray which revealed lung cancer.'

Carys massaged her temples. 'Maybe I should have phoned the GP straight away instead of writing up the discharge summary.' The crease between her eyebrows deepened as she looked at Dahlia imploringly.

Dahlia met her gaze and said, 'I don't think that would have made any difference as the GP gave the patient the x-ray form.' *Thank goodness she hadn't trained to be a doctor.* – All the agonising decisions to make, which patient to triage, when to switch off lifesaving machines and which investigations to request when patients gave you a poor history of their symptoms!

'It isn't the patient who's complaining.' Carys bit her lip.

Dahlia looked puzzled, 'Then who is?'

'His sister. But he agrees with her complaint. I assumed a patient with capacity would go to a follow-up. But medicolegally, that assumption was wrong. Patient autonomy does not extend to self-responsibility.' Carys took a deep breath.

'We have to expect to be sued every ten years in this country. She flung a newspaper on the table and pointed at a headline. 'Are you a victim of medical negligence?' Dahlia read further – 'You may be entitled to claim compensation. For free and confidential advice, contact us now.' Carys closed her eyes for a moment and said, 'This is how the media encourages patients to complain! My livelihood may be at stake. The Medical Defence Union would settle out of court. However, my standing would be tainted, to say the least. And let's not forget how dreadful I feel.' She looked down at the floor.

Dahlia took both of Carys' hands and squeezed them gently as she asked, 'How long is the process going to take?'

'It may take years to close the case or consider negligence proceedings. The media would hound me if they found out.'

'I'm so sorry Carys. You don't deserve this.' She watched Carys wring her hands. 'Come to Iraq with me.' She was surprised how quickly she uttered this request.

Carys looked at her with a mixed expression of shock and puzzlement. 'It's a war-torn area, Dahlia.'

'Well then, come to war-torn Iraq as a refugee from the NHS.'

Carys smiled for the first time. Dahlia's muscles relaxed at the thought of humans being refugees at different times of their lives. She almost chuckled.

Dahlia reached out for her hand again and clutched it with both hands. 'It's also a reminder of the biblical Babylon – the most famous city from Mesopotamia, a place of temptation.' She realised that she was trying to distract Carys, sooth her from her own trauma of a patient complaint.

She tilted her head to one side and looked at Carys, hoping she didn't look too coquette. Carys shifted in her seat, weighing up her options.

'You always say you wanted to join *Médecins sans Frontières* and travel. Now is your chance. And I'll be there to comfort and hold you if you fall!' Dahlia was amazed about the boldness that had entered her thoughts, even if it was temporary.

Carys withdrew her hand and focussed on Dahlia's dark red nail varnish. Dahlia felt the room spinning. What was she thinking? Would Carys risk coming to Iraq with a woman she had only just met a few weeks ago? The wait for an answer was unbearable. If Carys refused to come with her, their blossoming relationship would crumble under the weight of long-distance communication. She watched Carys intently, almost holding her breath.

'I've been agonising about my court case Dahlia. I have difficulty sleeping. Maybe you're right. A change of scenery would do me good. I'm not sure…'

Carys eyed her indecisively and in sudden mock-reproof said, 'You do know that biblical Babylon was also a place of threatened spiritual destruction.'

Dahlia suppressed a scream that was building up inside her. Babylon, Iraq was not only a place of destruction, even though it was portrayed that way; it was home to a rich heritage of poets, architects and handicrafts. It was the cradle of civilization! She could almost smell her favourite flower – Nergis, a blend of jasmine and hyacinth. The daffodils in Britain couldn't replicate that scent. She was overcome by a yearning to touch Carys, no better still to shake her. Dam, when would she find a way out of the maze of bewildered and excited feelings she had to hide? She got up to leave.

'Wait, when do I see you again, Dahlia?' Carys sounded

more focused on her now.

Dahlia tried to steady her breathing by leaning on the table for a second.

'Look at me, Dahlia.' Carys stood up, her napkin falling to the floor.

'Carys, I can see you need some time to think this move over. I'll give you a call in a few days.'

Dahlia hurried out of the café. She couldn't deal with two traumas – her own and that of Carys. Dahlia didn't dare to look at Carys again, beautiful Carys who would maybe abandon her in the end. Carys' skills probably wouldn't extend to her, and she had to admit, it was more than medical expertise that she wanted. She yearned for Carys to touch her entangled hair, again and again, and help her to find a way out of her present self-imposed torture and doubt.

11

After the argument with her mother and squabble with Carys, Dahlia felt the urge to confide in Jonathan, her mother's friend. She wondered what else she could call him: a colleague, an accomplice? She took the Central Line from Stratford to Holborn. The commuters looked weary, and outside the tube station, people were hurtling along streets as if immune to their beautiful surroundings. Dahlia was relieved that the Central Line was working well. A few days before, she had heard that a young man had thrown himself in front of a train. Traumas existed in every country, not only her own!

She sniffed the cold air outside the tube station and straightened the lapels of her black raincoat. How she missed the spring-time daffodils and the sunshine in Iraq! Even the simple chairs and wobbly table outside her home were etched in her memory as if they were treasures to cling to. Her family had known the true meaning of loyalty. There had been no discord until ISIS had arrived and distorted values and ideas. *Why did dreams have to turn into nightmares?* Dahlia shuddered.

Before entering the British Museum, she took out a photo from her handbag and touched it delicately, careful to preserve the happiness it brought her. A six-year-old girl, herself, standing on tiptoes between her parents, with her arm around her mother's waist. If only Dahlia could bring back that feeling of closeness with her mother. Dahlia had been wearing mauve baggy trousers gathered at the ankle and a knee-length dress of many layers in bright shades of red and green. The colours almost bounced off the photo. She also wore a sash at the waist and a short black, velvet waistcoat and revealed an almost toothless smile. Dahlia expelled a deep breath which she didn't realise she had been holding. What event had hurt her more – the invasion by ISIS or the current disputes with her anguished mother?

Dahlia entered the museum and made her way up the monumental staircase. She loved the sensation that she was being enveloped in history, an observer between times. No one could invade this building, no one could kidnap her or Coco her partridge here. She looked around for Jonathan. He was writing about the epic clay-tablets and he usually spoke about them while Dahlia listened willingly. *What a relief his simple life was*!

Jonathan came walking out of the Reading room. He had an assertive walk, always seemed to know exactly where he was headed. He didn't waver like her mother or move erratically like her brother Elias. Jonathan was taller than most men; his curator's uniform complemented his self-assured gait.

A young man who was wearing ripped jeans and a tattered woollen jumper stepped in front of Jonathan. Dahlia heard him speaking to the young man who had an American accent. She could hear the measured voice Jonathan always put on around students or visitors, the same voice she had heard and quietly admired when they first met right here in the Museum. *He was a non-judgemental and noble man, or was he?*

'These are the books I'd recommend on the history of writing. Let me know if there's anything else I can do to help with your thesis.'

The student thanked him. Jonathan nodded and looked past him. Dahlia smiled and waved. He waved back and walked towards her slowly, saying that he would refrain from rushing up the staircase two steps at a time in order to give her the chance to take in the wonders of the museum. Dahlia felt at home there. The Rosetta Stone, the Parthenon Marbles and Egyptian mummies fascinated her. Artefacts from Mesopotamia made her feel homesick and comforted at the same time. Cultures connected here instead of clashing like they did in her home country!

She didn't feel like a foreigner when she was here. Her culture was appreciated, and it contributed towards the success of the British Museum. The spectacular skylight of glass and steel was surreal. She felt proud when she stepped into its halls, especially when she saw the small statues, the intricate chairs created from wood and reeds and the mosaics in the Mesopotamian collections.

Dahlia and Jonathan headed towards the galleries of the Ancient Near East. He had been working in the museum for five years, allowing him now to move through the galleries smoothly and intuitively.

He explained that the museum had become a sort of home, ever since his wife had died from breast cancer a few years previously. The family dynamic had never been the same since. His son Daniel had been very close to his mother, happily spent time with her, helpful in the most mundane household chores, even sewing. A shadow passed across his eyes as he mentioned this. It had never sat right with him. After the passing of his wife, he encouraged Daniel to join the army 'to toughen him up, make a man out of him'.

This shocked Dahlia to hear. Why anyone should happily enlist one's son in the army was beyond her. Elias had been forced to join the ISIS forces. He assured her in the ensuing months that he had left shortly afterwards. He told her that he had felt blessed as a chosen leader of men and more importantly of women! Elias had been captivated by the devotedness of his ISIS family. However, the beheadings of Jihadi Jack had haunted him and so he escaped to join his mother and sister when they fled to Europe. Dahlia wondered whether he regretted his decision to run away from ISIS as they had enticed him with the promise to make a man out of him too. *What exactly did manhood mean anyway?*

She also noted with interest the small parallel in Jonathan's approach to household chores. It was deemed unmanly in her culture and wasn't spoken about beyond close family. Elias hardly did any household chores, or anything at home, come to think of it. She worried for him. He would be out until late most evenings, with never a hint of where he had been. She often held back from sharing too much about her brother and his strange behaviours. She didn't want to alarm Jonathan, to potentially spoil their relationship.

Jonathan and Dahlia crossed the little bridge that led to the 'Ancient Near East' department and walked towards the clay tablets from Iraq. Dahlia would sometimes visit these when she felt homesick.

Dahlia strolled the length of the glass cabinet containing the clay tablets. She was wearing a navy-blue pencil skirt with a white blouse underneath her black coat. Her dark brown hair hung freely on her shoulders. She felt like a Mesopotamian woman going to the market to buy food for her family but looked like a modern-day woman in Britain scanning

Mesopotamian artefacts.

How wonderful to have a voice here!

Jonathan straightened his uniform and placed himself in her path thereby blocking her view of the cuneiform tablets in the transparent glass-fronted cabinets. Dahlia met his bold gaze. He was slightly taller than her. His blue-green eyes looked mischievous.

'Have you come here to help me write my book and decipher the cuneiform tablets? They are the Mesopotamian Rosetta Stone!' Jonathan had a wry smile and cocked his head to one side, a dimple peeping out of his clean-shaven chin.

Dahlia admired his audacity. 'Well, as you don't speak Arabic, I suppose I may as well help you.'

Jonathan laughed. 'Arabic is not helpful for deciphering these valuable tablets. Only a handful of people can read this dead cuneiform script! There are more than 900 cuneiform signs. I want to unlock the secrets of the world's first civilization, Mesopotamia!' He beckoned for her to accompany him to the café. She looked around the open café to make sure Elias hadn't followed her. He was unpredictable since he had left ISIS. It was as if he had lost a limb or a family.

Jonathan watched her. She was quiet this afternoon. He broke the silence and asked,

'Do you speak Akkadian?'

'Akkadian?' Dahlia asked disbelievingly.

'Well, you said you speak a few languages,' which made her laugh. Jonathan explained that Akkadian was an extinct language spoken in ancient Mesopotamia. It was a broad term which comprised the Semitic Babylonian and Assyrian dialects. She watched the creases under Jonathan's eyes bunch up with fun. He enjoyed making her laugh, especially when she least expected it. 'We actually offer courses if you'd ever wanted to learn.'

Dahlia couldn't tell if he was joking or not. She enjoyed his boldness and didn't feel it was intimidating as it did with other men.

'It'd help you to decipher clay tablets which are the chief medium for cuneiform or wedge-shaped writing.'

Dahlia raised her well-groomed eyebrow defensively, 'Now, why would I need to do that?'

He shrugged and smiled. 'You seem quite keen on the clay tablets in my cabinets.'

The waitress approached them and took their orders.

Their English Breakfast teas arrived in dainty white china, Jonathan mentioned drinking tea from little curved glasses called *Istikan* when he had visited Iraq a few years ago.

'Do you miss the *chai* of Iraq?'

Dahlia started drinking her tea, and looking beyond Jonathan, was trying to envisage her life before coming to London. *Memories could be tasted.* Cardamom and sage generously sweetened in a warm and soothing blend. Life would always slow down ever so slightly with the first sip of that tea.

'Yes, I miss it. But I drink tea without sugar now. Much healthier.'

'You'd be right about that. Good thing we don't sweeten our tea as much here, we drink it by the bucket! Having a 'cuppa'. The ultimate pastime, cure-all, social activity. Guess it's something our cultures share, in a way.'

'I'll tell you what we don't share: You dress your pets in clothes. What's the point? They've got fur. Back home, we only had enough clothes for ourselves.'

She took a deep breath, 'And we don't share the same aromas. I miss the fresh flowers. *Nargis*, *Nasrin*… The flowers here don't smell as strong.'

Jonathan nodded his head, his eyes willing her to say more.

'I miss my family back home. The ones who are still alive, at least...' She trailed off.

Jonathan reached out for her hand.

'I don't miss the terrorism and the fear of war.' She was trembling.

'Do you want to talk about it?'

Dahlia shook her head. 'People here are demonstrating against Brexit. Who rallied against ISIS?'

Jonathan sighed, 'My son joined the army to help the Kurdish Peshmerga and Americans fight the extremists.'

'Weren't you afraid for his life?' He seemed nonchalant which surprised her. She had worried about Elias when he was in the ISIS army. Jonathan sipped his tea slowly. It was hot. He poured some more milk into it.

Dahlia shifted her position in the chair. Jonathan had no daughter and it made Dahlia happy that he had always wanted one. He was engrossed in his work as a curator. She smiled as he continued talking.

'Ancient literature helps us understand society today. Take the story of Gilgamesh, for example, a Mesopotamian myth of a tyrant King who is two thirds divine and one third mortal. He enslaves his population and molests brides. Therefore, the Gods create a rival, Enkidu, made from clay to interact with him. King Gilgamesh started his life yearning for immortality and power and after his dear friend or lover Enkidu dies, he becomes at peace with the finality of death. It gives him a maturity that he didn't know he could have.'

Jonathan hesitated, then said, 'Some scholars say, boys will be boys.'

He touched Dahlia's hand softly as if regretting his previous statement. 'I'm not like Gilgamesh. I'm a loyal man.'

Dahlia thought of the womanising Gilgamesh and couldn't help wondering about Jonathan's previous relationships. He held her gaze and she felt a warm feeling overcome her.

'Gilgamesh was obsessed by the 'wild man' Enkidu but he was more infatuated by his fear of death,' Jonathan said looking around at the visitors in the museum. 'Us humans should all learn to accept our limitations.'

She kept quiet. *How would she feel if she faced imminent death?* Jonathan looked excited and proud when he talked about the clay tablets in his display cases. Dahlia was happy that these tablets had brought them closer together and enabled them to explore and feel proud of her heritage.

'Every time I head out for another excavation in Iraq, we find more of the clay tablets. The clay preserves better in ruins of buildings. One day the Epic of Gilgamesh will be complete. We are grateful to the archaeologists who make the discoveries.'

Dahlia noticed Jonathan's pupils widen when he talked about his work. His curly brown hair was thinning at the temples which made him look as if he had a wide forehead. Dahlia could feel his excitement in the way he described the clay tablets.

Jonathan explained, 'The manuscripts of Gilgamesh are cuneiform, wedge-shaped tablets. The eleven tablets of the Gilgamesh Epic vary from over a hundred to over three hundred lines. The original work would have been about 3000 lines long. We still have many clay tablets to find.'

His mouth curved into a smile, 'This may mean another journey to Iraq. I would do ANYTHING to get hold of another clay tablet.'

Dahlia shuddered. *How far would Jonathan go to achieve his aim?* When would she return to the war-torn country? She had run away from it and would not run towards it so quickly. She was, however, interested in the stories depicted in the tablets.

Dare she hope that she might then form one harmonic piece of literature? She turned to look at Jonathan again.

'Which tablet would you like to gain more insight into?'

His face lit up, 'I'd love to fill in the gaps of the eleventh tablet, the Flood tablet. Hopefully, I can find an attractive archaeologist or translator to help me.'

He nodded in her direction and watched her smile for a split second. 'Look Dahlia, I'm learning how to decipher some tablets in this museum. Would you like to help me?'

She took a deep breath as Jonathan said, 'There is some more information on your ancestors in there.'

He pointed towards the railing from where they could look into the Reading Room.

'I don't give everyone this information. You have priority because of your heritage.'

Would her mother mind? She was secretly pleased and gave in to his offer,

'Okay, good, he said. 'It will have to be the end of the week as I've some other translating jobs to do before then. Let's say, four on Friday afternoon, in front of the Reading Room?'

Dahlia clasped Jonathan's hand softly. She gave him a chaste kiss on his cheek. He smelt of cedar-scented soap. Jonathan was bringing some light into her world and she badly needed it now. Elias was angry whenever they met, and her mother was talking in conundrums most of the time.

12

Dahlia longed to speak to Carys again but she needed to talk to Shirin first, a friend she had met through a colleague at the BBC. She hoped a period of peace and quietness with a person who might understand her ordeals better than anyone else would possibly rescue her from her spiralling sorrow and confusion about Yasmine. *How did Shirin deal with her own haunted past?*

She walked through the hip streets of Hackney Wick, taking in the warehouse buildings covered in graffiti. She passed one bearing the transgender flag, in light blue, pink and white. It made her think briefly of her friend Jennifer, who had recently told Dahlia that she had started the process of transitioning. It had come as a surprise to Dahlia. She had never spoken to a self-identifying transgender person before.

Jennifer was pansexual, which, she joked, made her spoilt for choice – but in all seriousness this was interesting for Dahlia to hear about. *It was such a taboo at home growing up.* It opened up a dialogue which she could never have with her mother about her own thoughts on femininity, how her mother's expectations for marriage felt so incongruous with her happiness.

Dahlia sighed; she didn't dare introduce her friends to her mother. They were worlds apart and sometimes she felt like no amount of words would make her mother understand her lifestyle. It was sad to think that the scars on her arms were an easier means of expression than rebuilding a connection with her mum. The scars were fading, growing old and forgotten the longer she knew Carys. She was the only person who brightened up a conversation, but she appeared too frivolous at times.

She may have felt herself opening up to Carys' warmth and affection, but she was still reluctant to fully open up to Carys about her past in Iraq. As a white woman, how could she possibly empathise with her grief, her trauma? Hence why today, she needed to see Shirin. She would be able to relate, having also contended with racial trauma.

They had arranged to meet by the Aquatics Centre in the Olympic Park. Zaha Hadid, the famous Iraqi architect, had designed the Aquatics Centre for the 2012 Olympic games. It was empowering to remember that great talent could come out of Iraq, despite its deep-set political division and terror. The Aquatics Centre resembled a wave sliding into the rest of the park. She yearned for restorative waters, but she hadn't ever been inside the swimming pool itself; she didn't want anyone to see the scars lining her arms.

Shirin came walking slowly towards her from the shopping centre, the other side of the Olympic Park. Shirin was as old as her mother, mid-fifties but less well-dressed. She wore a faint blue eyeshadow that also reminded Dahlia of the Aquatics Centre. It made her eyes gentler and larger, like a lake where any cast-away debris could float. She recognised the usual shuffle of her walk, an old injury incurred at Halabja in Iraq.

'Shirin! Thanks so much for meeting me at such short notice. It's so good to see you.'

They hugged. 'Not at all, sweetheart! I had the day off work today.'

'How has that been recently?' Dahlia knew that Shirin's work as the manager of a care home was often tiring. Sometimes they would go weeks without seeing each other, demanding as the job was.

'It's been… a lot. The care home has filled up quickly again. We've got a waiting time of about six months. And it's not always easy with the ones already in our care, we've been so short-staffed. They get emotional when I go on holiday for a few days, may Allah bless them.'

They headed back towards the canal by Hackney Wick, with its colourful boats. Each boat told a different story, an eclectic collection of decorative pot-plants, old furniture, bric-a-brac, some now had solar panels. Dahlia smiled as she thought of people living such a simple life, not seeking glamour or wealth, the last remaining community to survive the gentrification and commercialisation of Stratford, where new high-rises were rapidly expanding. She was relieved that they had left the shops behind. She had felt a bit nauseous walking past the shoe shops with hundreds of various shoes on display – growing up in Sinjar, Yasmine, her school friend, had often walked bare-foot.

'So, what's on your mind, Dahlia? What did you want to talk about today?'

'I've been… . I've been thinking about my childhood a lot over the past few days. I feel like you're the right person to speak to about this sort of thing. Shirin, do you ever think back to your time in Halabja?'

Shirin kept her eyes on the canal. 'Of course, my dear. I don't think I'll ever forget.'

'Can you tell me more about it, if you're comfortable?

What are the memories that resonate, what refuses to fade?'

'Yes, my dear. I've made my peace with it now.' She paused, then began: 'The sixteenth March 1988 – more than thirty years ago now. I was with my best friend, a Yazidi neighbour, called Gulan. She was loved in the village for her kindness. She'd hand out food to old widows and knit clothes for the children of poor parents.

'I was preparing *biryani* rice for my daughter and I, listening to the radio. The Iranians and the Peshmerga, the Kurdish Freedom Fighters, had just attacked military outposts around Halabja, forcing Saddam Hussain's soldiers to retreat. Gulan and I assumed that an Iraqi counterattack was looming. I remember Gulan regretting how the Kurdish community were once more caught in the middle of the Iranian-Arab conflict, knowing that neither side signified safety for her and her family.'

Shirin took a deep breath and inhaled the slightly musty smell of the canal in front of which they were standing.

'I heard the rattling of helicopters overhead. It wasn't the first time – by now we knew to rush to the basement. But Suzanne, my daughter, was playing outside. I had to run to find her, she was only six years old, she wasn't old enough to understand.' Shirin buried her face in her hands. Then, she looked up again.

'I could sense that something terrible was about to happen. I heard a clinking sound like pieces of metal dropping without exploding. I saw smoke clouds a short distance away, in the Jewish neighbourhood. I ran and got Sozanne inside the house. There was a pungent smell in the air. I couldn't quite place it. It smelt of rancid garlic and apples and was starting to make Sozanne cry. I folded my apron around her. Through the window I could see cows lying on the grass, sheep and goats dying. A mother was clutching her child who was barefoot.'

Dahlia put her arm around Shirin and waited. *How could she bear this grief?* It was impenetrable and threatened to spread its ugly fingers through both their bodies, permeating them like poison ivy and clinging to them like cobwebs. Oddly enough, it also brought them together.

Shirin covered her eyes with her hands. 'I felt my eyes stinging and Sozanne started crying and vomiting. The house was going to be a gas chamber if we didn't leave.'

Dahlia felt her own throat tightening, her thoughts widening through space and time from Hitler to Saddam and Halabja. Time and again, poison was used to achieve purity. How ironic! Future dictators would be born, imposing their psychotic ideals on vulnerable peoples.

'I picked up Sozanne and put some kitchen foil over our faces with two small holes to see through.' Shirin glanced at Dahlia to check this was not too overwhelming. 'I told her it was a game. It was sickening to turn this nightmare into play, but she was young, she wouldn't have understood.'

That little girl Sozanne was about Dahlia's age now. It was gruelling, listening to Shirin's description of the white powder that had formed a film on the ground, how some people had drunk from a contaminated well. Bodies were strewn, motionless in front of their houses, the front doors left opened, never to be closed again by the families. Shirin grimaced whilst telling Dahlia about the skin discolouration, the transfixed eyes and the greyish slime oozing from some mouths. Hands were twisted and legs lay lamely.

Dahlia thought of the cubist painter Picasso and his work influenced by the Spanish Civil War. Halabja was the Guernica of the Orient. Dahlia thought of Mount Sinjar and the mass graves that she had encountered there, hoping that Yasmine was not in one of them. *But it was easier, for now, to deflect her thoughts to Shirin's story.* Shirin reached out to hold Dahlia's hand.

'A young man was laughing hysterically and waving his hands, flinging off his *sharwal* and linen shirt until tremors seized his body and he, too, fell. That I was still standing was a miracle – Allah had saved us. My throat was tight, and every breath took a huge effort. My only option was to stagger to a collective settlement on the outskirts of town. As I made my way, I saw old Yazidi and other Kurdish neighbours collapse, their children orphaned there and then. Sozanne kept trying to tear off the silver foil. She said she couldn't breathe, she felt needles in her eyes.'

Dahlia felt her own eyes sting.

'Having left the town behind, the sounds of a town in agony became more distant and I now heard a truck pass us by, with a handful of surviving passengers in the back. Thank God one of the passengers was my uncle Omar who begged the driver to stop so we could jump in. As we travelled further up into the mountains I looked back and could see heavy clouds of gas choking the village.'

Dahlia and Shirin passed a family with a pushchair and a rosy-cheeked young child walking along the canal, all cushioned in thick knitted hats and scarves against the crisp midday air. *How lucky these children were!*

Shirin paused until the family had passed. 'I could hear the driver moaning more urgently – the other passengers didn't even seem to notice, so strongly were their lungs seized by the hostile air. We were at the foothills of the mountain, and the truck lurched to and fro with every bend in the road.'

Dahlia sensed an internal squirm as Shirin continued, 'We

couldn't afford to crash now. I placed Sozanne into uncle Omar's arms and with every ounce of energy I could muster, climbed into the front passenger's seat from the back of the truck. The driver, I recognised him: he was the son of a market stall keeper. His cries were intensifying, his words unintelligible, losing control of his voice, his arms, the vehicle. We were losing him!'

Dahlia watched the shifting patterns of sunlight on Shirin's face, grateful for the distraction from this horrific story. Shirin pulled the sleeves of her coat down.

'Dahlia, the driver turned around another curve in the road and something within me sensed that he would not have the physical strength to make the next turn. I did something I had never done before – I thrust myself onto his lap and slammed my foot on the brake. The truck came to a halt.'

Dahlia held her breath. She hadn't expected tales of sturdy palm trees, wrapped in fairy lights. But this story was unbearable. Shirin scanned the surroundings as if to make sure nobody else could hear her story. Then she continued, 'The adrenaline quickly drained from the driver's body and with that, his life and soul. His head slumped to the side and I felt the muscles in his lap beneath me grow lax. We had no choice but to place him at the side of the road without a burial.'

Only then did Shirin's voice catch and she gulped. *What a formidable woman to recount such a tale.* Shirin's story echoed her own trauma that Dahlia still failed to put into words – to therapists, to Carys. The exodus of the survivors from Halabja was less than thirty years ago. Taking flight from oppression and ethnic cleansing was as old as the Bible.

'Another few kilometres along the mountain path, the truck shuddered to a halt – no more petrol. We had to start walking. Here, the air was more tolerable. I noticed a woman sitting on a rock, breastfeeding a six-month-old baby. The more the baby sucked, the more the mother weakened and swayed. Their eyes were closed.'

Dahlia had once asked her mother how long she had been breastfed. She had answered that there had not been enough milk to do so. *Was this the real reason?*

'I was mesmerised by the baby's attempts to continue sucking despite the fact that the mother had fallen to the ground.'

Dahlia was not surprised. A baby or child would always try getting back to its mother and the source of its life, even if abandoned. Look how she was trying to reconnect with her mother!

'What happened to the baby?' she asked, frowning.

Shirin smiled briefly. 'I stroked the baby's thin tuft of soft hair and put my fingers into its mouth, easing it away from the dead mother. The baby continued sucking my finger peacefully, oblivious to the fact that it was not its mother's nipple.'

Dahlia felt a yearning come over her. She would love to drink up some comforting liquid, draw up some warm fluid in a straw. She wanted a source of nurture. Dahlia suddenly thought of Carys. The carefree way she drank her cappuccinos, unlike Dahlia's somewhat hesitant sips of coffee. Dahlia was afraid of their burgeoning relationship; fearful she might syphon off Carys' energy or swallow her enthusiasm. Dahlia suddenly realised that she had stopped listening to Shirin. She quickly turned away from the canal.

'I now had my daughter Sozanne sleeping on my right shoulder and the baby on my left arm.' Shirin let out a weak, defeated laugh. Delicate tears traced down her cheeks, taking her make-up with them. 'Then, the baby loosened its grip on me. I was holding a floppy body.'

Dahlia squeezed Shirin's hand. She noticed the way Shirin was so able to express her emotions, whilst Dahlia's mother hardly revealed her feelings.

'I was waiting for a cry, even a cry of hunger. But *bebeke* was silent. She looked angelic.'

Dahlia knew that *bebeke* was an endearment for a baby. Most probably, Shirin didn't even know its name.

'I had to put the baby down on a patch of grass.'

Dahlia thought of the exodus of the Yazidi people from Sinjar. No seeds were sown in the fields of those homes, where Yasmine had lived. Graves were dug instead. Who did the earth belong to? Did the Yazidi have no right to live in their native surroundings, the land of their ancestors stretching back centuries? She had longed for the United Nations to rescue them, but in vain. *Why had she not run down the mountain to try and find Yasmine?* She imagined the same disillusion and utter exhaustion felt by Shirin at her age. She turned to give her a hug.

'Shirin, I'm so sorry. Your whole life turned upside down just like that, within minutes. I think I can relate. I hardly open up to anyone about this but… I think you'll understand. When Yasmine was kidnapped from her home, the sky turned black within a few minutes. The stars were falling down. I knew what would await her with the ISIS soldiers.'

Shirin's tears slowed and dried, and she looked on at Dahlia, willing her to speak on.

'I prayed to God – the God living within all our nature. I prayed to the God of Christians, the God of Muslims and of Jews to help me. I never felt more alone.'

Dahlia was gripped with a wave of overwhelming sadness as she thought about all the pain endured between these two women alone, the pain of Kurdish families, Muslim and Yazidi.

Shirin took a deep breath and said, 'We've been betrayed, relentlessly throughout our history. We wouldn't have endured this if we had a country of our own, a government that represented us. Western colonialists promised us Kurds our own country in the Treaty of Sevres after World War One, and what did we get out of their next treaty? Just the opposite.'

Dahlia worried that if history was cyclical, then the Kurds would be betrayed again even after joining Americans fighting ISIS. Politics was not a love affair; it was transactional and transient.

'Shirin, what happened next?'

'We left our prayers with the baby's corpse. The journey further up into the mountains was arduous. The others didn't have the strength left in them to make it; my uncle Omar included. Sozanne and I were the only two to eventually reach a place of safety on the other side of the mountains, an Iranian hospital. My husband managed to reach us, having returned from the Iranian border where he had been working as a doctor. He'd brought an Atropine syringe to counteract the cyanide poison gas… but there was only one.' Shirin said flatly.

One syringe! Who would the syringe be used for? Shirin or her daughter? Dahlia tensed up as she waited for Shirin to continue.

'I was furious with my husband! He knew that we would need two injections. I felt nauseous and it wasn't only because of the chemicals. I was shocked that my husband wanted me to decide who should have the injection.'

Shirin was silent for another minute. 'I decided Sozanne

should have it.'

What an impressive woman! She couldn't begin to imagine how difficult such a decision would have been to make, risking her own life for that of her daughter. She tried to stay focused on Shirin and her story but for a second could not help but wonder whether her mother Hannah would do the same. Dahlia drew Shirin closer. How she would have loved to have her as a mother.

'Of course, there were implications for me…' Shirin trailed off. 'I could never have any more children because of the side-effects of the poisonous gas. But Sozanne was saved. I remember the jagged peaks of our proud Kurdish mountains. I even miss the dirty roads and ruts we had to pass while we were running away to Iran.'

For a moment, grief melted from Shirin's eyes. She reached out and took Dahlia's hand. 'The flight to Britain was the steppingstone to the rest of Europe. Iraq had torn families apart. Europe would save us,' Shirin said emphatically. 'Thankfully, it was goodbye to larger-than-life posters of Saddam Hussain in military uniform, Savile Row Suit or in traditional Arab dress.'

Dahlia decided this might be the best time to ask the question she had been longing to ask. 'Shirin, I've been thinking about that night in 2014 when ISIS came for the Yazidi community. Why were the Kurdish militia, the Peshmerga, told to retreat? Did they panic? The name Peshmerga means 'those who face death!" She would never have retreated if she had known what would happen to Yasmine and the other Yazidis. She would have to keep telling herself this, but how long would this false reassurance last?

'I'm so sorry Dahlia. Not all the Kurdish leaders are sympathetic towards the Yazidi. Some of them won't even eat at the same table as them.'

Dahlia felt insurmountable frustration bubbling up within her. Shirin gave her a kind, tired look that shared the same disillusion as Dahlia. 'I know sweetheart. Religion should never be weaponized, nor human rights politicised. But it's important to remember that eventually some Kurdish organisations like the Syrian Kurdish troops, the YPG, did help Yazidis to escape from ISIS, where they would otherwise have been wiped out. Syrian women with Kalashnikovs battled their way up to Mount Sinjar and built the escape corridor for many Yazidis.'

Thank goodness, her gut muscles were beginning to relax. The interaction with Shirin had been heavier than she had expected, but difficult conversations were often followed by a clearer headspace. They sat perched on a bench in a comfortable silence for a few moments.

'You know, I miss the fields and forestry by the mountains of Suran and Balumba. I miss the sweet floral scent of *yasmin* and *raski*. If I hadn't become infertile, I would have called my next daughter Yasmin or Dahlia.'

Dahlia rested her head on Shirin's shoulder. She missed the abundant cypresses, fig trees, and pomegranates with which her mother would cook red rice. Her favourite flowers had been *nasrin* and *nergiz* which blossomed in March.

'I can be your Dahlia.'

Shirin smiled faintly. 'You need to speak to your mother, my dear.'

'When I speak to her, she doesn't seem to hear me.' Dahlia said ruefully.

'Keep talking to her. One day, she'll listen to you.'

Dahlia nodded and reluctantly decided to meet her mother again. Maybe this time she would be successful in opening up to her. Her lack of understanding was making her sick. She had to try harder; until she felt her mother's full acceptance. Here she was in London, a colourful cosmopolitan heartland in which she still hadn't found her footing.

13

She was waiting for her mother by Old Compton Street. Her mother had initially refused to meet somewhere where she had to dodge rickshaws carrying tourists and people queuing outside the theatre. Don't get her started on its tight alleyways with raucous men in tight trousers, she had told Dahlia.

Elias had been acting strangely recently. He seemed more watchful, irritable, and when he was in the room with her, his long, viscid silences were pricked with disdainful comments about her. He had urged her to wear a headscarf for the first time and stormed off when she so much as questioned him. He seemed to know where she had been during the day even when they hadn't spoken. She had started to look over her shoulder more often.

Her mother would always hurry towards her when they'd meet, almost convincing Dahlia that she still enjoyed their time together, like a flawed replica of their relationship when she was younger. Dahlia yearned for the simpler times she had spent with her mother as a toddler, when Dahlia would laugh at the cows and donkeys from their field who'd lost their way and end up with neighbours.

She crossed the road and hugged her mother briefly. Dahlia smoothed out the fluffy burgundy coat she had bought her to make her look more feminine in order to please her mother. Yet she held herself awkwardly, arms floppy.

'How has your day been?' Dahlia asked.

'Productive. I did some reading in the British Museum.'

'Research with Jonathan, I suppose?' Dahlia raised her eyebrows.

'Bismillah! I'm only helping Jonathan with some translations.'

'What? Jonathan's nice. I mean, he seems like he could be good for you. And he's intelligent.'

Dahlia laughed remembering Jonathan's gentle eyes and astute way of talking about the beloved Mesopotamian clay tablets he was studying.

'Yes, well. There are plenty of intelligent men around – you work with them! Why do you never introduce any of them?' Her mother looked at her, despair in her eyes.

Dahlia recoiled at her comment on her male colleagues. It was the influence of those friends of hers, none of whom she liked, telling her mother she 'needed a man'.

'Actually Mum, there's something I'd like to have a word about – but not out here. Let's get something to eat. I've got a place in mind.'

So, they waded through the bustling street, her mother glowering at the pubs, observing some same-sex couples along the way like she was at the zoo, in both vague interest and revolt. One man emerged in a garish sequin dress and tacky high-heeled boots, his long hair in a bun. It appeared he was meeting his – boyfriend? girlfriend? – already out on the street, whom he kissed, arms sliding around their waist. 'Nonsense,' her mother muttered under her breath.

But Dahlia heard her. 'What do you mean? She walks better in those heels than you could.'

Easily triggered, her mother snapped, 'What do you mean, '*she*?', though this came out a little louder than expected and they both received a deathly stare from the couple, still within earshot. Her mother scurried ahead.

'We've been living in London for five years, Mum. Surely this isn't the first time you've seen a drag queen. I mean it's not for either of us to assume that person's pronouns.'

Her mother opted to glare on in place of a reply. Then she stammered, 'I hope none of our relatives can see how they are behaving here, an utter disgrace.'

A few heavy paces later, Dahlia gestured towards the Admiral Duncan Pub and said, 'You know, back in 1999 this pub was bombed. Three killed.'

'Oh dear – who was behind this bomb, then? Another US-backed invasion was it?' her mother joked darkly.

'It was a homophobic attack, Mum. See the rainbow flag?'

'Right. Yes.' She huffed. 'Anyway. Where's this restaurant? I'm getting hungry. It's starting to rain and, lacking an umbrella or hooded raincoat, I'm not keen for my hair to get ruined. I'm hoping to drop by Jonathan's place later again today.'

Dahlia shook her head and led her to a trendy-looking restaurant where the décor looked better than the food probably tasted, the façade lit up by pink neon, and 'GLUTEN FREE AND VEGAN FRIENDLY!' well-advertised on the door. An effeminate male waiter with sculpted brows swayed over to show them to a table by the window. Dahlia was relieved to sit down, so tiresome this ordeal had been so far. Her mother placed her Radley handbag next to her and eyed the place suspiciously.

'Dahlia!' called a voice from a few tables down. A blonde in faded jeans and an oversized shirt came over and pecked

Dahlia on the cheek. It was Jennifer! Her mother pretended to be browsing the menu to avoid a peck coming her way too.

Dahlia's face lit up, 'Jennifer, this is my mum.'

'I can see where Dahlia gets her good looks from,' Jennifer joked, turning to her mother.

'Mm yes. A pleasure to meet you.' Her eyes scanned Jennifer's hands. No rings – unmarried.

'Having some mother-daughter quality time, are we?' Her mother pointedly busied herself with the menu again before Jennifer got the hint and left them to it.

'You haven't mentioned Jennifer before.'

'Jennifer and I actually used to be… very close.'

'Come to think of it, you don't seem to tell me about anyone in your life these days. Friends, partners… I imagine it's not as easy finding someone at your age. But don't worry. I have a plan. Remember Noor who moved back to Jordan? She was on the phone the other day saying she knows some handsome young men who are keen to marry a British girl-'

'Mum! I don't need the stress of a marriage only for the groom to clear off once he's got a British passport.

'Dahlia, for once would you just cooperate. I'm doing this because I know what's good for you. You have no idea how hard it was for me as an unmarried woman when your dad died. You're lucky you've got me, because I won't always be around to help you out and Elias has enough trouble looking after himself at the best of times.'

Once more, her voice was louder than she realised. Jennifer shot a concerned look at Dahlia. Her mother drastically lowered her voice and said menacingly, 'Also, for what it's worth I don't like the way your friend is looking over here. Nosy cow.'

'That's enough!' Dahlia interrupted, her cheeks reddening.

'And completely uncalled for. I can't take this anymore – it's actually what I brought you here to tell you.'

'Excuse me?'

'Jennifer, I used to date her.' Her voice was hushed but steady. 'I'm... I wanted to tell you that I'm attracted to women.'

Separately, each word was meaningless, harmless, but as her mother began to process what she had just said, she grabbed hold of Dahlia and said, 'What a joke. What utter disrespect after all I've done to propel you forward through life, sparing every penny to support your education, motivating you to find one internship after the next until you had a job only others could dream of.'

Dahlia could feel the hot scalding blood, pulsing through her heart so powerfully it could burst.

'So... not only have you led me into this trap where only the most crooked, clownish riff raff come, but you mean to say that *you are one of them*?'

The space on the table stretched out for miles between them. Dahlia could not muster a response. Within two blinks of an eye, her mother waltzed through the door, out into the shower of rain and hailed a taxi. On the way, the torrent relented, producing a rainbow in its wake. Her mother screamed '*For crying out loud.*'

14

It had been two weeks since Carys had seen Dahlia and she couldn't stop thinking about her. She had tried keeping herself busy at work, she'd even accepted to do some extra on-calls, which had meant she'd seen a lot less of Phil at home. Admittedly this didn't bother her at all – since Brynn had left home for university, they had stopped trying to keep up any pretence of a happy family.

When had it all gone wrong in their marriage? For all the complacency and monotony that characterised their estrangement today, she could never forget the excitement she had felt at the start of their romance in university. When they met in medical school, she admired how comfortable he was with himself, how confidently he could speak to others, and reach out to strangers. It had rubbed off on Carys, initially a little shy, soon to be as boisterous as her lover. But eventually, having come into her own, Carys began to resent his extroversion. It seemed increasingly like a staggering sense of entitlement, arrogance, satisfaction with the knowledge that he could make anyone like him!

She had become pregnant in medical school despite using contraception. This had caused some complications as sleepless nights with the baby had led to failing some exams. Phil, on the other hand, had immersed himself into his studies, excelling quickly. She frowned but then thought of Dahlia. She loved how Dahlia was naturally so humble. Any time she learned something new or impressive about Dahlia it would always be by accident. Carys liked how Dahlia wasn't a people-pleaser. *It was no-bullshit, authentic.* Getting to know her was slow but it was organic and worth the wait for the blossoming result at the end, a bit like her floral namesake.

Coming to the end of a particularly taxing shift, Carys left St Thomas Hospital and got on her bike home, pushing the stress of work away with each thrust of her pedals. Dahlia had recently bought a bike too after a long, stimulating chat on the climate crisis. Carys fastened the strap of her yellow and red helmet – a present from Dahlia, who had pointed out the *Matisse-esque* colour contrasts and collaged shapes. She was impressed by Dahlia's intelligence, her interest in art from all over the world, her curiosity for the stories of others when she alone was enough of an interesting story in itself. She couldn't imagine the strength and endurance Dahlia had needed to pick herself up and kept going after her experiences back in her homeland. Dahlia was stronger than she realised. Carys wanted to be the one to help her see that.

Parking her bike and sliding her keys into the door, she wondered what Dahlia saw when she looked at her. Mindful that Carys was ten years her senior, she hoped she wasn't a substitute-mother. *Work was shit today. Are you free?*

Only moments later a response pinged through. Beautifully fast replies, another thing she loved about this woman. *Snap! My day was pretty shit too.* A sardonic winking emoji. *Where do u wanna meet up?*

Carys smiled into her phone as she typed: *Meet u at that restaurant on the South Bank.* She glanced down at the old corduroy trousers and tea-stained V-neck she had on, but it would have to do for now.

Carys hopped on her bike again and cycled through the evening smog, wondering if she should have worn a mask like some urban dwellers did. The first to arrive, she waited for Dahlia at the table nearest the door of the restaurant. She smelt Dahlia's Lancôme perfume before she saw her and turned intuitively to meet her, kissing her on the cheek like a French greeting, though perhaps slightly longer than was the social convention in France! Her skin was so soft. A coral necklace complemented her slender neckline and her red blouse made her cheeks appear more flushed.

Sitting down, Dahlia asked 'Won't your husband be waiting for you?', more playfully than genuinely concerned.

'He's on-call, supposedly. Won't be back till tomorrow morning.' Then Carys added, 'Weirdly enough, he always seems to come back the next morning smelling of our younger registrar's perfume. She's young, single, and brunette. Pretty much the opposite of me.'

'Oh… How long ago did you pick up on that?'

'A couple of years back. But you know what, I feel no way about it. I'm not even sure why we're together anymore. We held it together for Brynn but he's off at uni now probably not paying us much thought.'

They ordered a cocktail each and, swirling the crushed ice around with her straw, Dahlia said, 'Your marriage is my mother's dream life for me. Was there ever anyone other than Phil?'

'There was someone… a girl.' They locked eyes. 'Things didn't work out. We were both seventeen and times were different back then. There was no way I could introduce her as my girlfriend to anyone. I just wasn't comfortable enough.'

Leaning forward, Dahlia uttered, 'I understand,' in a way

she'd never heard inflected with more compassion and empathy. Plates of tapas arrived at the table. 'So, tell me. What made work so bad today?'

'Patients thinking they know better, It's exhausting. Today's episode was from someone playing up a whiplash injury for compensation from their insurance. She demanded a neck X-ray when it wasn't necessary and wouldn't have changed the medical treatment. In the end I gave in – I'm more wary of getting complaints ever since that obnoxious patient Thornton.'

She took another sip of her cocktail. 'A polite approach doesn't seem to get me far in the hospital. And then, even once I've left, at home I've been busy every evening getting ready for my yearly appraisal. Since Dr Harold Shipman's murder cases, every doctor has to get revalidated regularly. They get you to reflect on your clinical experiences then you're assessed by ten other colleagues and lots more patients. But it's tedious bureaucracy, not even a fair evaluation. You can choose the people you ask for feedback, so Dr Shipman would have passed his appraisal with flying colours.' *Dr Shipman was more popular with patients than herself!*

Suddenly conscious of her frustrated monologue, she broke off. 'Sorry for the rant.'

Dahlia's doe eyes looked on kindly, softened with jade eye-shadow. She didn't need mascara – her eyelashes were long enough. 'Not at all. Get it off your chest.' She took a slow sip of her cocktail.

The hours passed quickly, empty cocktail glasses accumulating on the table between them, and with the conversation meandering from one thing to another, from earnest to giggly and back again. Carys told her about Phil, about how within their conversation, Carys and Dahlia had already exchanged more words than she and Phil had in months. Carys realised she looked forward to Dahlia's shy glances when she thought Carys wasn't watching her. *Their relationship seemed to have something clandestine about it.* She was aware that this stirred her emotions.

'Going back to what you were saying before. About struggling to keep your patience at work. I've struggled to keep my patience today too,' Dahlia said.

'Talk to me.'

'Things have been difficult with my mother lately. I feel like she's played such a huge role in my life, she wants to be involved in every part of it, yet she refuses to hear me when I try to open up to her about… certain things.'

'Like what?'

'For starters, she's been trying to get me to go to Germany for a special type of counselling. There's a course funded by the German government for survivors of the Yazidi abuse, where the psychotherapists are from the Yazidi culture.' She paused once more. 'Forgive me if this is heavy… I'm not usually an over-sharer, but I feel like I can trust you.'

Carys warmed to her words. 'Who qualifies for the therapy your mother proposes?' Carys probed carefully.

'Primarily Yazidi women who have escaped from ISIS captivity… with evidence of severe abuse and psychological consequences. I would like to try and understand what Yasmine went through when kidnapped.'

Carys watched Dahlia shift in her chair. 'I guess you can't change your experiences of the torture, but only your thoughts towards it. Your mum might be right about therapy.'

She watched Dahlia roll her eyes slightly. It wasn't for her to decide when, or how, but she wanted Dahlia to voice her trauma, to help her process, to understand her story.

They paid for the bill and headed to the terrace, the cool wind already clearing Carys' head. They must have stood there for ten minutes, in comfortable silence, before Dahlia said, '2014 in Iraq was a hellish time to be alive. Living here now, sometimes I can't even fathom how I went through what I did.'

Carys willed her to speak.

'Yasmin phoned me a few weeks ago! She said she was sold at a Sabaya Market labelled as Girl Number Twenty-One, to an ISIS husband.' Dahlia massaged her temples. 'Yasmine kept making excuses when she was asked to crawl into the four-poster bed of her captor... She told him that she had a migraine, that she was pregnant, that she had an STD.'

Dahlia took a deep breath. 'The only response she received was for her to be locked up. Then after a few days her captor took her to the doctor in the compound, to check she wasn't pregnant and had no STDs. He was thrilled with the fact that a female doctor testified that she was a virgin.' She paused and averted her gaze.

'One night, he pushed Yasmine towards a wall and told her to undress... she had worn the same clothes for the past few weeks and not showered, hoping it would stop him from wanting to come near her. That night, he forced her into the shower and waited outside the *hammam*.'

Dahlia hesitated before gradually unfolding her story, Carys listening soberly, her eyes fixed on the same spot on the river, her mind transported to Iraq. Dahlia continued. 'when she came out of the *hammam*, Yasmine's husband dragged her into the bedroom and started touching her breasts. All she remembers are his bloodshot eyes and his bushy eyebrows.'

Dahlia shuddered. 'Yasmine says she pushed him back, scratching his eyes, biting his wrists. He kicked her until she was too weak to run away then tied her up with ropes he had kept underneath the bed…'

It was hard to know what to say. *What rupture from one's own body…* She pictured the sinking feeling of helplessness against a kind of violence that extended beyond the fleshly, being inflicted on Dahlia's whole sense of integrity. Carys reached out to hold Dahlia's hand and waited a few minutes before asking, 'Do you remember a time when you were happy?'

Dahlia replied in a low voice, 'When I was back home, before it all happened. Times were simple but I felt so alive.'

Carys pointed at the oak tree outside the restaurant, standing tall at the shore of the Thames. She said, 'Look at that oak tree, it loses its leaves every year in winter. What happens then?'

Dahlia followed her gaze thoughtfully. 'The tree grows more leaves in spring.'

Carys nodded. Dahlia's response had been more cheerful, her deep-set eyes gleaming. She watched the flicker of flames in her dark eyes and longed to find out what else would ignite those blazes. Whatever it was, Carys was willing to wait. She decided to change the subject.

'I'll visit you in Germany if you go,' she said, placing her hand over Dahlia's which were wrapped over the railing. 'But only if we go out for some apple strudel.' She added with a wink.

'Deal.' Dahlia said, gaining her composure.

15

In the taxi home from the dinner with Carys, Dahlia was mentally resolved to fly to Germany. More than a thousand Yazidi women and children had been brought to Donaueschingen in Germany for treatment through a special programme funded by Baden Württemberg in the South of Germany.

She felt guilty at her own reluctance towards the treatment – she kept having to remind herself that she ought to be grateful for the funding as she wouldn't be able to afford private psychotherapy. One day, she would try and rescue Yasmine and tell her about the therapy. *For God's sake, Yasmine would need this therapy more than her!*

Her thoughts turned to Carys. She had given Dahlia a Welsh love spoon before she left. Dahlia enjoyed tracing her fingers over the traditional decoration of hearts, lock and wheel. The lock represented security. *It would keep her safe.* The wheel apparently represented support. Dahlia couldn't doubt that Carys would help her whenever she could. There was only one heart on the wooden spoon. Apparently Welsh tradition dictated that two would mean love was reciprocated. Dahlia's thoughts wandered off. Who held the key to the heart on the spoon? Carys was caring, but would she continue to care if she realised just how complicated Dahlia and her family were?

Dahlia wondered if her mother would make cultural demands on Carys. Dahlia's first language Kurdish should have been an integral part of her social and cultural identity. But it was fading! She could not identify with many of the ideals she was born into and was fed up with the match-making tendencies of her stringent community. How would they know who suited her best?

Dahlia wondered whether her mother was right about the foolishness of unconventional love. Political ideas could be brushed away, but inner scars of unrequited or uncertain love would linger and burn like fire. *It was safer to stay guarded, even with Carys.* She had other problems to sort out. But she couldn't help daydreaming about her, how she laughed unrestrainedly, kissed her gently on her cheek and gazed into her eyes with a mixture of wonder and concern. Dahlia felt she needed to put her weary head on someone's shoulders. She sighed. Carys had an onerous job and a husband of some sort. Dahlia castigated herself about her fantasies of a life together when Carys lived with her husband and possibly still had feelings for him. Dahlia was afraid to ask her more about her husband. She was frightened Carys would reveal the intensity of feelings she had for him. *Would Carys be able to adore or even love two people at the same time?* Was this what people called polyamory? How complicated feelings could be!

When Dahlia went for walks with Carys, she felt the present was more vibrant than with anyone else. Carys would point out woodpeckers, magpies and pigeons and marvel at the surrounding nature. Dahlia had never known there were so many types of birds! Anyhow, in order to open up fully to Carys, she would need to declutter her hazy thoughts and feelings; unpick them rather than pick at her arms!

Hopefully the psychotherapy sessions would be soothing. She touched her left lower arm subconsciously. She hadn't allowed Carys to inspect her arms. It would upset her. Dahlia herself was used to the sight of the horizontal lines on her arms. Sometimes, they shone brightly like sparks from a fire. At other times, they were more like ashes, faint and sombre.

16

She had enjoyed the train ride to Stuttgart, passing luscious green fields with cows grazing peacefully. She chuckled as she thought of the cowbells dangling noisily from their necks. *Unlike herself, they couldn't hide anywhere!* Carys had told her to visit the Black Forest and Lake Constance after her six weeks of psychotherapy in the clinic. Dahlia hoped, no she longed to embrace Carys again after her therapy i.e. If she got out of it unscathed after baring all her secrets to a stranger!

How exciting it felt to be near the Swiss border. During the Second World War, it had been a source of rescue for persecuted Jews. If only the Yazidi had had such a neutral country to which they could have escaped from ISIS.

She clutched the key to her room in the white building which was to be her home for these few weeks. Carys had told her she would try and visit, but Dahlia knew that she would have to go through the actual psychotherapy alone. She shuddered and hesitated as she stepped into her room. It looked almost too clean, sterile. A single bed with a white duvet was laid out for her. The bedside cabinet was next to a table with a single wooden chair. The laminate floor was so spotless you could have eaten from it. She felt her stomach churn and couldn't remember when she had last eaten something.

Dahlia sat down on the solid bed and looked through the brochure. A swimming pool, sauna and creative facilities such as painting, ceramics and music were offered outside the therapy times. But would she have the time and energy to pursue these hobbies? She doubted it. The mattress felt firm. She hoped she'd be able to sleep well as she didn't want to stammer when she met her psychotherapist. Her first session was scheduled soon after the physical assessment in two days' time. Dam it. Why did she have to consult a therapist? Surely it would be an aggressor who needed one – the psychopath who was walking around freely after his heinous deeds with Yasmine!

Dahlia turned her attention to the bare table to the left of her bed. A sheet of paper was laid out explaining mealtimes and a diagram of how to find one's way around the various departments of the building. She frowned, preferring to stay locked up in her own room.

A painting of the surrounding hilly landscape hung on the white wall. *Would frugality enable her journey inwards?* She took a deep breath, wondering how much she would be able to open up to her psychotherapist. It might even prove too much for the therapist herself to handle, all of the secrets considered.

Dahlia had been relieved when she was told it would be a woman treating her. She hung up her few belongings in the cupboard and wondered how Carys was coping with her GMC enquiry in London. Even for a strong woman like her, it must have been debilitating to have a complaint lodged against her, especially as she was in the caring profession. She doubted whether Carys would have gone into the medical profession if she had known that the compensation culture was so rife and that it might destroy her.

Where was the apology from Yasmine's ISIS captor? He would never be able to reverse her torture and unlike the complainant against Carys, there was no compensation for her. She pined for justice. Maybe the therapist would help in some way. She didn't feel she would be able to reveal the full extent of her guilt in not being able to help Yasmine to any other person, professional or not. It would burden them and embarrass her.

In the few weeks and months following her escape from Iraq, every other night, she'd feel stifled by the vividness of her experiences. This had gradually become less frequent over the past two years, but she would still sometimes be struck by panic in the night, would wake up in a sweat, her heart palpitating. Since then the night terrors had dulled to a constant unease.

This bare room and the alien nature of her surroundings were bringing on surges of memory. No sooner had she put her pyjamas on and tucked herself into the freshly made bed, than her flashbacks began to set in again. She saw a snippet of a bearded man at the top of a staircase looking down on her. He didn't speak to her but motioned for her to enter his bedroom. The man held a Kalashnikov across his broad shoulders. Dahlia felt herself breathing quickly, trying to forcefully exhale the poisonous memories. It had been Yasmine who had been violated, and yet Dahlia felt disabled as if she were the broken one.

Her recollections were like a tumour waiting to spread to every cell of her body and mind. Dahlia felt she would be too feeble to coexist with this malware inside her body. She thought that she'd never escape the spiral of worsening flashbacks, when suddenly she felt the hug Carys had given her before leaving. It had been gentle, undemanding and yet there was a magnetic force behind it that Dahlia could not ignore, and she yearned for more.

She fell asleep dreaming that she was on a trip with Carys. They were both mermaids, had escaped a shipwreck and landed on an unfamiliar island in the Pacific. Dahlia felt elated in her dream. She felt beautiful with her large breasts covered by long, red hair and seaweed tugging playfully at her ankles. Carys and her were far away from pirates with their menacing swords.

*

Dahlia was suddenly awakened by the shrill sound of the telephone on her bedside cabinet. She jolted and lay awake for a while, heart racing. Her throat felt parched. The receptionist reminded her that it was time to get up for her first therapy session after an early breakfast. Dahlia rubbed her eyes and washed and dressed quickly. She didn't want to disappoint her mother or Carys. They were both hoping it would help her.

Her brother Elias had just laughed at the prospect of her healing – to him, she was 'damaged' and western therapy would serve nothing other than to 'brainwash'. *A bit rich coming from him,* she thought, *given how quickly he had fallen to the coaxing words of ISIS.*

Dahlia had been told to wait for 'Mariam' outside room twelve and did so obediently. How long would she have to play the part of the dutiful woman adhering to her culture? Looking at other woman her age was an unsettling endeavour – her friends seemed to have outgrown the insecurities from their teens and twenties and were making families of their own by now. Yet at this moment in time, peevishly looking down this ridiculously clean corridor that resembled the kind of mental asylum that only existed on film sets, she felt that she had failed.

A middle-aged lady with dyed, dark hair slowly approached Dahlia. She was slightly smaller than her mother. Mariam had black, high heeled shoes on and a blue suit which reminded Dahlia of a blue river she used to walk past near Sinjar. Her eyes were almond-shaped and gentle, framed by a round face, unlike her mother's pointed one. There was a hint of curiosity mixed with professional formality in her look. Dahlia felt her neck muscles begin to tighten.

'Hello Dahlia. My name is Mariam. I was looking forward to meeting you.'

Dahlia was silent for a few seconds. Mariam nodded toward the room that had been allocated to them. 'Let's go inside. We have an hour together. What language do you want to talk in?'

'I'm afraid my Kurdish isn't good enough for that. What about English?'

'No need to be sorry, Dahlia. English is fine with me.' Mariam smiled.

Dahlia was wary of her slow movements. She followed Mariam into the small room. Her psychotherapist moved towards a black leather chair and Dahlia presumed the plain chair opposite her was for the client. Dahlia didn't like that word. She didn't want to be a patient or a victim. Either way, it was too late to leave now.

Mariam held her gaze for a moment, waiting for her to speak, she supposed. *Where do I even start?* But the lady looked on patiently and Dahlia felt quite safe in her presence. It made a change to the constant monologues of her mum, her dominant presence, her outbursts and drama that with every word left another dent in Dahlia. She felt that nothing she said would distress Mariam.

Dahlia tightened her lips and watched the slow and measured rising and falling of Mariam's chest. She realised suddenly that her anger was hiding feelings of wanting, longing for acceptance.

'My school friend Yasmine phoned me a few weeks ago. I failed her as a Peshmerga fighter and as a friend.' She buried her head in her hands. 'She was sold at a Sabaya Market. ISIS called her Girl Number Twenty-One. She lost her name and respectability. I kept mine.'

Mariam watched her patiently, then said, 'Your name is Dahlia. Do you know the symbolic meaning of the Dahlia flower?'

Dahlia shook her head.

'It means finding inner strength, remaining graceful and changing in a positive way.'

Dahlia's eyes welled up with tears. This woman with the soft brown eyes was acknowledging the pain Dahlia had been through. 'Yasmine kept making excuses when she was asked to slink into the four-poster bed of her captor… she told her ISIS husband that she had a migraine and that she had an STD.'

Mariam was observing her carefully. Except for Carys, Dahlia had never told anyone about this experience in such detail. Her mother had never wanted to know the details of Yasmine's captivity. Maybe it would be too much for her to bear. She licked her parched lips before she started speaking again.

'Yasmine's ISIS husband locked her up after a few days. And then, he made her have some check-ups with the female doctor in the compound. He found out that she had no STDs. He was thrilled with the fact that she was a virgin!'

She hesitated. Mariam waited for her to continue talking…

'One night, he pushed her towards a wall and told her to undress… she had worn the same clothes for the past few weeks and not showered, hoping she would stink so it would stop him from wanting to come near her. That night, he forced her into the shower and waited outside the *hammam*.'

Dahlia hesitated before she continued the story she had told Carys a few weeks ago. It was a burden only Carys and her psychotherapist would be able to bear.

'When she came out of the *hammam*, her husband hauled me into the bedroom and started fondling her breasts. She shuddered at the sight of his glazed, bloodshot eyes and pushed him back. He was bald and she couldn't pull his hair, so she slapped him. He booted her until she was too weak to run away. She dug her long fingernails into his wrists. He squealed and finally pushed her onto the bed. Then he tied her up with some ropes he had kept underneath the bed. She couldn't resist any longer…' *What would she have done if this had happened to her?*

Dahlia covered her face as she felt her tears escaping into the corners of her mouth. Mariam gave her some tissues on the side table and waited for Dahlia to stop crying.

Dahlia dabbed her eyes with the tissues. She felt compelled to speak about the ordeal she had been through.

'Yasmin said her captor looked like Humbaba, the monster who guarded the pine forest in the Epic of Gilgamesh. His face was as contorted as coiled intestines.'

She noticed Mariam blink twice, but she didn't say anything or look shocked. Dahlia felt the wailing of her younger self flooding her brain. She felt stuck in thick mud. *She needed the fluidity of water.* It would help her escape. She looked around the room. A picture of an old man sitting near a waterfall caught her eye. The bearded man was smoking a pipe and reminded her of her late father. He had taken her to the waterfall near their village when she was a toddler. She had squealed with laughter as a bleating goat had been splashed by the waterfall. Dahlia felt Mariam follow her gaze as she asked, 'Do you remember a time when you were happy?'

Dahlia replied in a low voice, 'When I was back home, before Yasmine was abducted. I felt alive.'

Mariam waited a few seconds, then asked, 'Is there a time when you feel alive now?'

Dahlia felt Mariam was able to walk in her shoes, feel her fatigue and her joy. She looked at the painting on the white wall and answered, 'Yes, when I'm painting my self-portraits.'

Mariam waited for her to elaborate on her feelings.

'Mariam, I love painting various shapes of my face, my body, my soul.'

Mariam's eyes were gleaming as she said quietly, 'My work is like your paintings, reframing, reshaping thoughts and feelings.'

Dahlia couldn't help smiling. It was odd how quickly a bond to another human being could take place. She enjoyed the analogies. Dahlia felt the solitude of the room, the inaudible peace that ascended on her and the non-judgemental eyes that followed her every word.

'Dahlia, would you like to listen to another tune, alongside the sad one?'

Dahlia crossed her arms. She tried to catch the expression in Mariam's eyes. There was no sarcasm in them. She thought she could hear the tinkling of water droplets when she met up with Carys. It was the sweetest tune.

'I feel happy when I'm with Carys.'

Dahlia scrutinised Mariam's face. It revealed a gentle curiosity. She decided it was safe to elaborate on her relationship to Carys.

'Carys is my other half, the optimistic, beautiful woman at my side.'

Mariam took a sip out of her thermos of tea and looked as if she was contemplating a deep issue,

'Hmm. Splitting Carys and yourself into good and bad. What makes you think you're not the beautiful, hopeful woman, deserving love from yourself?'

Dahlia sighed. How she wished she could be a gorgeous woman, deserving admiration and love. Mariam had already mentioned her name which signified a lovely flower. *Could it be that she saw something else in her that she herself had failed to see till now?* She kept quiet. Carys was still at her side, despite the meddling tendencies of her family. Carys would easily be able to find another woman to go out with. Yet she stayed with her. Dahlia realised suddenly that she was the one who didn't have enough confidence to love herself. She looked up at Mariam and said in a louder voice, 'Carys is my anchor.'

Mariam smiled and cocked her head. 'Your heartbeat is your anchor too.'

Dahlia doubted she had enough resources in herself to overcome the unsurmountable pain she felt when thinking of her past. Her feelings for Carys were littered with obstacles that appeared too heavy to push aside. She couldn't help feeling bewildered.

'I feel vulnerable, Mariam. My mother only sees one version of me, the obedient one.'

Dahlia massaged her temple as she waited for Mariam to reply.

'How would you like to reveal yourself to her, set boundaries, challenge her?'

Dahlia felt emboldened by this thought. She felt her eyes gleam with hope. 'There's going to be a Pride Parade in August.' She smiled inwardly and explained to Mariam that her time would come soon where she would disclose herself as never before. Meanwhile, thanks to Mariam, her healing journey had begun.

17

Carys had changed an on-call duty to join Dahlia in Germany. This had led to a row with Phil who had shouted at her, saying she was heartless to leave him alone to care for his widowed mother for a whole weekend. Carys had repeatedly brushed his gaslighting aside. With her away in Germany, he wouldn't be free to run off to his mistress – Yes, he could look after his own mother!

And now, here she and Dahlia were on an hour's train ride, travelling from Donaueschingen to Lake Constance. Carys turned to Dahlia as they got off the train.

'Dahlia, this was a great idea of yours to travel here to the Bodensee. Weren't the views of the pines and lush meadows on the way stunning?'

Dahlia nodded with her customary dreamy look about her. Carys hoped she was coping with her recent thought-provoking counselling. Some people felt worse before feeling better.

'I'm so happy you came, Carys. I wanted to show you the largest lake in Germany, the Bodensee or Lake Constance as you call it in English. There's a clear view of the Alps and semi tropical gardens flourish on Mainau, an island in the Lake…'

Carys touched her arm lightly, 'You do know that I only came for the apple strudel.'

Dahlia stopped walking and stared at her blankly.

'Actually, I almost wanted to get off the train when I saw the vineyards,' Carys relished in Dahlia's confused expression. *How attractive she looked with her flushed cheeks!*

Dahlia smiled and said, 'Ah, I see, one of your jokes. Well, we'll get some apple strudel later on. Let's first enjoy Niederburg, the neighbourhood of Constance.'

Carys looked around her. The city had a mediaeval charm about it, and she loved the winding alleys and half-timbered houses. Her beige Ugg boots made walking on the cobbled streets easier. She admired the blue Giesswein shoes Dahlia had bought in Donaueschingen. They were made from soft boiled Merino wool and Dahlia had told her how comfortable they were.

Dahlia tugged at Carys' sleeve and said, 'Let's have a traditional German or Austrian dish like Schnitzel, Knoedel and Spaetzle.'

Carys felt her mouth water. She wanted to walk quicker but they had already fallen into a comfortable stride together.

'You have to earn your dessert.' Dahlia said mischievously, her eyes lighting up.

Carys stopped and put her hands on either side of Dahlia's face. *Till now she had given Carys the impression that she was struggling to escape a straitjacket!* Could it be possible that the counselling was beginning to help her?

'Oh, I do like your cheekiness, Fraulein Dahlia Aziz!' She drew Dahlia closer to her. She buried her face in her neck and felt the slender collarbones. As she backed away, she said, 'And how can I earn my dessert, my lovely?'

'Hmm. A trip to the Island of Mainau would be one possibility. We could swim there.'

Carys frowned in mock reproof, 'I haven't grown webbed feet yet.'

Dahlia grinned, 'I heard the Island has beautiful tulips.'

'And 200 000 dahlias,' Carys said triumphantly, having read the brochure, 'Imagine all those dahlias bursting into colour.'

'Um, there's a butterfly garden too,' Dahlia said blushing.

'Well, I can't catch a butterfly, but I can try and entrap a Dahlia.'

Dahlia shook her head, but a smile crossed her face. She appeared to be more at ease with being teased. Carys felt a stir of pleasure as Dahlia's smile lingered. The underlying sadness of her expression vanished when she smiled and Carys had a glimpse of what Dahlia was holding back on, life and love. She felt like caressing that smooth skin, but would also nurse her scars, if she had any hidden ones.

They paused and watched each other, each of them weighing up what the other was thinking. There was a bite in the air. It was Dahlia who broke the silence.

'I can breathe with you.'

Carys nodded. Dahlia had obviously felt asphyxiated. If she ever had the chance, she would caress her gently, first her shoulders, then her lower back and finally her legs. One day, Dahlia would hopefully open up to her.

She turned to look at the glittering Lake Constance, nestled in the foothills of the Alps and straddling three countries – Germany, Austria and Switzerland. The international border passed through the middle of the lake. Carys wondered what nationality a baby would have if it were to be born in the middle of the lake. Dahlia had told her she would love to have a baby. She chuckled inwardly. *Boundaries on a lake and in their relationships* – were Dahlia and herself floating alongside or against each other?

The lake emanated a certain calm. But who could imagine

what undercurrents it was hiding? *Just like Dahlia, stillness on the outside and a storm on the inside.* Carys felt an irresistible pull as if a magnet was propelling her forward, towards this woman. It was difficult and complicated, and she didn't know where this friendship was leading to, maybe a relationship or a disappointment. But then again, how long did one have in this crazy, beautiful world? She had seen many patients die without having chased the dreams they had wanted to follow.

Suddenly, her cell phone vibrated. She muttered her apologies as she took the call. It was Phil.

'Hi Phil. Yes, I'm at Lake Constance with a friend.' She shuddered as Phil raised his voice.

'No, I'm not coming back earlier. You're perfectly capable of dealing with your mother yourself.' She ended the call frowning. Mothers! His mother, Dahlia's mother; all these dysfunctional families. At least she had been a loving mother to Brynn, reading him stories at night when he was a child, taking him to football and other hobbies, despite her time constraints.

'I'm so sorry, I'm causing you problems with your husband.' Dahlia's face was ashen.

'No darling, you keep me alive,' Carys said with alacrity.

Dahlia had a startled expression on her face. Carys let the sentence dangle for a while.

'You must know how I feel about you?'

Dahlia fidgeted with the lapels of her coat and replied, 'Maybe, but I don't want to cause the breakdown of a family.'

Carys held her gaze, 'Sometimes it's necessary to break down a family in order to build up a new one.' She wondered if there was a tear in Dahlia's eye. So, she pulled her closer, closed her eyes and felt the soft hair brush her cheek. Her body thrilled and her breath quickened. It was as if Dahlia's breathing had entered her and they had become one. Carys let her go gently and peered into her dark eyes. The pupils were dilated. *Was this in fear or arousal?* Hope was enough for the time being.

18

Dahlia clenched her fists in tense anticipation ahead of the meeting with her mother, that habitual knot in her stomach from their previous unfruitful encounter in Soho. This time, she had deployed Shirin as a buffer to their Cold War, a shield from her mother's inevitable criticism. She remembered how Shirin had only chuckled knowingly when Dahlia had plucked up the courage to 'come out' to her.

Henceforth she had trusted Shirin with the ins and outs of her blossoming relationship with Carys, confessed her excitement and her pragmatic fears of disappointment. She paused on that last word. *Disappointments for whom exactly, her mother or herself?* Dahlia walked through the shopping mall briskly, semi-nauseating at the indulgent clothes on display, remembering the rags Yasmine had to wear when under the roof of her ISIS husband.

She thought of Carys, and always the memory of her eyes, azure eyes evoking once more a boundless river seeping into the ocean. No need for the two of them to be boxed, cartooned or labelled in unrelenting plastic; as simplistic and pure as their relationship. Oh, if only her mother would share this perspective!

She sighed. It would be prudent to start the conversation with her mother about her experience of the counselling – a more neutral starting point than relationships, she thought sardonically. Dahlia approached the café and stopped to watch her mother before entering. She was staring at a young woman in a mini skirt with a tattoo of a sailor on her arm. Her mother had the usual look of aloof contempt on her face, ready to criticise any woman outside her self-constructed norm. Her mouth curled into an encouraging smile as she caught sight of Dahlia, no doubt keen for a fresh target. Dahlia wondered why Shirin was late. Anyway, there was no turning back now. Her mother waved at her. Dahlia felt an ache in the pit of her stomach.

She forced a smile and walked towards her mother's table.

'Hi Mum. How are you?'

'I'm fine. Just worrying about Elias and you. Family is the most important thing in life.'

Dahlia tried to gauge the expression on her mother's face. She was not so much relating to a fact, but wasn't she rather trying to convince herself that a blood family was worth more than any other relationship?

She sat down opposite her mother and smiled obediently after ordering orange juice and a fruit salad.

'How was your counselling?'

'My psychotherapist Mariam was very good. She didn't allow me to indulge in self-pity or wallow in hurt.' Dahlia looked at her mother hopefully, 'We went through methods of self-help together like meditation, self-journaling and yoga. Oh, and she asked me if I knew what the *ferman* was.'

Her mother shuddered, 'The ferman was like the Holocaust but against the Yazidis. In the past over a million Yazidis have been killed.'

Dahlia nodded, remembering the crimes on a hot day in August 2014, near the sacred mountain Sinjar where Yasmine and 7000 women and children had been abducted. She focussed on her sessions with her therapist Mariam. *She needed to calm down.*

'There was no psychotherapist for the Yazidis hundreds of years ago,' her mother said. and folded her serviette.

She added decisively. 'ISIS is just one example of our trauma. I'm sure you remember what Shirin told you about the massacres of Saddam Hussein in 1998 by poisonous gas.'

Dahlia nodded. Shirin had almost died and suffered from infertility after the poisonous attacks.

'This German funded project of treating abused Yazidi women is a very kind one. Some of the women who were treated wanted to return to Iraq. A few women committed suicide, but a lot of them decided to stay in Germany because they felt more accepted as women.'

'How could the ISIS soldiers mistreat the Yazidi without any remorse? Yasmine was my best friend. Why have women become things they can exchange in their eyes and gay men be thrown off rooftops only because they love another man? We cannot forget.'

Ghastly memories made her stomach churn and the only relief she had was when she 'pricked' her arms. She dug a nail into the back of her hand and picked up her glass of orange juice to take a few sips.

Dahlia wondered whether acknowledgement by international courts could offer atonement of the stress disorder Yasmine had been suffering from, a bitter retrospective justice, just like the Nuremberg trials had been. Yet institutional validation of that suffering was not all that she yearned at present. *Surely her emotions towards Carys were natural.* They should not be weighed down by shame or disgust. When she was with Carys, her feelings spanned the spectrum of pain, sorrow, anger, relief, pride and exhilaration.

Dahlia stirred her orange juice thoughtfully. She kept quiet for a few seconds, then in trepidation, made her first move. 'But you're right, I've been fortunate. The psychotherapy sessions were really helpful. I even had time to speak about my desires and… um… inclinations.'

Her mother straightened her posture. 'Your phantasies are not involved in the issue.'

'You're not listening to me, Mum. I don't want to keep talking about the trauma concerning my Yazidi friend Yasmine. Surely you've seen Eros's statue in Piccadilly Circus… !'

'Keep your voice down, Dahlia. People are turning around to look at us.'

Dahlia leaned across the table and looked at her mother wearily. 'Is that all you care about? Whether people accept us? I want you to look at me.'

Her mother looked startled. She clasped her hands.

'Maybe I haven't been clear enough, Mum, but that's because you won't hear me. I deserve to decide what's good for me and what isn't.' Dahlia couldn't mute herself anymore. Therapy had helped her understand the baggage that her own mother was encumbered by. She loved her mother but couldn't keep denying herself the joy of flying the nest, feeling the loving hands of another woman, *calling love by its name.*

Her mother genuinely looked flummoxed. 'I came all the way to this café to make up with you. Isn't that good enough?'

'Oh yes, I'm grateful, Mum. Thank you for coming to meet me. But your physical presence here isn't enough. I want you to listen to me, to what I want and need as an individual. I yearn for emotional warmth, someone to lean my head on, to share my anxieties and laughter with. I need a woman to be my oasis in the desert, my shining star in the universe, the person I turn to when I feel as weak as a crumpled daffodil.'

Dahlia was physically shaking with the shock waves of her own words of empowerment. The young couple at the neighbouring table had fallen silent and were unreservedly watching the spectacle enfold. Dahlia pressed her lips together. She had said enough for now. Her heart was beating faster, the knot in her stomach was getting tighter.

Her mother stared past her, a frozen look on her face. Then she suddenly smiled and waved at someone. 'Shirin, my dear friend, at last!' Her mother sounded desperate.

Dahlia turned around, relieved to hear Shirin's name. Then her heart skipped a beat. Oh no! The tall woman at Shirin's side was Carys. She was smiling confidently and looked stunning in her dark blue faux fur coat. Dahlia's mouth felt dry. What was Shirin thinking, to suddenly spring Carys on this preemptively strenuous negotiation with her mother? She had only told Shirin about Carys a few weeks ago, trusting she would be discreet about her revelations.

'How are you Shirin? We couldn't wait for you to arrive!' Her mother didn't wait for an answer as she nervously scrutinised the companion at Shirin's side. 'Is this lady your work friend?'

'You can ask your daughter that question.' Shirin winked at Dahlia, willing her to open up to her mother.

Dahlia's heart jittered as Carys watched her expectantly. Dahlia could hear her own breathing. She focussed on it, trying to blot out the outside noise and the situation she found herself in. 'Mum, Carys is… um… I think… Shirin's doctor,' she heard herself say in a low voice.

Carys glared at her, 'Having trouble with your memory? There's the little matter of you and me. What about *us?*' She turned to observe Dahlia's mother who peered at her suspiciously. 'Oh, I see, a woman partner for your daughter doesn't suit, Mrs Aziz. Maybe you would prefer a besuited man? Hmm, perhaps I should go and buy a dinner-jacket.' She waved her arm in the direction of the shopping centre.

Dahlia glanced at her mother who appeared perplexed and said, 'Am I in the wrong film or what?'

'Come on, Dahlia, look at me.' Carys said imploringly.

Dahlia reluctantly turned towards her. The fun went out of Carys' face, it flushed with anger: 'Do I have to pretend I'm here in some professional capacity, Dahlia? Maybe you should tell your mum that I'm your fairy Godmother!'

Dahlia flinched when her mother said, 'What's going on here? Sit down and explain! Isn't there enough space at the table?'

'No need to worry, Mrs Aziz.' Carys swayed her shoulders as if she was beginning to dance. 'I can sit and be straight at your table, and I can swing the other way! I know what you would prefer.'

Dahlia felt mortified. Bewilderment and fear ricocheted across her mother's face. A second of silence passed by agonisingly slowly. The neighbouring couple looked on, mesmerised; it was a free night's worth of entertainment for them, Dahlia's scathing inner voice couldn't help but remark.

'Dahlia, darling,' Carys said in a softer tone. 'Do you want to lie to yourself? My mother thought my left-handedness was abnormal just because it wasn't the norm; only ten per cent of the population is left-handed. It was referred to as my *sore* hand. Despite all tries to wean me off this perceived deviation, I'm still left-handed and am doing well without all the conditioning!'

Dahlia fidgeted in her chair while Carys continued in a

louder voice, 'What would we have missed without our left-handed Leonardo da Vinci, Marie Curie and Aristotle?'

Dahlia watched her mother quickly switch her cappuccino from the right hand to the left hand. She wouldn't have minded belonging to *that* group!

Carys turned to look at Dahlia's mother and said in a gruff voice, 'Are you afraid I'm going to corrupt your daughter and dive into a hot tub with her? Too late for that!'

The line had been crossed. Her mother gasped. Dahlia felt herself retreating. 'Carys, Mum doesn't know what you're talking about.'

'What the fuck!' she heard Carys say, 'she doesn't want to know! Is this your only purpose in life, to fit in with what other people want? Always being what others think you should be instead of being what you could be?'

Dahlia didn't dare look into Carys' eyes. *The smouldering fury would have killed her.* The dreams she had of 'coming out' with her evaporated into shapeless clouds.

The last thing Carys did before striding out of the café was to thrust an object onto the table. It was the wooden Welsh spoon with the traditional decoration of hearts, lock and wheel, the one she had given to Carys to carve her name on.

Dahlia's mother ran her hand through her well-groomed wavy hair and said, 'What an extraordinary woman! Probably deranged! Fancy flinging a spoon on the table like that and spoiling our mother-daughter get-together. And what was she talking about?'

She stared at Shirin for an explanation. Shirin shook her head, picked up the spoon and said in a loud voice, 'Hannah, when will you listen to what your daughter is trying to tell you?'

Dahlia winced as she watched her mother snatch the Welsh

love-spoon off Shirin.

'This ridiculous spoon should be a gift from a man, not a woman! Oh yes, Shirin, I think I understand what that woman was trying to say but I can't see how it concerns my daughter.'

Dahlia felt like sobbing. She was afraid of being torn, of floating or drowning in an ocean which knew no end! She picked at her arm with her long fingernail; it distracted her from the pain in her stomach whirling like a tornado with no space to turn to. She stood up, without looking at her mother, horrified by her own cowardice and Carys' justified rage and set off to walk towards Hackney Wick. Still canal water might cool her being which was full of bubbling anger.

19

After the dispute with her mother and Carys, Dahlia felt compelled to go to the British Museum again. She felt like she was entering Switzerland during the Second World War, a neutral territory! Complicated emotions weren't involved here.

She watched Jonathan pacing outside the Reading Room of the British Museum. Having been away for a few weeks, she felt listless with not having been able to talk to him, especially after the heated discussions with her mother. She felt like a toddler craving for her mum's love!

Her feelings for Jonathan were less complicated. She remembered the sadness in his blue eyes whenever they said goodbye to each other. They were framed by white eyelashes like reeds standing tall on a river. He never made crude jokes like her brother Elias.

Her friendship with Jonathan was bound by their love of Gilgamesh and the clay tablets; it bordered on being a transactional bond because she spoke Arabic and was able to help with translations from Arabic journals but he was in awe of her knowledge of Gilgamesh and she needed that overwhelming admiration after arguments with her mother! She walked towards Jonathan slowly, aware of the half-worried expression on her face.

The image of Carys flinging the Welsh love-spoon kept appearing. She brushed it aside. The soft hue of love would only lead to disappointment. The present was confusing. The museum was just the right place to travel back in time and witness the feelings of her ancestors thousands of years ago! Dahlia yearned to reassemble the ancient clay tablets and help Jonathan decode them.

He moved towards her. 'Are you here to hear the Ancients? Do you feel their souls stirring?'

'Well, I saw their treasures at the Pergamon Museum in Berlin last year. They themselves were sleeping. Must be old age.' She was surprised to catch herself joking with him. Jonathan made her feel light-hearted in a way that was not possible with her mother.

'We can't go to the Reading Room as we have to be quiet there. Let's go to the coffee-house across the road.'

Dahlia realised she had not yet met Jonathan anywhere except near his workplace. After entering the small café across the road from the Museum, they sat down and ordered their lunch.

'Jonathan, my heart feels heavy when I think that the Ishtar Gate and Processional Way have been taken out of my country and placed in the Pergamon Museum in Berlin. The Ishtar Gate is the most splendid gateway that penetrated Babylon's walls.'

Jonathan ran his hand through his hair like he usually did when frustrated or embarrassed. He said, 'We may have taken a few items of the Ancients, but we left big things like the Acropolis. It was too heavy to carry.'

Dahlia rolled her eyes and couldn't help smiling. 'At least 8000 treasures have been looted from the Iraq National Museum by Iraqis as well as people from other nationalities and are untraced till now. Many items have been stolen from archaeological sites in Nimrud and Babylon.'

'Yes. I heard that some artefacts were located and retrieved in surrounding countries such as Syria, Kuwait, Turkey and Iran.' Jonathan frowned. 'There was some confusion as to whether the British Museum had been involved in the lootings. But the Museum staff had only emptied cases of transportable goods and hidden them in secret storerooms before the war broke out.'

Dahlia enjoyed watching the apologetic look spread on Jonathan's face. She had never touched it. *It would feel soft*, she mused, scanning his face for scars or blemishes and seeing none. Her late father had had a tanned face with lots of wrinkles from being out in the fields, keeping an eye on the vegetables they grew. Jonathan had been watching her hands. She was glad she had cut her nails and admired Jonathan's unblemished hands. Her late father had involuntarily hurt her with his dry and rough-skinned hands.

Jonathan had started talking again. 'The Cultural Objects Offences Act of 2003 means that anyone trading in illicit objects faces up to seven years in prison,' he said in a low voice, almost sounding frightened and hesitated a few seconds before he added, 'I would think twice about taking anything out of Iraq without permission.'

Dahlia was surprised about the vague look on his face and touched his restless fingers as they tapped the tablet. She didn't want him to feel his work was illegal or unwanted.

'I know Jonathan. Don't worry. If you didn't preserve these objects they would be destroyed anyway.'

Jonathan heaved a sigh of relief as she brushed back a wisp of hair that had fallen into her eyes.

'I brought you something that may help with deciphering

the clay tablets.'

Jonathan opened the brown paper bag she offered him and smiled. In it he found something that looked like a bookmark. It had the cuneiform alphabet on it. He took her hand and squeezed it.

'This looks colourful, but I don't think it is quite that easy to decipher clay tablets with this small toolkit.'

Dahlia let out a laugh in agreement. Then she fell silent for a minute, contemplating her next words carefully.

'How would you feel if you had a new clay tablet of the Gilgamesh Epic to decode?'

She trailed off, watching him closely.

'I would feel like Alan Turing when he decoded signals during WWII. He had to bear all the oppression he faced as a gay man, yet he still managed to help us during the war.'

Dahlia felt her jaw muscles tighten. He watched her smiling. 'But I have friends who are gay, and homosexuality isn't a problem with me.'

'We could look for new clay tablets.' Dahlia said, relieved.

'How would *you* know where to look for them?' Jonathan looked puzzled, then said, half apologetically, 'My late wife was a primary school teacher. She was never interested in my work, clay tablets or my writing. Maybe I was married to the British Museum, not my wife.'

He cocked his head. 'She was too busy with our son Daniel. As a child, he stuttered for a long time. The speech and language therapist helped him overcome the impediment and advised psychotherapy. He didn't need a shrink, just toughening up!'

Dahlia put her cup of cappuccino down and said, 'I would love to meet him.' *Now, why did she feel she had something in common with him?*

Jonathan sat up in his chair, looking puzzled. 'Hmm..., I always wanted a son who was interested in playing football. Instead, Daniel honed an obsession with Jean-Paul Gaultier's fashion ideas, such as seductive sailor collections!'

'Not everyone has to be strong and masculine like John Wayne, my mother's favourite actor.'

'Well, if you don't mind a camp gait, I'll try and arrange a meeting. He may understand how important my work is if he meets you.'

Dahlia looked at him aghast.

'Sorry, I shouldn't keep mentioning my work in the British Museum. We were busy with pottery, copper and bronze in Britain while your civilisations were well in advance of ours.'

Dahlia relaxed and let out a chortle. 'Indeed, they were, curator, sir. I'm glad you're aware of it.'

She preferred the witty Jonathan, although she admired his intellect. Her father had been solemn and they had hardly laughed together. When Elias had caught a mouse in a jar, proudly presenting it to his father, his father had slapped him in the face and ordered him to kill it. It would eat the cheese they needed; he had told the crying boy. Elias had to go outside the house and pick up a boulder to throw at it.

Dahlia had looked away, but remembered the tears welling up in Elias' face. He had looked at his mother reproachfully. She had not stopped her husband from slapping him. Dahlia tried erasing that hurt look from her mind. She wondered if that was the reason Elias was full of disdain for her. *Had she failed to protect him from his father?*

She watched Jonathan run his fingers through his brown hair. It was thinning at the sides and grey strands were clearly visible. Nonetheless, his confident stride gave him a youthful look. She smiled as she observed him smoothing the crumpled bookmark gently.

Her father had never been interested in writing or books. She was surprised that her parents had been married for so long. It had been an arranged marriage. Some of her friends were content with their arranged marriages. She yearned for a deeper connection. Jonathan's eyes sparkled as he spoke about what he loved most.

'There were more than 600 cuneiform signs in the beginning. It's easier now, with twenty-six letters in the alphabet. There are only about seventy five people who can read cuneiform fluently!' Jonathan looked at his bookmark with Sumerian signs. 'This bookmark is strongly simplifying the alphabet,' he chortled.

Dahlia nodded her head in agreement, waiting for him to elaborate.

'At first, Dahlia, the signs were written from the top downwards, in boxes arranged from right to left.'

She touched his hand and said, 'Arabic is still written from right to left.'

Jonathan beamed at her and said, 'Your hand is lovely and warm.'

Her hands were not usually that warm, except when she was near Carys. *The fluttering inside her stomach,* she mused, *the expectant look in Carys' eyes.* Her childhood had been so different to hers.

Dahlia had been a quiet child. Weddings didn't seem to excite her, even when her friends were present. Elias had been a defiant boy. He had to be reminded about his chores, except when Dahlia was involved. Then he would willingly accompany her to the well to get water, smiling and singing on the way. She removed her hand. 'I was engrossed in your explanations. Go on…'

Of course.' He grinned. 'It was between 2400 and 1600 BCE that the method of writing gradually changed from left to right, in successive lines. By then, the shapes had lost their resemblance to pictures.'

Jonathan paused for a few seconds. She filled the silence as she said, 'You know a lot about the origins of writing.'

'I am intrigued by the ancestors. By the way, didn't you notice my longer hair? I try to fit in with the Ancients.'

Dahlia giggled. She was beginning to laugh more in his company. She noticed his brown suit looked creased; the trousers had not been ironed properly. Although his hair was thinning at the temples, the gleam in his eyes told her that he was still an active man. She wondered whether he had been with other women after his wife's death. She could see herself in his pupils, looking up at him expectantly.

She loved talking about the origins of writing and clay tablets and admired his intellect. Her ethnic origins made her more receptive to the culture of Babylonian writing. Whatever the reason, she felt entranced listening to him; it made her feel closer to her origins, more than her own mother!

'Dahlia, we offer some courses on clay tablets and cuneiform writing in the Museum. If you would like to attend, I could arrange that.'

'My mother thinks I'm more interested in the history of women.'

Jonathan laughed and put his cup down. 'You may be interested in both histories.' He winked at her. 'New pieces of the Gilgamesh Epic are appearing all the time. A fragment of Tablet XI, the Flood tablet, only came to light in the nineties.'

Her late father had talked about the Gilgamesh Epic and

his quest for immortality. She sighed. What use was immortality if life was full of violence and suffering? She was intrigued that a Westerner like Jonathan was just as moved by the Epic as people had been back home in Iraq. Maybe Jonathan was even more charmed by it.

As if reading her mind, Jonathan sat up and exclaimed, 'I'm helping to decipher the Epic of Gilgamesh.'

He was like a little boy excited about a new adventure he was going to undertake. 'Cuneiform clay tablets were used for over 3000 years, Dahlia. As we delve into deeper research of Gilgamesh, we'll uncover more about the epic. One day, the Epic will be complete, just like it was two thousand years ago!' He leaned forward in his chair with animated eyes.

Dahlia beamed and said, 'Imagine, it would be the discovery of the Millennium!' She was glad they shared a similar dream, wherever that would lead to. As they leaned in closer to continue their chat, she felt drawn by the smell of his aftershave. It reminded her of the Bergamot orange fruits they grew back home. She brought her mind to the present. 'Jonathan, when are you travelling to Iraq to find the missing clay tablets?'

He tilted his head to one side as if to tease her and said, 'You know very well that Iraq is in the middle of a civil war. It would be too dangerous to go there now.... as a civilian.'

It had been years since she had last visited her country. She didn't want to succumb to the images that kept invading her mind. She sighed and looked outside to see if the rain had stopped. It was still raining heavily. Jonathan followed her gaze.

'I'm afraid you'll have to stay here a bit longer. Women don't usually run away from me so quickly.'

Dahlia answered quickly, 'I'm still here because I love the

Gilgamesh Epic. I admire Gilgamesh for the maturity he achieves after so many setbacks.'

'Hmm. I need to take a leaf out of his book.'

Dahlia looked at Jonathan thoughtfully. Gilgamesh brought memories of a world before Christianity and Islam. Before the Yazidi religion. Before the Crusades and before ISIS, wars had still been waged about religions. People had been killed in the name of God. She shuddered. Instead of connecting people, religion had divided them. Stories such as the Gilgamesh Epic brought different communities together.

This epic was a thousand years older than Homer's Iliad. He had captivated the Greeks with stories of the Trojan War. But this was the oldest story in the world. The quest for immortality was embedded in the Epic. No doubt this wish would never die, no matter which generation thought about it.

'Dahlia, you look pensive.'

Dahlia touched the tip of Jonathan's hand and said, 'I was thinking of home, I mean back home with my relatives… or what remains of them.'

Jonathan squeezed her hand and said, 'It must be terrible. Have you got many relatives back home?'

Dahlias 's gaze took on a distant look as she replied, 'I have an uncle who survived Abu Ghraib prison, a few aunties and uncles, and traumatised cousins…'

'Are you able to contact them?'

'We ring them as often as we can, but the connection isn't always easy. I'm still afraid of ISIS.' Jonathan pushed his chair back abruptly as he said, 'Those barbaric ISIS terrorists!'

Dahlia moved closer to him and beckoned him to keep quiet.

'Why am I supposed to keep quiet?' Jonathan protested.

'They're the criminals. Their day will come. Mark my words. No genocide has succeeded in wiping out a whole ethnicity.'

Dahlia watched his pale skin take on a purple-reddish tone. Silence ensued. He took a few sips of his tea and faced her again. 'Sorry about the outburst. I care about you and I don't want to see you hurt.'

She stood up quietly and said, 'Jonathan. You mustn't raise your voice like that. I still don't feel safe from ISIS. Not even here, in this country.'

Jonathan got up from his chair and took her hand as he said, 'The bastards would have to get past me first.'

She took her hand away as she scanned the dining area quickly. 'You're not making it easy for me, Jonathan. I think I should leave now.'

Jonathan reached out for her hand again and said, 'Listen, Dahlia, I'm sorry. I've been more keyed up than usual; I've been stressed with my son Daniel lately. He's a soldier.' Jonathan's face was now ashen.

She looked into his pain-filled eyes and hesitated. How she longed to have someone to help her understand her own mother.

'I hope my son will never have to kill someone while he's a soldier… Even more so, I hope he will not be tortured himself.' Jonathan looked down at the round table at which they'd been seated at and put his arms on it to steady himself.

Dahlia realised that if Jonathan lost his son, he would have no one left from his immediate family. She remembered how he had told her his wife had died a few years ago. 'I'd like to meet Daniel and I'll help where I can, Jonathan.' She took out a ten pound note out of her black purse and put it on the table for the waiter. Jonathan pushed the crumpled note back into her hand.

'I need to go now.' She smiled wryly. She stood up and was about to turn around and leave when her gaze fell upon a pair of polished black shoes. Her heart missed a beat. They were her brother's. Even when he had very little money, he would make sure the shoes were immaculate. She looked up as he waited behind her.

'Is this what you call your research?' A stern voice asked.

Dahlia saw the disdain in her brother's eyes. 'I was just about to come to the entrance, Elias.'

She felt her mouth drying up. Without looking at Jonathan, she faced her brother and said,

'This gentleman is Jonathan, Elias. We became acquainted at the British Museum where he's writing a book on Gilgamesh. He's also interested in the cuneiform tablets that originated in our very own country, Elias!'

She turned to Jonathan, 'This is my brother, Elias.'

Elias grunted in disbelief as he took in Jonathan's placid presence. 'We don't need him or any other British person to tell us about our history.'

Dahlia looked into Elias' eyes which were ablaze with anger and hurt. She tried to put her arm on his shoulder to pacify him, but he pushed it away.

Jonathan intervened, 'Now look here son, don't speak to your sister like that!'

'Who are you to talk to me that way? I'm not your son. I know her better than you and trust me, meeting up with some old, white man is the last thing she needs right now.'

Elias stepped closer to Jonathan. He was slightly smaller than him but not as trim. 'She's my sister. We're from the same country, a place you and your army bombarded senselessly.'

Dahlia felt her pulse quicken. She tried to walk past Elias.

But he blocked her way.

'The West is a violent disease.' He spat his words out. 'Do you know what the US women did to my Muslim brothers during the Iraqi invasion? Our men were forced onto boxes that had electrical wires connected all over their bodies. They were threatened with electrocution if they fell off the box.'

Jonathan kept quiet as Elias spat out the following words: 'We weren't the terrorists during the Iraq invasion. Your soldiers were acting against the Geneva Convention.'

It became clear to Dahlia that she could never tell Elias that Jonathan's son was a soldier. She glanced at Jonathan; his gentle nature was accentuated in the presence of fiery Elias. Was he responsible for his country's actions? Were they not all born into their communities?

Jonathan said in a measured tone, 'I'm sorry you feel this way. I had no involvement with the war – I'm not too political, just an archaeologist and a humanist.' Dahlia was grateful for his careful choice of words. He wasn't a confrontational man. She felt safe in his company.

Elias was not to be stopped. 'They made our prisoners crawl around the floor naked whilst riding them like donkeys. They pissed on one of my ISIS friends and the guard threw acid on his leg wound!'

Jonathan had paled. Dahlia tried to hold Elias' arm again. A young couple on the next table had stood up to leave, shaking their heads in disbelief.

Jonathan looked anxious but his firm voice said quietly, 'These torturers have been punished. This is what we do in a democratic country.'

Elias snorted. 'Even *women* paraded behind the naked prisoners and one held a dog leash around the neck of one of them. The men were paraded around like circus animals.

Sickening women.'

Jonathan held his gaze and replied that all violence was disgusting including the rape of innocent Yazidi women. He added, 'The American and British soldiers were supposed to use reasonable interrogation techniques. They shouldn't have tried waterboarding or…'

Elias brought his fist down on their table and said, 'Reasonable control techniques? They treated our soldiers like vermin. They acted like a bunch of Nazis.'

Dahlia felt herself freeze in her position. Jonathan would hate this analogy. She felt her temples beginning to throb.

Elias was oblivious to anyone else in his surroundings, just like he always was when wrapped up in his own anger.

'And what about the Yazidi women?' Jonathan interposed. 'You don't think the Yazidi women felt humiliated when they were raped?'

Elias jumped forward and grabbed hold of Jonathan's jacket as he hissed, 'Don't mention the Yazidi nation. You have done nothing to help them.'

Dahlia moved towards the two men to separate them. Elias was about to punch Jonathan, but he dodged him. A waiter came running towards them. Dahlia heard a plate crashing.

Elias let go of Jonathan's tunic just as the waiter arrived at their table. He decided to run away but not before shouting at Jonathan, 'You're not Lawrence of Arabia. *Kefir.*'

Dahlia put her hand to her mouth to stop herself from screaming. Jonathan was sweating. When the young waiter arrived, he looked uneasily at Jonathan and her, 'Is anyone hurt?' She looked at Jonathan imploringly. She didn't want her brother implicated in anything. Elias was in enough trouble trying to keep his job as a postman and he had few friends.

She touched Jonathan's tunic gingerly. He frowned and told the waiter that it was a family dispute which would be resolved in due course.

The waiter looked at him in disbelief. Jonathan tried smiling to keep the waiter away and said the boy had been annoyed about his sister's new friend. Dahlia pressed her lips together. She was grateful that Jonathan was playing down the incident. Elias was suffering and needed help. He would surely realise that. She wiped her forehead with a tissue from her handbag.

Dahlia turned her attention to Jonathan who had sat down again. He asked the frowning waiter for a glass of water as she took her place next to him. He kept quiet till the waiter walked off again, before saying, 'It can't go on like this, Dahlia. I'll lose my job if Elias continues to harass me here.'

She took her hands off the table. 'Oh, Jonathan! Is that all you care about?' Her eyes welled up with tears again.

Jonathan hesitated. 'Of course not. I...'

Dahlia wondered what he was going to say. *Would he brush aside their delicate relationship?* She didn't want to lose her brother, but she didn't want to lose Jonathan either. She took a deep breath.

'Please excuse me, Jonathan. I need to leave.'

Jonathan looked as if his life had been drained out of him. She walked towards the stairway. When she looked back, she saw that Jonathan had his hands cupped around his face and was massaging his temples.

20

It had been a few weeks since she had heard from Jonathan. She kept thinking about the confrontation with Elias and how Jonathan had felt threatened. Jonathan had phoned Dahlia to clear the air and had suggested a meeting with Daniel who would need some help with Arabic as he was probably going abroad.

Jonathan had told her that he felt he was straying into delicate terrain every time he met up with him. The lad never seemed happy with himself and Jonathan couldn't quite fathom what he needed from him. He had topped up his army wage, helped him to buy a car and paid the deposit for his flat in Hackney, amongst his many other gifts of money.

She felt a warm wave engulf her. Daniel needed shielding, like herself. She would try to be like a good sister. Hmm, *would her loyalties have to lie with her brother Elias?* He belonged to her blood family as her mother kept telling her!

Jonathan was standing outside the Reading Room in the British Museum, hands in his pockets, trying hard to look relaxed. Daniel waved his hand elaborately as he approached his father. Jonathan's eyes fell upon his son's old moccasins and he winced. Thin arms grasped him hungrily.

'I see you're punctual for a change.'

Daniel's arms slackened. 'Dad! What a warm welcome.'

His eyes narrowed. 'It was you who asked to meet up here!'

Jonathan nodded his head slowly. 'Yes. But not in those moccasins.'

Daniel raised his eyebrows. 'But why?'

The curves in Jonathan's mouth straightened. 'They're old and…' Dahlia took in Daniel's slender fingers lying loosely at his side. They appeared too long. His arms were like those of an octopus, hungry and lonely.

Daniel said, 'The moccasins are soft, and they match my blue jeans. It's nice to feel some comfort, even if it is just from an old pair of jeans if it can't be a human.'

Jonathan stared at his son. This meeting was not starting off well, Dahlia thought frowning.

'You'll have to get used to the discomfort, son. You survived the Iraqi invasion. That must have taught you to wear a uniform and how to be a man.'

Daniel looked around the indoor courtyard of the Museum and his tight jaw-muscles relaxed suddenly as he caught sight of her. His jeans were too slack for him and a button was missing from his shirt. He was clean shaven, and his fingers were long and thin. The rucksack he was carrying appeared to drag him down. *Was this a man who had been to war?* She smiled at him.

'Your father wanted me to meet you.'

'Daniel. This is Dahlia. She's helping me write a book. We're doing some research for it here. She's from Iraq. I thought you'd have something in common.'

Dahlia and Daniel caught each other's eyes and laughed out loud.

Jonathan looked taken aback by their amusement. Dahlia patted Jonathan on the shoulder and said, 'Just because Daniel went to Iraq as a soldier, it doesn't mean we're soulmates.'

Jonathan winced as Daniel shook her hand with carefree pleasure. Dahlia added quickly, 'But, from the look of him, I do think Daniel could benefit from some good Kurdish cooking.'

Daniel patted his tummy and smiled at Dahlia.

Jonathan nudged Daniel and said, 'Let's go to the restaurant upstairs and start with tea, or *Chai* as you would say in Iraq.'

'Is this an offer or an order?' Daniel responded, raising his voice to match his father's.

'Whatever your gentle soul needs at the moment.'

Daniel looked as if he couldn't make out whether his father's remark was meant as sarcasm or was merely neutral.

Jonathan added, 'The Great Court we are standing in is a realisation of the Enlightenment ideals. Did you both know the British Museum is more than 250 years old?'

Daniel winked at Dahlia and whispered, 'Sorry if this sounds like a headmaster speaking. He does this with me too.'

She smiled and replied, 'Don't worry. We can stop him when it gets out of proportion.' Jonathan had already continued speaking.

'To our left is the pedestrian bridge connecting our restaurant to the galleries of the North Wing which consists of the Eastern civilisation findings.'

'Connecting East to West.' Dahlia heard herself say aloud.

'Not divisive like ISIS.' Jonathan said looking pensive. Dahlia kept quiet and stared into space.

'Sorry, Dahlia. I didn't mean to upset you or remind you of anything unpleasant.'

'Well, you did, Dad. As always.' Daniel scowled at his father.

Jonathan took Dahlia's hand and squeezed it. 'Let me invite you to some refreshments.'

She nodded her head as they moved towards the restaurant, which was housed in the upper level on the right-hand side of the bridge. She looked up at the geometrical roof. It looked stunning, fragile and powerful at the same time. *Somehow, the image seemed to merge, reflecting Jonathan.*

They sat down and looked at the menu. Jonathan said, 'The £100 million project to restore the Courtyard opened in December 2000 and took just two and a half years to complete.'

'That's enough, Dad!' Daniel threw his menu back on the table, not knowing whether to laugh or to cry.

'Ah, yes. But you must know that the Great Court is the largest covered courtyard in Europe.'

Daniel picked up his father's menu and put it back into his hands. 'Tea-time, dad.'

'Okay. Okay…', Jonathan answered. 'Dahlia, I'd recommend the apple tart.'

Dahlia let out a laugh and decided it would be easier to talk to Daniel on this occasion.

'When did you decide to join the army?'

'Actually, Dahlia, I wanted to be an artist or a musician. But my father didn't think it was manly enough.'

Jonathan, who was sipping his tea, put his cup down and said, 'Few artists earn enough to live on.'

Dahlia turned towards Daniel. 'What type of art are you interested in?'

'I love Impressionism even though they may not be as old as the Ancients that dad worships.'

He grinned at his father briefly. 'But they're just as compelling for me, if not more.' He added, 'Hippocrates said Art is long, life is short.'

Dahlia watched Daniel as he scowled at his father. 'Daniel,' she said quickly, 'I've been to some exhibitions recently. Monet is my favourite impressionist.'

Jonathan mumbled, 'Let's talk about my next lecture on Iraq. I have a few students who may quiz me on that.'

Dahlia leaned back on her chair and took a deep breath. 'Okay Jonathan, hardly tea-time talk but we all knew that the fall of the dictator Saddam Hussain didn't mean democracy would come smoothly. We're pleased that Saddam Hussein and his Baath Party have been beaten. But the De-Baathification will take a long time because of Al -Qaeda and ISIS.'

'Our boys will hunt down the remaining insurgents.' Jonathan patted Daniel's shoulder. Daniel winced and moved his shoulder away.

Dahlia said, 'It wasn't only Saddam Hussain who was responsible for mass murders, you know. His cousin, General Ali Hassan Al Majid, got his nickname, 'Chemical Ali', from the gas attacks he mounted on the Kurds in 1988. They have found mass graves from these killings and... General Ali used to entertain party guests with a game that involved shooting prisoners tied to metal posts in their gardens.'

Daniel cringed and said, 'I hope these criminals will be tried in court, just as the Nazi criminals were.' He clenched his fist. Dahlia sipped her tea before continuing. 'So yes, we're glad that Saddam Hussain was caught and killed and then the UN sanctions were lifted. But, before the fall of Saddam Hussain, 5000-6000 children died each month as a result of UN sanctions. This is what UNICEF estimated.'

'Oh God, it's awful in the telling,' Jonathan said. 'And we know that without the English army, children would still be dying.' He took his glasses off to clean them and said, 'Well now we need to show the remaining insurgents that we're in control.'

'Yes. But are you in control?' Dahlia asked.

Jonathan remained silent. Dahlia answered her own question. 'Iraq is caught between vicious insurgency and…'

'Previous unloved occupation.' Daniel added. 'My job may be to search landmines in Iraq. I won't have anything to do with fighting Iraqis.'

She patted his hand. 'It's okay, Daniel. You don't have to defend yourself to me.

I'm just worried about you going there.'

'Well, nice to know that someone is worried about me,' Daniel said with a wry smile.

'I'm a journalist,' she told Daniel, 'I may go back to Iraq.' Her voice trailed off. Jonathan leaned in towards her and held her hand. 'To be seen writing there would be dangerous. Journalists are kidnapped and if their ransom isn't paid, they're killed.'

Daniel nodded in agreement., 'There may still be some insurgents left in the area.'

She sighed. They were so far away from Iraq and yet they were involved in its problems, politically and personally. *Would there ever be peace?*

Jonathan said, 'Tell me about the current tensions between Sunni Muslims and Shi'a Muslims, Dahlia.'

'Oh dear, it's such a bitter story. Tensions between them have existed since the beginning of the Islamic Era. The Baath party was based mainly on the powerful Sunni Arab minority at a cost to both the majority Shi'a Arab community and the Sunni Kurds.' She frowned. 'All because of a political dispute in the seventh century A.C.E. over who deserved to be the Prophet Mohammad's successor or Caliph. Both communities were Arab, but they mistrusted each other.' Daniel appeared to be waiting for some more clarification.

'The Sunni Arabs represent less than twenty per cent of the total population, while the Shi'a Arabs represent about fifty five per cent. The rest are mostly Sunni Kurds.' Dahlia added.

Jonathan turned to his son and said, 'Some Sunnis had closer ties to the British than the Shi'a, at the time of the Arab Revolt in the desert. Their forces were strengthened by T.E. Lawrence, better known as Lawrence of Arabia.'

Daniel looked surprised at the mention of Lawrence. Jonathan noticed this and said, 'Lawrence spoke Arabic. So, there's still time for you to learn, Daniel.'

Daniel snarled, 'You always find fault with me, dad. I'm fed up with your reprimanding me. It seems I can never live up to what you'd like me to be.'

Jonathan held up his hand involuntarily, but Daniel hadn't finished speaking, 'For your information, Lawrence preferred men. How about that Dad? Did you know he was homosexual? Do you still want to hero-worship him? Or are you going to drop your respect for him like a hot potato?'

Jonathan turned to Dahlia, looking embarrassed. He heard Dahlia's voice as if from afar, saying, 'Jonathan, as far as I know, Lawrence of Arabia spoke very little Arabic. But he got by.'

She smiled at Daniel and said, 'Shall we learn a bit of Arabic together?' She watched Daniel's muscles relax and his mouth curl upwards, in a half-smile.

'Hannah, I'd love to learn a bit of Arabic with you. I may need it if I'm sent back to Iraq.'

She nodded her head. 'We'll do that, Daniel.' She didn't want to remember the ordeals she had been through in Iraq, but the Arabic language was not at fault. Language was just a vessel but, in some instances, humans used it as a weapon. Dahlia wanted to start using it with love. She squeezed

Daniel's hand and they smiled at each other. Jonathan called the waiter to pay the bill. She got up to leave.

Jonathan stood up with her and said, 'I'll see you again, won't I Dahlia?'

She looked at Daniel and said, 'I did say I would teach Daniel a few words in Arabic.'

Jonathan heaved a sigh of relief and Daniel got up to go with her. They had already formed a bond and she felt they both yearned for a family, other than their own one, a water family – a fluid family.

21

Dahlia looked out of her sitting room window. She could see the Olympic Stadium and Canary Wharf skyline. Shirin had wondered why Dahlia would want to leave this safe area. Dahlia felt she had no choice. A magnet was pulling her towards her homeland and danger.

She had told her boss at BBC Headquarters that she would write some articles on how the dictatorship of Saddam had heralded a new era once he was beaten. In April 2003, the pictures on television had shown jubilant crowds in the streets watching the toppling of Saddam's giant statue while Firdouz Square in the heart of Baghdad had been surrounded by tanks. Waving protesters shouted abuse at the fifty-foot statue of Saddam. Many months later, his own people had found him hiding in a hole in the ground.

Saddam had instilled fear in his people, and it was deeply rooted. His regime, the Baath Regime of Pan Arabism, employed power and fear to drive its ideology.

ISIS had formed itself after the Americans had left Iraq. It was now the extended arm of Al-Qaeda. Democracy? Dahlia pondered on the flavour of the word and licked her lips involuntarily. The word tasted like a delicacy which would only be served in the best restaurants. If it had a colour, it would be a luscious green, like the grass one would find near wells, bluish-green grass like the paintings of the impressionists her mother loved.

Dahlia sighed. She would need to distance herself from her mother for a while. They were arguing more often than before. She loved her mother but felt her body dismembered almost every time they met up. Carys made her feel whole and energy would flow to the tips of her fingers, through her body and hips till the toes. Finally, Dahlia had summoned enough courage to ask Carys if she would come with her to Iraq for a few weeks but sadly had not received an answer yet. Perhaps Carys was waiting for the hospital management to agree to a sabbatical. It would get her away from her distressing court case.

Dahlia got up from her chair which overlooked the Westfield shopping centre, to look for the self-portrait she had drawn a few days previously. She pushed aside the stack of clothes lying on the dark laminate flooring in the sitting room.

She found the portrait in the kitchen on top of her microwave and picked it up. A pair of questioning eyes peered at her. The dark shades underneath her eyes made her look older. She could use eyeshadow and foundation to look more youthful.

How could Carys have been interested in someone as complicated as herself? But since the therapy, she was beginning to think kindlier of her body. She walked tall and wore more colourful clothes. She bought a dark green dress to complement her slim figure.

For her birthday, her mother had given her a glossy red Isfahan carpet of soft cork wool for her sitting room. It had a bird and floral motif and a central medallion surrounded by red flowers on an ivory background. Dahlia liked stretching out on the smooth carpet whenever she felt lonely. She loved its silk highlights. Carys had silky hair.

Dahlia flung the portrait aside and walked to the phone which stood on her television table. She dialled Carys' number.

'Hi Dahlia. What's up honey?'

No wonder she sounded worried, Dahlia thought. It had been two weeks since she had contacted Carys. Not that she hadn't wanted to, but she needed the solitude to work out her feelings. She felt loveable and more attractive, although at the same time somewhat confused. She didn't want to label her feelings, but she realised she wanted to be near Carys. She was drawing more portraits since meeting her, felt more alive and her portraits were becoming more colourful. Black was being used less frequently. The portraits transformed and illuminated her face from different angles, just as writers would do in their stories.

'Hi Carys. I'm so sorry about the episode in the café with my mother. I just wasn't ready for a confrontation yet. Shirin didn't tell me you were coming. I wasn't prepared to introduce you to my mother yet.

There was silence at the other end. 'Ok, Dahlia. Maybe I was coming on too strong. We can go slowly if you want.'

'Thank you, Carys. I'm not as brave as you yet. What about going abroad for a while?'

'Dahlia, you must be joking. Do you still want to travel to Iraq? Anyway, you haven't even got my up-to-date CV. Did the BBC give you a bullet-proof vest?'

Dahlia chuckled. 'I'm not ready to go to Sinjar and my greatest fear yet, but Al Yarmouk Hospital in Baghdad needs doctors badly and would be thrilled to get one from Britain.'

'Um… I'm still thinking about it. Give me a week or two.'

Dahlia smiled. Anticipation was enough for now. She would write an article about the dire situation in Baghdad which would make her bosses and her mother happy. It would give her time to contemplate whether afterwards she could go back to Yasmine's place of torture and trauma in Sinjar.

A trip to Baghdad, which was further away from Sinjar where ISIS still roamed, might help her to heal and enable her to observe Carys from a closer and more intimate angle. There would be some danger in Baghdad which would lead to tension. She felt she was becoming addicted to danger. *Would she and Carys be able to share strain and possible trauma?*

Family, politics, spirituality. What or who could be trusted?

22

Elias stroked his beard. It reminded him of his nom-de-guerre, Abu Farooq. Oh, how he had relished slinging his Kalashnikov on his left shoulder, checking how many bullets he had left in it and most of all, shooting the enemy!

He let out a chuckle when he thought of the catholic priest who had been forced to help build bombs for them. Enough with the pitiful crusades. The Jihadis would prevail. The caliphate would rejoice, if not now in Raqqa, then amongst the Infidels in Britain.

He eyed London Bridge from the shore where he was standing and wondered why he had targeted it amongst all the bridges in London.

'London Bridge is falling down, falling down

London Bridge is falling down, falling down

My Fair Lady.'

Elias scowled. There was no Fair Lady. Ladies were not trustworthy. Women were like cattle. You had to show them the way to live otherwise they would get lost. A man would give a woman a home, and all the other men would keep away from her out of respect. Dahlia would dress more modestly after being married. No one else would get a glimpse at her full breasts. They had been overflowing and too inviting.

He was waiting for Dahlia to arrive. She was half an hour

late and he was feeling the cold air. He tapped his foot impatiently on the asphalt.

'Hi Elias, sorry I'm late,' Dahlia said, as she came up to him. 'Work kept me. But never mind, it counts as overtime.'

She kissed him lightly on his cheek. He looked at her tight raincoat tied at the waist. Her jeans were also too close-fitting. She should be dressed more modestly. He loved the smell of her perfume, always had. She didn't know about his obsession with her perfume.

'Dahlia, if you had a man to protect you, the BBC wouldn't take advantage of you this way.'

Dahlia sighed. Elias raised his voice and said, 'The BBC doesn't release impartial news about the Muslim world; Pakistan, Uzbekistan, Afghanistan, Kurdistan, they're all vilified.'

Dalia scanned London Bridge.

'Look how the Mongols massacred Baghdad. Dijla turned red with the blood of the Muslims.'

Elias used the Arabic word for the Tigris River, Dijla. He had told Dahlia that he would refuse to use Westernised words as much as he could.

Elias raised his fists as he asked where the news was mentioned then. Dahlia looked taken aback. 'Elias. We're not in the Middle Ages! That was hundreds of years ago and Al Jazeera was not present then.'

Elias bared his white teeth. He hated it when she made fun of him. Disloyal, disobedient Dahlia. She was greedy and never put aside two and a half per cent of her income for zakat like he did. Shame on her. Men needed to lead women. Men had a purpose in life.

Women talked without waiting for a response, just for the sake of talking, especially in the West. Dahlia never read the Qur'an. Elias would teach her all about the Qur'an and the

Hadiths if she gave him time. But she never did.

It was that woman Carys who kept her away from him, he was sure. Carys with her white supremacy.

He would teach them both a lesson. But he would have to plan carefully. Dahlia was simple and gullible, but Carys was sly and arrogant. She forced his sister to be more English than the English.

He smiled as he glanced at London Bridge again. He would bide his time, do his research. Then he would make his move, before Christmas. That would be the best time. Elias turned to look at his sister who seemed puzzled and somewhat troubled.

'Say it now and be saved,' he said. 'There is no God but God. Those who follow the last prophet serve in the army of the lord. Declare the truth and be heard – there is no God but God. There is no God but God.'

Elias felt his chest expand, and his banging heartbeat. He thought of his suffering brothers back in Iraq, stripped of their natural rights, of fair hearings when in captivity. The shameful orange jumpsuits they had to wear and the torture – the waterboarding and drowning. The humiliation of his brothers when their wives ran away.

'Dahlia,' his voice was loud, 'in our caliphate there was no difference between rich and poor, between black and white.'

Dahlia recoiled as he tried to hold her arm. 'What about women?' she retorted, 'was there no difference between men and women?'

Elias pulled his arm back. 'Both had the same amount to eat! They could access the same doctors and go to the same lessons in school.'

Dahlia took a step back. Elias realised that she couldn't move any further. She had hit the railing. He had her where he wanted her. She needed to listen, to comprehend that there was no other way. He stepped towards her, breathing heavily. He would give her the respect and dignity a woman needed. He would be her protector. He pinned her against the railing and tried to embrace her. Dahlia's eyes widened, with a mixture of fear and disgust.

Elias hoped there might be love behind his sister's expression of repulsion.

'I'm your brother, aren't I? We're bound together by blood. No one can take that away from us, least of all that arrogant Carys bitch.'

Dahlia pushed him away. She looked horrified.

'*Stachffarallah*, Dahlia, are you thinking of someone else?' Elias snapped. 'You can't kiss your brother because you are dreaming of someone else?'

Elias felt his rage rising as she tried to push past him. The expression in her face had changed to anger and determination. He liked that. Her anger emboldened him. He would straighten her ideas out.

'What are you going to tell mum dammit? That you prefer a white prostitute to a man?'

Dahlia pushed him back as she cried out, 'You know very well which one of us has used prostitutes before.'

Elias felt his jaw tighten. She had no respect for him or his brothers back home. He was trying to uphold her reputation, her respect. Where was her gratitude?

She ran past him, while he was shouting at her. 'Don't worry! I'll find you and that fucking Carys.' He didn't care when he saw passers-by stop Dahlia to ask if she was okay.

Once again, he looked back at London Bridge and smiled a calculating smile. Yes. He would do his research. He would be patient.

23

Dahlia had told Carys she wanted to meet her in Borough Market on the Southern end of London Bridge. It was high time to find out whether Carys was willing to go to Iraq with her or not.

She loved markets. The previous meeting with her mother in Spitalfields had not resolved any issues. She had, however, felt at home with all the stalls selling fruits, cheese and meat just like in Iraq. Those were happy times. She walked towards the arranged meeting point.

Dahlia stopped at a cake stall; she eyed the various types of cake, chocolate brownies, carrot cakes, fruit cakes. She missed the Baklava from home. Her mouth filled with saliva as she thought of the pastry made of layers of filo filled with chopped nuts and sweetened with syrup or honey.

She thought of Carys, the way she stirred her cappuccino a few times and scooped up the froth with her teaspoon before licking it slowly. Everything Carys did was slow and insightful. There were hardly any reckless movements like her own. Carys was at peace with herself. *Oh my God, I hope this doesn't change after being with me,* she mused. Dahlia had only known her for a few months and yet she was sharing thoughts with her in a way that she hadn't with anyone else till now.

'*Bore da.*'

A boisterous voice caused her to turn around abruptly. She smiled when she saw Carys who was wearing black jeans and a paisley-print blouse with a teardrop-shaped motif which complemented her slim waistline. Wisps of hair were flying into her round face.

'Well, aren't you going to answer?'

'Bore da.' Dahlia answered, proud that she knew this Welsh expression.

'How did you know it meant 'good morning'?' Carys smiled, revealing her dimples.

'I've been googling some Welsh expressions.' Dahlia blushed. She didn't want Carys to know how much she had been thinking of her.

'Let's form the Welsh-Kurdish alliance.' Carys took Dahlia's hand and squeezed it. *Was this a reflex or pre-planned?* She returned the squeeze. They strolled through the maze of narrow passageways of the oldest market in London, which was not too busy as it was early on this Wednesday morning.

Coconut pancakes, duck wraps, various spices and products from plantations in Kerala, farms in Mauritius and from Kashmir were on display. Dahlia felt Carys was leading the way to somewhere slowly and she was following willingly. They wandered into a nearby Starbucks and Dahlia was happy that it was half empty. They sat near the window overlooking some food stalls. Carys ordered her usual cappuccino and a croissant. Dahlia opted for a filtered coffee.

'How did you manage to get away from work?' Dahlia wanted to know.

'I've taken a day off to prepare my yearly medical appraisal portfolio. So, tell me, how are you?'

Dahlia shifted in her chair and took a sip of her coffee before answering. 'I'm well but I had an unpleasant meeting with Elias a few days ago.'

'Does he still want to play Guy Fawkes and blow up the houses of parliament?' Carys took a bite of her croissant and chewed it slowly.

Dahlia froze for a second, conflicted. Carys' melodramatic words cut below the surface as Dahlia prepared herself for what she had to say next.

'My mother told me Elias was asking her to buy acid.'

'What?'

'Some sulphuric or nitric acid.' She muttered. 'I don't know anymore…'

Carys' cup clattered onto the table and she shot Dahlia a look of concern, mixed with fear.

'Dahlia, do you know what that's used for?'

'I know it's used for cleaning purposes.'

Carys' eyes were fixed on her. 'You know very well what sick people do with acid and it's not cleaning a goddamn toilet.'

Dahlia cleared her throat and said, 'He needs help with the housework.'

'What the fuck?' Carys thumped the table, bristles up. 'Stop being so naïve. Your brother is quite literally psychopathic and you're making blind excuses for him?'

'*Blind* excuses?'

'He's a sick *incel* who's turning his disgust for women on you, can't you see that?'

'You don't know anything about the trauma he's endured! Behind his rage is grief so strong that he doesn't know what to do with it. He's not an artist or a writer, just a boy who used to be my bodyguard when Yasmine and I would go to collect water from the well in Sinjar.'

There followed a long silence. She wanted to defend her

brother, to continue to believe that there was still a gentle boy in there somewhere from before ISIS brainwashed him. But it was too late for that now. She couldn't accept her toxic brother any longer. Carys' candour was what she had long needed to hear. Tears filled her eyes.

Carys took her hand. 'Dahlia, I'm sorry. But you can't pretend your brother is well when your life's at risk. You know what he's trying to do. Whether your mother knows it or not, he's using her, trying to get her to collude in his plans to harm you. Something needs to change, before he does something he'll regret. How many more scars can you take, Dahlia?'

Dahlia pressed her lips tightly together. 'There was actually something else I wanted to ask you about today. My bosses need someone to write up a piece on the aftermath of the occupation in Iraq. They've asked me if I'll agree to this. It will be the first time I've been back since everything…' her voice tailed off. 'I was… well, I was wondering if you might want to come with me.'

Carys didn't answer. *Waiting was agony.* Dahlia felt as though the whole café was enveloped in silence. They had been holding hands over the table for so long enough now that she couldn't feel which hand was hers and which one Carys'. 'Um, Carys. Did you hear me?'

'Yes.'

'Oh, and?'

'Yes. I'll come with you. Mostly because I want to understand you. Dahlia, you have no idea how much I care about you.'

For the first time since Dahlia could remember, she felt truly safe and whole. Carys offered more than protection to her. To have someone care about you, with no ulterior motive, to be loved, listened to, truly understood. Wasn't that what anyone wanted, at the end of the day?

'Thank you.' She drew Carys' hand to her cheek which was damp from her tears, then kissed it.

And there they sat for an hour or two, discussing the logistics of the venture. Carys would take a sabbatical and help out at a local Baghdadi hospital. Dahlia's article would focus on the lives of medics in post-war Iraq. She said she would contact a hospital in Baghdad later that day to arrange their trip immediately. For now, planning for the trip offered a cathartic release; she could channel her energies and emotions into this project. But in the recesses of her mind lurked the image of Elias.

24

Gunfire thundered outside Al Yarmouk Hospital in Baghdad. Carys wiped her forehead with her right forearm wearily as she turned around to speak to Dahlia.

'You didn't tell me I would be dodging gunfire here.'

She pretended to be ducking missiles as she waited for Dahlia's response; she realised that she hadn't felt so much exhilaration in years! Her husband didn't like travelling, let alone to war-torn countries, and he hadn't protested when Carys had told him about her plans.

It had been obvious for some time that he didn't care where she went or what she did. She had got used to the hurt. Dahlia did care and Carys felt it wasn't only because she wanted to support her with this visit to her country. She hoped Dahlia welcomed this experience because she was doing something meaningful with the woman she loved.

'Hmm. Well, at least you don't have to listen to complaints by patients who think the NHS is in shambles,' Dahlia said, 'they could do with seeing what present-day wartime disasters are like.'

Carys raised her eyebrows, half bemused, smiling, and half serious. Dahlia appeared to be more self-assured in this city of turmoil and civil war, probably because she was far away from her oppressive family in London. *If only she would con-*

tinue to assert herself.

'Yes,' she said, 'the patients are not swearing at me, only their relatives.' Carys smiled and pushed some broken glass aside with her foot. A window had been broken by a looter the previous day when he came to steal a hospital bed.

'Dahlia, we don't have enough operating theatres here. Four aren't enough for the ninety percent of war injury cases we have.'

A piercing scream sliced the air and they saw a crowd of people storming towards the hospital carrying a boy of about ten years of age. Carys could see that he was covered in blood which appeared to be coming from chest wounds. Her heart started racing. A woman wearing an *abaya,* maybe his mother, was held back by some relatives of the boy whilst they put him on the only empty hospital bed left in the hall. Carys ran towards the pale-faced boy. Her throat felt dry. Dahlia listened to what had happened and translated quickly.

'The relatives say he was hit by shrapnel as he was returning from an errand to the shops. A car bomb exploded outside the shops and ten people were killed. They call the dead 'Shahid' or Martyrs.'

Carys wiped her damp forehead and tried to remove the fused clothes from the boy's skin. His face was partially blackened, reminding her of previous miners' accidents back home in Wales. Their accidents and black faces had been as a result of their jobs. This child had not asked for his suffering.

He winced when she removed his clothes. She had never experienced such injuries in children in London. She shuddered and glanced at his mother hitting herself at the end of his bed. The self-flagellation disturbed her; she was a mother too. Brynn... what would she do if Brynn... ? She dragged her thoughts back to her present situation.

'Dahlia, get me the antiseptic gauze.'

Dahlia ran to look for the cream, leaving the relatives to pin down the boy. There was no anaesthetic to ease his pain. Carys frowned at the thought of having to insert a chest drain without any anaesthetic. Dahlia returned with the antiseptic cream and they smothered the boy's blisters with it and then covered them with gauze.

The boy protested and screamed as Carys tried to insert the chest drain. A shockwave moved through her body. *She had to stay calm.* The boy had to be held down by four men; his mother was sobbing nearby. A relative covered her head with her hands. She was held back but broke free a few seconds later. She ran toward Carys shouting in Arabic. Carys recognised the words '*Amreeka, Britannia*'. Then the mother screamed in English.

'Bring back Saddam. Bring back Saddam. He didn't harm children. My son do shopping for me. He not political. Take our oil. Take all Iraq. Just leave us in peace!'

Carys closed her eyes for a split second and took a deep breath in an attempt to control her feelings. The helpful relative forced the mother backwards and she collapsed into a chair.

'We'll have to manage the treatment here. The boy may die of septicaemia if we take him to the operating theatre. The hospital has no means of sterilising the medical instruments.'

Dahlia conveyed this to the wounded boy. His name was Yusuf. He didn't respond but he continued wriggling to free himself from the relatives who were pinning him down. One of the relatives spoke to Dahlia who nodded her head in acknowledgement and nudged Carys,

'I think you should have a look in his ears. The relatives say there was a loud explosion and Yusuf doesn't seem to be hearing well.' She picked up the otoscope on the nearby table. Carys took the otoscope from Dahlia's hands and looked into the boy's ear canals.

'You're right. Both eardrums are perforated. But this is the least of our worries now.'

An hour later, Yusuf was lying asleep in bed, exhausted by his ordeal. The relatives surrounded him, and his mother held the hand where Carys had inserted a drip. Carys heaved a sigh of relief. Dahlia took her by the arm and led her to a small room which was adjacent to the treatment hall. They badly needed a cup of tea.

They entered the room followed by another doctor. He turned to Carys and said in an apologetic voice, 'Please don't blame the woman for screaming in such a way. It is true circumstances were very different before the invasion by the Allies.' Carys nodded her head, too weary to talk as the doctor continued.

'Until the mid 1980's, Iraq had one of the most advanced health care systems in the Middle East. It also had the highest percentage of female doctors.'

Carys noticed Dr Ali had seated himself on a chair that had springs spiking out in all directions. His gaze was flitting between Dahlia and herself. She frowned. Dr Ali had already aired his views on Yazidis by telling Carys that they were devil-worshippers. He had asked Carys why the two of them were in Iraq when they could be enjoying themselves drinking wine in London. He had an inquisitive glint in his eyes.

Carys hoped he didn't think they were informants for the British intelligence services in Britain. She didn't feel it was her place to tell him about the plight of the Yazidi, she would rather concentrate her efforts to relieve the anguish of the patients in the dilapidated hospital.

Dr Ali sipped his *chai* after putting four teaspoonfuls of sugar into it. Carys saw his eyes lingering on Dahlia's curvaceous body for a second time. She would need to keep her safe. Why on earth had she agreed to come to Iraq's capital city?

Dr Ali put his *Istikan* down after slurping the tea loudly. 'When sanctions were imposed on us by the Allies, we had babies dying of dehydration from gastroenteritis. There was no oxygen for the incubators. But nothing compares to the situation in Iraq now.'

Carys frowned. She had worked in paediatric wards in Great Ormond Street where there was always enough oxygen for the babies.

'Porters in this hospital have to spend the night here because the fare back home is too expensive,' he said.

Carys thought of her own accommodation in the Al-Rashid Hotel. She hoped they would get back there before darkness.

Dr Ali sneered at Carys. 'Most families have lost relatives, and whatever accusations are made about this country, no one can say that weapons of mass destruction have been found.'

Dahlia said something to the doctor in Arabic. Carys beckoned her to stop. 'It's okay, Dahlia, I understand Dr Ali's concerns but I'm a doctor. I'm not a judge and I'm certainly not a politician.'

Dr Ali's expression was half-contempt and half-bemused. Perhaps he was wondering how Carys as a Westerner could distance herself from the decisions her leaders made.

'I admire your courage,' he said, 'but be careful. Many doctors here carry guns for their own safety.'

Carys laughed indignantly, 'I didn't come here to work as

a soldier.' She disliked Dr Ali's supercilious tone.

He got up and said, 'I have an AK-47, a Russian style gun. You may need to borrow it one day.'

Carys got up and nudged Dahlia. 'Time to go back to our residence.'

It's better not to tell Dr Ali where we're staying, she mused. Dahlia understood and smiled. At last they could go back to their hotel and relax. Carys felt irritated and realised that she had not smiled at Dahlia once since Dr Ali had come in. She felt restless, not knowing whether to keep her feelings for Dahlia quiet in this country or enter a more heart aching, deeper relationship to her.

25

Dahlia watched Carys waving her hand towards the television in the stark room at the Al Rashid hotel. They were seated on an old sofa and Carys looked agitated while watching a documentary on living conditions in Iraq after the war. Everything in their hotel room was creaky: the bed, the table and the wooden flooring.

How weary, she felt, a contrast to Carys who was still energetic despite her ordeal in the hospital. Dahlia saw Carys form her mouth into a disgusted and contorted expression as she turned towards her to whisper, 'It's sickening! When you think that, at the end of the invasion, Saddam was found hiding in a blinkin' hole in the farmyard of his former cook near Tikrit, where he was born! And yet, his arrogant aura permeates the hospitals and doctors.'

Dahlia touched Carys' hand lightly. 'Keep your voice low. There are still loyalists to the Arab Baath Party around. Many of these rooms are bugged.'

'The bastards. That doctor in Al Yarmouk Hospital could have been happy I was there to help out after those explosions.' Carys had already told Dahlia about her unease and mistrust on meeting Dr Ali.

Dahlia sighed. 'Is that the only reason you came here, Carys?'

Carys leaned in and gave Dahlia a chaste kiss on her cheek. Dahlia felt the sweat on Carys neck. It had mingled with the soap she had used to wash herself. She smelt like dates mixed with almonds. Dahlia felt she didn't need to hide anything from her. That is except for the tingling feeling that overcame her whenever they were close.

She yearned for their bodies to touch, not only pecks on the cheeks or gentle hugs. She brought her thoughts back to her work and sighed, 'The BBC team I work for all express themselves freely. We are reporters. But we still have to be careful.'

Dahlia thought of the journey through the Jordanian desert which route they had chosen as it would be less conspicuous than flying to Iraq directly. They had travelled with a group of German and French reporters who had stayed at different hotels once they separated in Baghdad. The trip had been tiring and very hot. However, the Jordanian police had been friendly towards the reporters.

Dahlia noticed that their sofa was dusty and frayed at the edges, almost like herself. She and Carys sipped their cups of milk, sweetened with honey.

'Dahlia, don't you want to contact your mother now that we have good connections to the satellite phone?'

Dahlia pursed her lips. *It was better not to disturb their togetherness by thinking of her mother.* She was surprised Carys had asked her to contact her mother, especially after the confrontation in the shopping mall in Stratford.

'I'm not sure she would appreciate hearing from me.'

'She might. You're her daughter and share the same background, the same problems that arise from it.'

Dahlia rolled her eyes. Yes, her mother was Kurdish like her. But that was their only similarity.

'It's enough that you came to Iraq with me. I appreciate your support in this venture.' She felt her eyes well up with tears. Carys pulled her towards herself gently.

Dahlia felt that something had shifted in their relationship, it was deeper than camaraderie. She caught her breath and her pulse quickened. Carys massaged her shoulders with her hand in small, accelerating circles. Dahlia pressed her mouth onto Carys' cheek. Her lips parted, an infinitesimal, involuntary movement. And there were Carys' full lips so near to her own. At last! She could not tolerate the mounting tension in her body.

A vision of pleasure and pain stabbed her senses followed by a surge of tenderness when she glimpsed the tiny scar underneath Carys' lower lip. It was as faint as the scars Dahlia had on her lower arms. She kissed the scar, then felt a hot surge take control of her own limp body. There was still time to stop and make excuses for this.

But they didn't stop. Carys moved her mouth closer to Dahlia's, waiting for the next kiss. Dahlia felt herself drawn by Carys' magnetism. As she teased Carys' mouth open, she tasted milk and honey which Carys had been drinking earlier on. Their kiss surpassed all boundaries of time and place, becoming more forceful and frantic. Just as Dahlia was about to gasp with the intensity of her experience, they heard a persistent tooting of cars outside.

Carys drew back quickly and turned towards the window. Dahlia followed her gaze. She sighed, trying to gain her composure.

'We don't need to worry Carys. The rooms may be bugged but there are no secret cameras here.'

'How do you know?'

'I searched the room an hour ago.'

That made them both laugh, and Dahlia felt her muscles lose some of their tension. She was tired. Danger and pleasure mixed freely in this country of her mother's. However, it was her country too. She took a deep breath and reached out to pick up a glass of water on the table.

'Carys, how did you feel when we were kissing?'

'I was looking for your soul.'

Carys whispered the last word and Dahlia laughed.

'I think my experience with *Médecins sans Frontières* will be well appreciated here,' Carys said and tucked away some stray strands of hair which had fallen into her face.

Dahlia smiled. 'You know, Doctor,' she said archly, 'you looked quite attractive in your blue headscarf today.'

Carys smiled. 'I had to wear that to blend in with all the headdresses there.'

'You should do that more often in London.' Dahlia touched Carys' hair teasingly. It felt soft, despite the heat and sweat.

Carys laughed, relieved to have something to be amused about. She slumped back onto the sofa.

'I have to finish my report by tomorrow, Carys. The BBC was banned from Iraq during the war. Now is our chance to report openly.'

Dahlia put her glass of water down. She had needed to drink something cool after their kiss. The curved contour of Carys' almost ginger-coloured eyebrows suddenly gave way to an angry, tortuous form.

'The patients are not only suffering from a lack of food,' Carys raged, 'but also from a lack of hygiene! Infections are rife and the smell of cheap detergent is suffocating.' She wrinkled her nose as if she could still smell it.

'Some of my colleagues who work in war-torn countries

have told me that they protect themselves with guns; they said that looters are always looking for an opportunity to attack.'

Dahlia watched Carys gravely. *Did she regret coming to Baghdad?*

'Take me with you to the hospital again. I will bring a cameraman with me. We have no other assignments.' Carys shook her head.

Dahlia grasped her arm, saying, 'I know you don't like reporters meddling with your affairs, but I can translate for you and people back home in Britain will have a better picture of the turmoil in Baghdad.'

Carys smiled wearily, 'Tell me a bit more about Baghdad first.'

'Okay. If it means I can come to work with you tomorrow.'

From the wooden table near the sink, Dahlia picked up one of the articles she'd recently written. She began to read the first paragraph.

Baghdad was captured by the Turks in 1534 and was ruled by them for about 400 years. After the First World War, the British came to claim the territory and defend the oilfields against the Turks. They assigned King Faisal I to govern the country in 1921 but the monarchy ended when it was overcome by the military coup in 1958. King Faisal and his family were shot dead.

Carys listened carefully. Suddenly, she put her fingers to her lips, motioning Dahlia to stop talking. Dahlia followed her gaze to the door. She instinctively knew it was better to keep her flow of words moving.

'Carys, you'll have to get some sleep now. I am sure you'll have lots of work in the hospital tomorrow.'

They both moved towards the door stealthily. Dahlia picked up the knife she had left on the cupboard next to the scratched mirror. She glanced at the mirror. Her hair looked dusty and the expression in her eyes was a mixture of fear and hope.

The door burst open and three bearded men forced their way into the room, guns in their hands. 'Stop moving! Both of you. On the ground, now!'

Intuitively, Dahlia went to thrust her knife into the first man's leg, but he caught hold of her wrist and twisted it. She cried out and the knife clattered to the floor. It was picked up swiftly by one of the henchmen. Carys rushed to her side and held her hands up in the air to show that she was unarmed.

The door was closed. The men encircled them. Dahlia recognised a man from the hospital who had been talking to Dr Ali. She wished she had been friendlier towards him. He must have been an informant for these men, whichever political group they belonged to.

Things moved fast. They were made to sit down. In one charged, single breath, the man issued orders to Dahlia in Arabic, whilst the other two held Dalia and Carys at gunpoint, the glint of the AK47s winking at them, threatening them. He told them that his commander was seriously ill and needed a doctor. Carys was to come with them immediately and wait for further instructions.

'Please, let me come with my doctor-friend. She doesn't speak Arabic and I can be of help.' Dahlia begged.

'No. You stay here.'

The first man who appeared older, motioned them to keep quiet. Dahlia moved to draw the curtains. She realised that she couldn't put up a fight with these men and turned towards Carys to explain what was going to happen. 'You are to go with them and I'm to stay here.'

'What? For how long? What do they want from us?'

Dahlia looked at Carys pleadingly. She knew her country and its machinery of torture if disobeyed.

'Carys, it's not me they are after. It's you they want because you're a doctor.' Dahlia ached when she saw Carys' face grow pale. Her freckles appeared more marked now and her eyes were overcast by clouds of terror.

'Is it because I'm white? Tell them I'm not an agent! That I went on strike against the war in 2003!' Her eyes spanned the room. 'I'm a mother. My child needs me. My patients in the hospital too, they –

'That is all we need. Your skills as a doctor,' the leader spat out, for the first time in English with surprisingly little accent.

'Carys, listen. These men belong to Shia insurgents. One of their leaders is ill and won't show his face in the hospital you're working at.'

Dahlia suppressed her urge to hold Carys in her arms. Any display of emotion would have an adverse effect now. 'They're taking you straight to their camp.'

Carys gulped before answering. 'What if I can't help him?'

'You're a good doctor. You need to do your best.' Dahlia held a measured tone whilst her heart pounded in her chest. 'Our lives depend on it.' She glanced at the two men who were watching.

'The plan is that I'm to leave with two of the men. If anyone stops me, I'm to say that they are my cousins and that they are escorting me to my auntie's house. After ten minutes, you're to leave the Al-Rasheed Hotel. Remember the tea shop in Rashid Street where I did an interview for the BBC a few weeks ago?' Carys nodded.

'Well, walk to the tea shop and get into a black Chevrolet parked outside the teashop. I'll be waiting in the car. The men have decided that I should translate for you.'

At their command, Dahlia stood up slowly. She felt disgusted with herself. Maybe she should have listened to her mother about not coming to this warzone. She wiped the beads of sweat off her forehead, trying to cast away her doubts at the same time.

Journalism was the first draft of history. That was what she had been told when she had started her profession. She was proud of it. Carys had been to other dangerous areas in Afghanistan. Was it Carys who had insisted on coming to Iraq with her? Dahlia tried telling herself that there was no need to feel guilty. One of the men motioned Carys to stay seated and told Dahlia to leave with the two remaining kidnappers if she wanted to see her friend alive.

Dahlia understood. The insurgents were everywhere. She remembered trying to convince Carys to leave the Al-Rasheed Hotel for the Palestine Hotel. She should have gone along with that idea. Dahlia ran towards Carys and put her arms around her waist. She had always looked upon her as a strong woman. Now, she appeared lost and out of her depth. Her beautiful, deep-set eyes were downcast.

Carys broke away without saying anything. Dahlia watched her scribble a few lines on a notepad. She read the note slowly while looking over Carys' shoulder.

'Dear Brynn, my only son,

I love you very much and I know it was always your dream to be in the army. I urge you to continue studying instead. It's difficult trying to bring democracy to longstanding dictatorship regimes. It is not worth losing your life for. You may ask why I am writing this. I know that I may be facing death. Please remember, life is precious…'

Dahlia looked at her watch. It was time to leave the hotel

with the kidnappers. She took Carys' hand and kissed it gently. She would need a lot of affection now that they were in the hands of the insurgents. Also, her Decree Nisi had been finalised a month ago and Dahlia knew old memories of happier times would be flooding back.

Dahlia had no memories of happier times. Being with Carys was what made her feel passion flowing through her veins and her blood feel steamy. Dahlia cupped Carys' face in her hands and said, 'We'll get through this together. Believe me.'

But then, she doubted it herself. Belief had never got her far in life. She had already taken steps to remedy her sense of herself but her awareness of belonging anywhere had evaporated many years ago. *I'm in exile, even in my own country,* she thought.

Dahlia didn't say this to Carys, just slipped out of the room quietly with the two kidnappers who appeared restless. She smiled at the hotel receptionist so as not to appear suspicious whilst leaving the hotel.

26

Carys quickened her pace once she was out of the hotel. There were no guards to stop her. She hoped the receptionists wouldn't be suspicious of her leaving the hotel without a companion. Her shoulders felt tense. She didn't want to let Dahlia down who was the only person needing her support. *But, was she ready to die for her?*

Brynn, her son, led his own bohemian student life. Her husband, well, the latest news was that he already had a steady partner and, and as she knew, patients would always turn to any doctor when in need. She looked at her watch. The curfew would start soon and then any movement by car would pose a danger of being stopped or shot by army patrols.

Dahlia had already told her all about this Rasheed Street which ran parallel to the river Tigris on its Eastern side. The book shops and tea shops had been her favourite spots when on holiday in Baghdad as a child. She'd peer into expensive boutiques but didn't have enough money to buy anything. Poor Dahlia. These same buildings were now browned and dilapidated.

They had planned to visit Al Mutanabbi Street full of bookshops, located in the old quarter of Baghdad. Dahlia had told her that it was named after a tenth century poet and housed poetry readings. Well, right now, she wished she was somewhere else. A Thousand and One Nights narrated by Scheherazade but morphed into Dahlia had been in her dreams!

Carys felt sweat beads trickling down the sides of her face. She didn't dare wipe them away. She approached the café Dahlia had told her about and caught sight of the waiting Chevrolet. There was still time to turn back. This wasn't her country. This wasn't her war. She was here for humanitarian reasons. The thought made her mouth twitch with a faint smile.

Then she remembered her son. Brynn would be devastated if she was killed by Iraqis. He regularly gave small donations to charitable causes such as the Red Cross and Oxfam. If something terrible happened to his mother, his beliefs and philanthropism were likely to go up in smoke!

She saw the silhouette of a woman in a headscarf sitting tensely in the back seat of the Chevrolet. One of the bearded men, whom Carys had seen earlier on, was looking in her direction grimly. Carys leaned forward slightly to make sure that the woman in the car was Dahlia.

Dahlia met her gaze and Carys recognised the defiant glare in her eyes, like when she first met her in St Thomas Hospital. It was mingled with fear which made her large eyes appear hollow. *Still beautiful,* Carys thought, stepping into the car. The man in the front seat was twice as large as the man in the back. He was darker in complexion and watched her cautiously in the mirror of his car.

She heard the rumble of a lorry coming from the opposite direction. The astute eyes of the men were sure to be watching her. She pulled her headscarf tighter over her partially wet and sticky hair, hoping her freckles would be half covered by her scarf. The young men would be very suspicious of a European lady getting into an Iraqi car.

The Chevy drove off quickly. She tried to catch Dahlia's eyes as she leaned forward an inch. The bearded man opened his left hand to reveal a hand grenade. Carys sat back in her car seat as he gave instructions to the driver in Arabic. In the past, reporters had been killed after only a few days of futile negotiations. Carys tried to size up the strength of the men. The back-seat man spoke a few harsh-sounding words to Dahlia.

'Carys, Abdullah our Shia captor says you should stop looking around and keep your head still. It'll attract attention and endanger our lives. We'll soon be leaving Rasheed Street.'

Carys stifled a rough remark and decided to stop any jerky movements in order to appease the men.

After a few minutes, the Chevy passed the 'Hands of Victory' monument. Dahlia had told Carys that Saddam had decided to build a Triumphal Arch to celebrate his 'victory' over Iran. Carys looked up at the enormous arch which was formed by two scimitars. The Iraqi flag was caught on a pole where the two large blades met. Iron forearms grabbed the two blades. Carys felt herself stiffen. A pyrrhic victory, as futile as a plastic trophy.

Iraq's war with Iran had lasted eight years and had ended in 1988 with Iraq having suffered 200,000 fatalities. The two large stone hands of the monument formed fists ready to explode with aggression. Carys trembled.

She observed the driver's clenched, white knuckles: They were smaller versions of the monument's two large hands. She wiped her forehead. The air weighed like lead, particularly heavy and oppressive in the Chevy.

The car took a sudden swerve into a narrow alley. Carys

had to grip the door handle to stop herself lurching onto Abdullah's clenched fists. She glanced at Dahlia who was staring out of the window. The car came to a halt. A pack of possibly rabid dogs were howling, looking for food in empty bins. *What skinny, fearsome dogs*, she thought. *Not like the ones in London.*

Abdullah prodded Carys to get out of the car. She opened the door quickly feeling very hot in her headscarf. The heat was negligible compared with the fear that froze every fibre of her body. She hoped the dogs would not smell the kebab she had eaten for lunch as the scent must be oozing from under her armpits. Dahlia was ordered to stand next to Carys. She was shivering despite the heat.

'Are they going to execute us?'

Carys tried to read the answer on Dahlia's silent face. She put her arm around her, pushing her face under her neck. The scent of her familiar deodorant had evaporated.

'I don't know, honey.'

'You need to reassure the men, Dahlia, keep them docile.'

Carys felt her anger stir. Surely, they were the ones that needed to be reassured. Not these villains.

Dahlia talked to the men in Arabic, trying to sound level-headed. Carys only understood a few words such as *tabib*, which meant doctor and *atakalam englisi* meaning *speaks English.* None of these words formed a coherent sentence in her confused and tired mind.

After a few minutes of debating in the sweltering sun, Dahlia squeezed her hand.

'I've told the men that you are an A&E consultant in London and that your skills are unique.'

Carys could barely stand upright and nodded.

'I also told the men that you're Welsh and have nothing to

do with the politics in London. I emphasised the fact that you speak Welsh.'

Carys wondered if she did indeed still speak Welsh as her head felt foggy. She didn't know where she belonged and what she portrayed in this strange country.

Dahlia said quickly, 'They agree to our release if we help them with their sick leader.'

Carys lips felt parched and sore.

'Oh. Something else...'

Carys sighed. How much longer could she survive in this heat?

'I'm to report on their political issues favourably on Al Jazeera TV.'

Carys didn't dare to disagree.

'Dahlia, you can write that they're as cute as Mickey Mouse.'

Dalia flashed her angry eyes at her.

'I need water, Dahlia. Otherwise I won't be capable of doing anything, let alone save a man's life.'

Carys was drenched in sweat. Dahlia quickly translated what Carys had said. She omitted the Mickey Mouse comment. The men pointed to a van which was parked at the end of the alley and pushed the women towards it. When they reached the van, Carys was given a bottle of water. She drank it voraciously. It almost spilled over. Dahlia watched the fluid longingly.

Carys looked up and gave her the rest of the water. Dahlia drank less quickly. Carys presumed that her time with the Peshmerga soldiers had hardened her to basic needs such as water or food.

After a few seconds, one of the men gestured for them to get into the van. Once they were seated, they were blindfolded. Carys felt the sweat collect under the makeshift dirty rag over her eyes. She didn't dare to raise her hand to remove it. The van drove off quickly. It smelt of dead bodies and vomit. Carys wrinkled her nose. She was used to going to the morgue to certify death in St Thomas Hospital in London, but this smell was void of detergents and formaldehyde. Carys decided to breathe as little as possible.

'Inhale slowly,' she told herself, 'that's what you tell your patients. Hyperventilating will only make you dizzy.' She would have to have all her senses about her when she met the leader of the kidnappers.

The van's bumpy ride came to a halt and the two women were let out. Carys felt her eyes twitching underneath the blindfold which was beginning to hurt. Suddenly, she felt some cool air, maybe from air-conditioning and the burning sensation in her face began to cool down. She and Dahlia were pushed onto what felt like a sofa. Carys could feel the springs, which she was already used to, and were no cause for concern just now.

A pair of rough hands yanked the blindfold off her. Carys rubbed her eyes gently and opened them. Her gaze fell upon a bearded man in a bloodstained white shirt. He lay very still on what looked like a hospital bed at the end of the small room. Carys bit her lips. It was probably one of the looted beds! She waited for instructions.

Abdullah spoke to Dahlia in a torrent of Arabic. She nodded her head acknowledging submission as Abdullah ended his monologue with *tamam* which Carys presumed was, 'understood?'

'Carys, the leader of this Shia religious group was hit by a bullet yesterday. He was close to a car which was driven by a suicide bomber and there was a collision by a van in the last minute. The car exploded. The men would like you to treat him.'

Carys refrained from shaking her head. 'I can examine him but how on earth am I supposed to treat him? I haven't got my surgical instruments or anything medical with me. The kidnappers didn't exactly give me any time to look for my best instruments.'

The guard smiled and went into another room, which adjoined their own small room. The door was hanging on hinges as if it too had been blasted a short while ago. Abdullah returned with a canvas pouch of surgical instruments. Carys glared at him. She was disgusted at the thought of life-saving instruments being looted from hospitals in Baghdad but kept a face devoid of any emotion.

Abdullah looked at her proudly and held up the canvas pouch like a medal. He motioned her towards the wounded man. Carys approached the patient, tightening her headscarf. If these men were Shia, they would be very pious and as a woman, she was not sure of her status, even as a doctor. *Thank goodness her skirt covered her knees appropriately.* Carys also hoped the wounded man was not a cleric as he would most probably not be happy with a woman treating him.

Abdulla prodded her once again. She turned around and frowned at him. He prodded her to start again. Carys realised *fight or flight* would not be feasible now. She would have to comply. A glance at Dahlia's imploring eyes made her move nearer to the wounded man. She felt his pulse. It was weak but regular, not too quick. This was a good sign. Then she took his blood pressure. As to be expected, it was low. He had lost a considerable amount of blood. She moved all his joints gently. None of them seemed to be fractured. She couldn't help feeling vengeful at the thought of a wounded leader. It was symbolic for a wounded and fractured nation.

His vulnerability was evoking feelings of sympathy and revulsion in her at the same time. One of the men moved forward to mop the sweat off the leader's forehead. His clothes were partially stuck to his chest. A deep wound on the man's right thigh looked as if it had been made with surgical precision. She turned towards Dahlia looking puzzled.

'Who operated on this man? The wound looks fresh?'

'Carys, Abdullah has told me he used to work as a nurse in the hospital. He took a bullet out of the leg using the instruments he looted from the hospital. When Mohammad, the leader, didn't seem to recover from his wounds, they decided to kidnap one of the doctors. Unfortunately, there were no male doctors available. You were the only one who was present at the time.'

Carys stepped away from the wounded leader and said, 'What do you mean *unfortunately?*' She felt a blush stain her face.

'Carys, this is no time for taking offence.'

Carys took a deep breath and bit her lip as if to stop herself from saying anything offensive. She wasn't sure if any of the men spoke English despite their protestations.

She took a tube of antiseptic cream off the bedside table and motioned Abdullah to help her slather the wounds in cream. They then wrapped the wounds in gauze. Fluid was oozing from burns on the legs of the wounded man. He didn't groan.

'Mohammad needs to be rehydrated. Do we have a drip?'

She signalled a drip with her right hand and eyed Abdullah daringly.

'Carys, Abdullah says he tried to insert a drip, but Mohammad is so badly burned that the usual drip sites are difficult to get at.'

Carys nodded her head, careful with her words. 'I noticed. He has puncture wounds in the usual cubital and hand areas.' She looked at the bedside table. There was no local anaesthetic to be found.

'Dahlia, there is no local anaesthetic. I will have to cut down the skin to locate a vein in his arm. It may be painful. Ask the men if they would like me to proceed.'

She pointed at the leader's right arm. The men conferred quickly and decided that the procedure needed to be done as soon as possible. Carys moved towards the wounded man and picked up a scalpel. She cut down the flesh of the right elbow. She sweated as she tried to locate a vein.

The room was very still. As still as the wounded man who lay in the hospital bed in the middle of someone's dilapidated house. Abdullah held the arm tightly to ensure Mohammad would not move during the painful exploration process.

Carys' mouth was dry with fear. Their release depended on her success. Finally, she heaved a sigh of relief as she located a vein large enough to slip in a plastic cannula. Abdullah helped her to connect the drip and Carys stitched the cannula in place to ensure it would not loosen quickly after it had been connected in such precarious conditions. The saline drip entered the man's body, the colour changed slowly to a healthier one.

He moved his head towards the door which hung loosely on its hinges. His eyes opened and he caught sight of Carys wearing a dark brown headscarf. A tuft of her brown hair struggled to get out of its confinement. No doubt he was wondering why a woman was standing so close to him, she thought apprehensively.

Mohammad closed his eyes again. Abdullah motioned the

ladies to walk into the other room. Carys looked at him, barely disguising her abhorrence. Was she to be discarded like a paper bag, no longer needed after fulfilling her job? What now?

Dahlia seemed to read her thoughts and whispered, 'Carys, you saved Mohammad's life. Let's hope that this will be enough to save ours.'

27

The wounded man, Mohammad, had given permission for Dahlia to talk to Al Jazeera Arabic news channel. She had been ordered to speak favourably about their time with the Shia kidnappers. This meant that, although they were still kidnapped, they would stay alive a little longer. Dahlia looked around for any escape route in the small room that was their prison. The only window had been sealed off by thick cardboard that also covered a brick wall.

'We're recording in three, two, one...'

'*Allah uh Akbar.*'

The hooded guard's voice boomed towards the small camera that was filming Dahlia and Carys. They sat slumped against a dirty wall which was splattered with blood. Missing bricks conveyed the brittleness of the building in which they were being held hostage.

'This is a message for the *kafir.*'

Dahlia squeezed Carys' hand. She could smell the sweat emanating from her, no more a mixture of milk and honey but more like old almonds. She closed her eyes for a second trying to conjure up the image of their first kiss. It tasted like milk and honey, innocent and sensuous at the same time.

The glare of the spotlight shining on her wet face made her wince. She held on to her chair, hoping it would be just as easy to hold on to her dear life, and gulped as she glanced at the kidnapper. The man had covered his face with a black and white scarf. He looked up suddenly and pointed his gun in her direction. Dahlia's experience asserted itself. She looked into the camera serenely.

This recording would be broadcast on Al Jazeera television. Then the West would get hold of it. Dahlia didn't dare to wipe the beads of sweat off her forehead. She was aware of the humming noise from the swirling ventilation of the ceiling fan. In the hospital, she had compared it to whirling dervishes. But here, it was more menacing. There was not much air about to be circulated. She wondered whether Britain would care about their whereabouts and hoped that Scotland Yard would not think they were here to join ISIS.

Were their lives worth saving? What had the kidnappers demanded in exchange for their lives? All she could do was offer the camera a haggard nod of the head. One of the kidnappers motioned her to speak into the camera.

'The insurgents would like the American and British invaders to admit that they have not found weapons of mass destruction here in this country and never will. They don't exist,' she said then added, 'Dr Carys and I are grateful for the kind treatment by the Shia insurgents.'

She glanced quickly at Carys who nodded and hoped she appeared as a genuine doctor on camera.

Dahlia continued to talk in Arabic, but she felt her throat dry up. Hadn't she seen a bottle of water somewhere on a table earlier on? Her mind spiralled. She didn't want to die of hyperthermia or dehydration. The men would hardly waste a saline drip on her. She would end her days hallucinating. Her voice stopped.

Carys noticed the silence and turned to look at her as she

had stopped talking.

'Do you need your asthma inhaler?'

Dahlia nodded her head. Abdullah started shouting. He raised his pistol and stormed towards her. He tried to point his gun at her temple. She stayed seated with a glazed look in her eyes. Carys screamed and pushed the guard's hand towards the ceiling. A shot was fired. The guard spun around and pushed Carys off her chair.

Dahlia covered her face with her headscarf and started to cough incessantly. Carys lay on the floor and watched a lizard bemusedly, as he tried to scurry through a crack in the dry wall. Dahlia wondered when Carys would realise that she was in trouble.

Carys scrambled up from the dirty floor as soon as she heard Dahlia's laboured breathing. She raised Dahlia's head and drew it to her breast. Carys stroked her hair and she whispered into her ear.

'Darling, breathe slowly.'

She brushed Dahlia's ear with her parched lips. Two of the men next to Abdullah started shouting at each other. One of them tore Carys away from Dahlia and pushed her towards the door grabbing her neck with one of his fleshy, stubbly paws. Dahlia heard Carys sobbing. She felt the guard's gun jab at her back.

Carys winced at the sudden light when the door in front of them opened. Mohammad stumbled his way into the room using his two crutches. He had left his bed and stood in the guard's way. His eyes blazed angrily. Carys grabbed his arm and looked at him imploringly.

'Please don't kill us.'

Mohammad looked at her blankly.

'You're a good man.' Carys looked at him intently.

Mohammad looked around the room briskly. He spoke to the two other guards in a stern voice. Then he turned his attention to Carys.

'I'm a man of honour. We have no intention of killing you.'

Carys sighed with relief.

'Even though your country is killing thousands of us. Our innocent children...'

His voice trailed off and his face darkened. Dahlia was surprised to hear him speak in English.

'Sir,' Carys said, pulling herself up to a standing position, 'I came here to help the ill people in your country. I'm a doctor and I love my job.'

She turned towards the guard at the door, '... And I'm *not* a soldier.'

Dahlia was hoping that Carys might have saved their lives because of her occupation. She kept quiet. The guard's smile mocked her. Mohammad scowled at him. Dahlia noticed Carys' headscarf loosening, horrified that it would fall onto the floor like an errant leaf floating away from a mother tree. Mohammad narrowed his eyes and hissed at the guard closest to Carys. Dahlia noticed his eyes softening. Carys grabbed her headscarf and fastened it back on her head. She looked at Mohammad imploringly.

'Sir, my friend here suffers from asthma. She needs her inhaler otherwise she will suffocate.'

Mohammad watched her curiously. Then, questioningly he said, 'She must be a good friend of yours.'

'Yes, *effendi.* She nearly died at the hands of...' she hesitated. 'Bandits.'

Mohammad watched her in disbelief. 'What bandits?'

Carys weighed her words carefully. She wondered if these men formed any alliances with ISIS. There was not much sympathy for Yazidi women in Iraq.

'Robbers in the mountains of Sulaymaniyah.'

Mohammad eyed Dahlia suspiciously and said, 'Are you a Kurd?' Dahlia nodded her head and looked at the floor. It seemed endless.

Carys added, 'I met her mother in London, where Dahlia was being treated in my hospital. I promised her mother to look after Dahlia.'

Dahlia felt Mohammad's watchful eye on her. Her breathing was still laboured. Mohammad spoke to Carys again and said,

'My wife's mother was a Kurd. She was a good woman.' He paused for a long time, his pupils dilated, focussing on nothing.

'Very well. Bring me the inhaler for *ukhti*!' *My sister*, he called her. She had been called that by the hospital staff who had warmed to her.

An hour later, once the men were satisfied that their video recording relayed all their kindness, they left the room. Dahlia sat hunched on the small mattress. Her head rested on Carys' shoulder. Dahlia's breathing had eased after using the inhaler Mohammad had allowed. The kidnappers had surprisingly brought them a tray of aubergines stuffed with okra, hummus and naan which they had hastily eaten.

Carys put their tray aside and said, 'I don't know much about the Shia. Tell me something about them.'

'You know how there are two main denominations in Christianity – Catholics and Protestants, right?' Dahlia explained. 'The Muslims are Sunni and Shia.' Carys nodded.

'When the prophet Mohammad died, there was disagreement as to who should be his successor. It was decided that Abu Bakr, the prophet's father-in-law should become the first

Caliph. These people were the Sunnis. Another group of people were disgruntled with Abu Bakr as Caliph. They thought that this special status should go to Ali, the Prophet's cousin and son-in-law. Viz, the Shi'at Ali or the partisans of Ali, simply called the Shia.'

Carys fidgeted and looked into the distance. *A religion should make you more compassionate,* Dahlia thought, gritting her teeth.

'You survived your asthma attack,' Carys said, relieved.

Dahlia smiled at her and wanted to hug her, but she wasn't sure if the men were next door.

'Carys. I overheard the men speaking to Mohammad. They're negotiating our release with the British government. I don't know if they want money for us. I hope that means we're worth keeping alive.'

Carys almost hissed her words, 'Our families will fight for us. My son Brynn will have seen the video footage. Your mother will have spoken to Jonathan.'

Dahlia felt sad to hear that Carys didn't have the hope and optimism that she had shared as a young girl and added, 'So many British soldiers were killed in Iraq, senselessly.' Carys nodded. Dahlia felt angry that Saddam had been tolerated by the West for decades. Dictators had one thing in common – destruction.

In 1991 when there had been a nationwide uprising in Iraq, the West had decided not to move their armies up to Baghdad and not to topple Saddam. She suddenly felt a kernel of sympathy with her kidnappers and said,

'I was just thinking about the soap they gave us for the cold shower yesterday. It was so soothing. Made me forget about this whole mess for a few minutes.'

'How kind of them, huh? After the whole week they let us

go mouldy without showers?'

Dahlia sat up and caught the glint of humour in Carys' eye as she said, "It would have been more exciting if we'd been allowed to have a shower together.'

But Dahlia couldn't laugh. She put her hand up to stop Carys from continuing. This was no time for fantasy. 'Well, how about the newspapers and TV they've left us? That was kind of them.'

'Babe, the newspapers are censored beyond recognition. Get real! We were kidnapped. They almost killed us. They're playing mind games to keep us sweet, in case they decide to free us after talking to the British government.'

Dahlia was too tired to argue. She lay down on the mattress and very nearly succumbed to the uncomplicated tides of sleep but instead, she put her head on Carys' shoulder and said, 'Before I met you, I felt that all women I'd met were afraid of my frailty and my weaknesses.'

Carys stroked her hair gently and said, 'I know honey. I love you all the more for your vulnerability. I remember the first time I set my eyes on you, the frightened look in your eyes, like a deer about to leap away.'

Carys kissed Dahlia's forehead and sighed, 'You were like a dam waiting to be released and your beautiful, large eyes… shining like moonlight.'

Dahlia smiled and turned to face Carys, 'You're the first person who hasn't been engulfed by my anxieties and my past.'

She remembered interviewing Carys in St Thomas Hospital. 'I was mesmerised by your clear blue deep-set eyes, like a river, boundless and inviting.'

Dahlia felt Carys hold her tighter as she said, 'I felt like a bear who had been hibernating till I met you.'

Dahlia chuckled at the comparison, then said, 'I'm so sorry I brought you here. I should never have put you in this situation.'

She felt Carys' finger on her lips as she said, 'Honey, I would sacrifice anything for you. Isn't that what love is about? You have taught me to cherish my own feelings.'

Dahlia rubbed her cheek onto Carys' slender neck. She felt her mouth move towards Carys' lips, yearning to open them gently. There was no need to move slowly. She felt Carys' luscious lips open up to her hungrily. Dahlia fell back on the mattress. She could feel Carys rubbing herself onto her thigh. As Carys gasped, she rolled back onto the mattress, looking exhilarated.

Dahlia watched the door. None of the kidnappers had come into the room since the Al Jazeera interview and the following phone call with the British government. The banging of doors and arguments from the adjacent rooms had ceased. The men had clearly left the building. The only noise she could hear was the howling of a hungry dog.

She decided to risk her next move. Dahlia pulled up her white blouse and put Carys hand on her breasts. Carys looked at her knowingly. She took her hand away and moved her face towards Dahlia's breasts. The fondling, stroking and caressing of Dahlia's breasts with her tongue made Dahlia feel as if a fire had been lit next to her. Carys started leaving a trail of light kisses down to her navel as Dahlia moaned and surrendered herself totally.

'Hold me tightly,' she whispered as she waited for the remaining ripples of pleasure to slowly subside. She felt they had merged into one person, one life.

*

A few hours later, the two women were torn out of their sleep by the sound of gunfire and shouting outside their room. They held each other tightly. The house had been quiet for a long time. Even the lizards had been absent.

Dahlia kissed Carys' forehead. If they were going to die, at least they could have a last quick kiss. She kept an eye on the door. It was flung open. Three men stormed into the room, covering their backs as they came towards the two frightened women. They belonged to the US army!

'Are you okay?' One of the men tried to help Carys stand up.

'Yes,' she said, holding Dahlia tightly, 'Now that the kidnappers have left this farmhouse. Where have they gone?'

'It's an empty house, ma'am.' was the curt response. 'Let's get you two up – you're safe now.'

Carys and Dahlia were helped up, and the soldier guided them to the outside door. A van was waiting.

Dahlia shielded her eyes from the daylight and said, 'Wow! The insurgents let us go! They had a heart after all.'

Carys looked at her sideways and said advisedly, 'I think you need a good rest before you start talking to the press or to anyone else for that matter. You must be tired.'

Dahlia scrutinised the area as she stepped towards the van. Date palms and a farmhouse further away caught her attention. Surely, the people there would have witnessed the insurgents fleeing.

'Where are we going?' Carys asked one of the soldiers.

'The Previous Green Zone where our Embassy is.'

'Al-Mintaqah al-Khadra!' Dahlia exclaimed.

The soldier, whom the others called Sam, didn't look at her. What did she expect? Soldiers did their duty without questioning. Maybe they even resented rescuing two women, one of them being a native they knew nothing about.

'The US Embassy is the largest Embassy in the world, almost as big as the Vatican City. Ever seen the film by Matt Damon, *The Green Zone*?' Sam said wryly as he led the way to the van.

Dahlia was interested in the mention of the Green Zone which constituted an old palace compound. It had been a heavily guarded complex in the centre of the city, protecting it from bombings. Following the 2003 invasion by the United States, it had become a symbol of inequality and alienation in Baghdad. A few months ago, the barbed wire had come down and the checkpoints were taken away. It was opened to the public in December 2018.

She wondered whether they should call the rest of Baghdad the Red Zone as all the bombings, kidnappings and any form of lawlessness had happened there. The reopening of the Green Zone had come on the first anniversary of Iraq's recapture of the city of Mosul from ISIS.

'This area used to be a playground for Saddam's son.' Sam said. 'It was full of villas for 'Papa Saddam's' family, friends and Baath party loyalists. You are lucky you weren't here at that time otherwise Saddam's son would have captured you.' He eyed Dahlia snidely.

'You've no idea what Dahlia has been through.' Carys interrupted, almost jabbing Sam in the ribs and continued, 'She's as much a soldier as you.'

Sam stared at her, opening his mouth slightly. Then he decided not to say any more. What use was it arguing with women, he must have thought. A soldier said apologetically, 'The Green Zone was also used as a playground for Saddam's man-eating lions. They've been moved to the Iraqi National Zoo now.'

Dahlia stopped listening to the soldiers and looked back at

the place in which they had been held captive. It seemed to have been a farmhouse because there were some chickens wandering outside. Whenever the kidnappers had left, they had left in a hurry because some of their water bottles had been left behind. There were no medical instruments in sight.

From the corner of her eye, Dahlia could see Sam kicking a lizard away from the van.

'Oh, do stop! You'll hurt it,' she cried out.

Sam and his friends laughed out loud. 'You have other matters to worry about now,' Sam said mockingly.

Carys said, 'I'm sorry, captain. Dahlia has been through an ordeal. She needs time to regain her old self.'

Dahlia interjected, 'An ordeal? The whole business was an eye-opener, Carys. Taking everything into consideration, we weren't treated that badly by the kidnappers. They didn't kill us. We're alive.'

The soldiers looked at each other apprehensively. They probably thought she was cracking up. Dahlia wiped the beads of sweat off her forehead. She hoped she wasn't going to faint. She didn't understand the words that were coming out of her mouth. Her cheeks felt flushed.

'Dahlia needs medical attention.' Carys added quickly.

'We were told that you're a doctor.' Sam responded.

'Yes, I am. But she needs a specialist.'

'Sounds more like she needs a psychiatrist.'

The captain closed the door of the van and terminated any other possibility of conversation.

Dahlia felt the sweat threaten to pour down her face. She wondered what her mother was doing and whether she would be coming to Iraq to look for her. Suddenly, she realised that she needed her mother's approval as much as she craved the intimacy Carys offered her.

28

Hannah wrung her hands, glancing at the Sumerian and Babylonian artefacts in the corridor of the Baghdad Museum. She had not wanted to believe Jonathan when he had phoned to tell her that Dahlia had been kidnapped. Despite the altercations with her daughter, she needed to know she was alright. Her feelings about Dahlia were still confused but of one thing she was certain, Dahlia must realise that a man was necessary to support her. There was only one truth in life.

When she thought of Dahlia, it was with a mixture of reverence and loathing. She admired and hated her rebellion, especially when she was fighting against a woman's natural sexual tendency. *What was she thinking of, going back to Iraq with Carys?* The two women would have been sitting targets for kidnappers! Carys had put her up to this, endangering both their lives. Her daughter needed protecting, not perverting.

It was fortunate that Jonathan had been assigned to the Iraqi museum at this specific time. The two of them had made hurried preparations and travelled together to Baghdad. He had been chosen by the British Museum to assess the losses and damages at the Iraqi Museum and estimate the amount of conservation work that would be needed to repair the damaged objects. Surely he would find a solution to the kidnapping! Hopefully, Dahlia had realised the rashness of her actions and had come to her senses.

Hannah paced up and down the corridor of the Baghdad Museum, glancing at the artefacts but finding it difficult to focus on them. They were fewer in number since the British had looted some of the objects in the distant past. She met Jonathan and they waited impatiently for the Museum curator, whose name was Khalil, to come and start the collaborative restoration project.

Hannah's mind was on the distressing kidnap; she felt it had dealt the final blow to her delicate relationship with her daughter. Jonathan probably sensed her unease because he put his hand on her shoulder and slowly marched her through the Museum.

'You could have won a marathon at your previous pace!'

Hannah turned her head back swiftly. 'Jonathan. I can't stop thinking about Dahlia. I'm worried sick about her.' She knew her eyelids appeared puffy and darker than usual. For days she had left her hair unkempt, her eyebrows ungroomed. Her poor daughter was probably as thin as a stick of cinnamon! She was all too aware of the treatment Dahlia could be facing right now.

'Hannah. Darling. Slow down!... I know... It's dreadful for you; and the awful fact is that a hostage situation won't be resolved overnight. It's bigger than two desperate families. It's an act of war between countries.'

Hannah felt Jonathan's warm breath on her cheek. 'I'm sorry,' he said, 'I'm not trying to scare you.'

The faster her mind raced, the more she couldn't keep up with her own thoughts. Jonathan was right. *Slow down,* she thought. A statue on the other end of the gallery caught her attention. It was the statue of a headless lion. Hannah knew that the museum had been looted, the lion decapitated, and its head seized. The stone paws and limbs which remained could have passed for those of a cat, stealthily waiting for a moment to pounce on a victim.

Hannah shuddered. 'Is that what you want the kidnapping to end like?' She pleaded with the lion and flung her arms in his direction. A dreadful premonition raced through her body like a hot liquid brewing on a stove. 'Jonathan, what if…'

'Hannah!' Jonathan shook her shoulders and her body almost crackled like a leaf. She'd felt her muscles weakening since they arrived in Baghdad a few days ago.

'Listen to yourself. I doubt Dahlia is going to be decapitated by Jihadi Jack!'

Hannah felt her muscles relax. How could a mother stop her child from suffering when the child was running towards it?

'Sweetheart, look at me.' Jonathan shook her shoulders. Hannah was soothed by the refuge in his eyes. 'We're going to locate the kidnappers. I have a friend in the British Embassy who can help us.'

Hannah had hated having had so many arguments with her daughter. Here she was, as injured as that headless lion. Jonathan never seemed to be worried about his son, even while he was working in warzones. Maybe it was because she was a woman, Hannah thought. Nine months in a womb, sharing nutrition and warmth, formed a bond that men could only imagine.

The silence was broken by footsteps heading towards them. 'Mr Jonathan and Mrs Hannah!'

It was the Museum curator, Khalil, with whom Jonathan had been collaborating online with each other for the past two weeks. Hannah noticed his shapely pointed chin despite his burly appearance. His sandals were dusty and one of his eyes kept twitching. It was most probably daunting for him to meet a British curator.

'How are you doing? My name is Khalil,' He said pleasantly. 'I thought we'd take a look upstairs today. I'm afraid the statues of Eros, Apollo and Poseidon were smashed, and the heads stolen a few years ago.'

Hannah smiled at Khalil and said, 'Hello! Nice to meet you. The statues you mention are in the Hatra Gallery upstairs, yes?' She felt Khalil needed to acknowledge her acquaintance with the artefacts in the Iraqi Museum. It wasn't only Jonathan who was worthy of validation.

'Indeed. Shall we head over?'

In the Hatra gallery, Hannah almost slipped on the dusty floor of one of the new storerooms. There they were, shards of smashed ivories and pottery spattered across the laminate flooring, glass cabinets gaping open. Hannah worried about the lack of staff at the museum. No wonder lootings were taking place. What a contrast to the British Museum where there was enough staff and they all felt safe to work there.

Khalil began to tell Hannah and Jonathan the story of the museum. His twitching irritated Hannah. He needn't feel threatened or nervous by them. They were here to help. 'This museum was established in the 1920s by the British,' he said. 'Back then, it was secure and as proud as the lions portrayed in its galleries. Now, the museum is situated in this dangerous street, the Haifa Street, where outbreaks of violence are a regular feature. It makes us a vulnerable target for a heist.'

Hannah cast her eye bleakly across the gallery. Khalil continued talking in a low voice, looking around him as if to make sure no one else was listening.

'Since its establishment about 15,000 pieces have been stolen. You can sort the perpetrators into three groups: professionals who've stolen several dozen of the most valuable treasures such as the lions; random thieves who stick to excavation-site pieces and insiders who take pieces of jewellery.'

'Half of the items have since been restored, no?' Jonathan said.

Hannah couldn't help but feel a resentment building up towards Jonathan and what he represented. Here he was, an Orientalist, trying to justify the plundering of valuable artefacts by saying that they had been restored. She scowled at Jonathan and said, 'The Western greed for Eastern culture is the very reason why this Museum was plundered!'

Khalil looked uncomfortable and excused himself, saying he had to interview a new member of staff.

Jonathan stepped closer towards Hannah, hurt and indignation in his eyes. 'I understand your anger, Hannah. But I'm an archaeologist. I try to preserve ancient property, not destroy it.'

Hannah looked angrily at him and said, 'The army is too busy defending the oil fields rather than our cultural heritage. Oil is gushing out of the ground, right now.'

'I get that Hannah, I'm on your side.'

His eyes had clouded over. She wanted to believe him, the way he cared for and protected her. But she felt that sometimes he wasn't on her side and would never truly understand her love for her country.

'I've sat through countless conferences on preserving heritage sites,' Jonathan defended himself.

'And what have you achieved with your countless meetings? You don't get it, Jonathan. This is my heritage, not yours.'

'I know sweetheart. Your people have had to endure lots of hurt and humiliation. But my son Daniel has had to fight in a war he didn't believe in. Sacrifices are made on both sides, darling.' He hesitated, then said, 'But we cross all boundaries when we fall in love.'

Hannah let him draw her into his arms. He kissed her forehead. Her legs felt numb. She looked into his eyes and saw the reflection of a woman torn between doubting and wanting to trust.

'Hannah, we'll sort everything out and Dahlia will be freed by the time our UN plane flies back to Amman.' It was safer to fly back to London through Amman in Jordan and Jonathan wanted to visit the Dead Sea and the Citadel. They clung to each other before Jonathan broke away saying, 'I heard some good news from one of our members of the British Museum yesterday. The archaeological site in Babylon appears to be in a good condition. The only damage was to a Mushhushshu (dragon) figure in the Ishtar Gate.'

Hannah let out a laugh. She remembered her German friend Monica walking through the Ishtar Gate in Berlin, waving her hand around in wonder at the ancient artefacts. There it was again, the way that Jonathan managed to bring a smile to her lips, the way he made her feel less alone in the world. She knew she had been silly to doubt that earlier.

Suddenly, Jonathan left the gallery, saying he needed to get some fresh air. She hung around with Khalil before she made up a polite excuse and went to follow him. She scanned the grounds of the interior courtyard and there he was, emerging from behind a lion's statue. What was he looking for? From this distance it was hard to see what he was doing but she was sure she saw him closing his black leather bag hurriedly. He looked anxious. *What was he putting inside his bag?*

She crept towards him, taking care not to crunch the gravel under her feet. His head jerked up at the sound and met her eyes with a strange expression on his face. She hadn't seen him this way before. *Fear? Excitement? Guilt?* In a millisecond, Hannah spied the bulge in his bag but took care not to show that she had seen it. What could be the lump in his bag? She could only handle one uncertainty at a time. Her daughter came first.

'Jonathan! Come on, let's head back to the hotel.'

29

Adhamiya was located east central of Baghdad. It was one of the nine administrative districts in the city and was considered a no-go zone. However, once the defeat of ISIS had been promised, Dahlia was told it was a safer area. Her mother had chosen one of her auntie's houses for the unexpected reunion. It was near Sadr City, a Shiite slum where the kidnappers had come from. Debris had been bulldozed and heaps of rubble covered the ground around her aunt's house.

Dahlia had slept soundly after their rescuers had brought them to a small house in this district, East of the River Tigris. She was to wait there because her mother was coming to visit. *I feel removed from the world*, Dahlia thought. *But then, I always have been.*

She remembered refusing to play with some of her friends when she was a child because they loved to put on frilly dresses which she deplored. She was happy once she came to Britain and could wear jeans which were frayed at the ends and torn at the knees. Her biggest dream was to be true to herself. And now she had to face her mother.

She paced up and down the small living room, wondering how she would react once she was reunited with her mother. Carys had talked about her own mother, saying that she hardly ventured far from her home in a village in North

Wales. She only left it to go to a farm shop.

Dahlia thought of how her mother left her house every day, kohl across her eyelids and a Bohemian outfit, always conscious of how other people would perceive her and her daughter. Her mother clung to old, traditional values as if she were on a life-saving raft in the ocean. Carys didn't have to hide anything from her mother whereas Dahlia's sensuality had gone too long unshared and unnourished to the point that her own feelings had been alien to her.

She heard the latch of the door. Her auntie Roonak's house didn't have much furniture in it as she now lived with her daughter since her stroke a few months ago. Hannah's high-heeled shoes resounded in the empty corridor. The door was flung open and her mother rushed towards her, sobbing as she kissed the alcove of her neck. Dahlia felt her tears flow down her cheeks. She tried to break away from the tight squeeze, aware of the American guard standing near the door.

'Why is he still here?' She burst out. He ignored her.

'Darling,' Carys said, 'He was one of the soldiers who rescued us.' Carys tried smiling at the soldier weakly. 'Sorry. She's exhausted and still hasn't come to terms with the kidnapping.'

The soldier grunted his displeasure and shook his head, 'I'm on duty. And anyway…' He glanced at Dahlia and continued, 'Not exhausted or confused, like her.'

Dahlia was briskly led into an adjoining room by her mother who either didn't see or chose to ignore Carys who had been standing behind the wooden table in the sitting room. Her mother showed her some black and white photos on a mantelpiece next to the door.

'Dahlia, I haven't been in my sister's house for twenty years. This is a photo of your uncle Tariq. Look at his boyish expression. That was before he was imprisoned in Abu Ghraib.'

Dahlia's gaze travelled along the mantelpiece for other photos. She didn't recognise any of the photos and wasn't even sure she would be able to identify herself. Her hands felt numb.

Her mother said in a low voice, 'Darling, you've been through a terrible time. But be polite to that soldier. You don't want to be on the wrong side of him.'

'This is our country Mum. Didn't the Allies say they wanted to initiate a democratic regime? Well, if is democratic, I can say what I want.' Dahlia glared at her mother who kept silent. Then she continued, 'Freedom of speech is a dangerous gift, Mum. But it's still a gift.' She looked at her mother defiantly.

Her mother said softly, 'Democracy takes time to prove itself.' She took Dahlia's hand and squeezed it. 'Look how long it took East Germany to come to terms with the fall of the Berlin wall.' She hesitated, 'Tell me, how did you know you were free? Did the insurgents tell you that you would be released?'

Dahlia's eyes had lost focus. 'I have no idea how it all happened. There were three men who would bring us food, that's all I was aware of. The evening before the Americans stormed the house to rescue us, we were allowed to read the newspaper and watch TV for a while...' She looked at her mother, baffled. 'The next day, we were free, without any warning or discussion.' Hannah eyed her curiously.

'I do remember that there were more phone calls than usual the evening before the rescue.'

'What language were the phone calls in?'

'Mostly Arabic. I remember a phone call in English. I think it was a long-distance phone call as it was done in a loud voice.'

Her mother persisted. 'Did they mention any institution?'

Dahlia turned to look through the small window nearest to her. Her gaze fell upon the ruins of a building. The bricks scattered on the baked ground reminded her of a building in London.

'Just a minute… I remember… One of the men mentioned a museum.' Hannah jolted backwards.

'I didn't hear anything else though. It did strike me as odd that they were interested in a museum or a curator in the midst of civil unrest.'

'Dahlia, it wasn't the museum itself that intrigued them. Maybe it was someone in the museum they were talking about? Someone who works in the museum in London.'

Dahlia shrugged her shoulders. She smiled as she caught sight of Carys coming into the room.

'Mrs Aziz. I hope you recognise me. 'Carys said, cocking her head.

Hannah frowned. Carys moved forward to kiss her on both cheeks in the usual Middle Eastern way but Hannah broke away abruptly and said, 'My daughter has told me how caring you were with her asthma attacks. Thank you for being such a good doctor.'

Carys stifled a laugh. 'Mrs Aziz, I'm more than just a doctor to Dahlia.'

'Yes. I know. You're an idealist.'

Carys laughed out loud. 'Goodness me. Haven't you figured us out yet? We're in love.'

Dahlia felt like hiding behind Carys who moved towards her and touched the small of her back lightly. Dahlia's eyes softened as she realised this was the first time Carys had challenged her mother. She felt the fluttering of her heart as she walked towards the door and asked, 'Iraqi chai or English breakfast tea with milk? I'll get it. I need to stretch my legs a bit.'

Happy to escape the confrontation with her mother, Dahlia stumbled out of the room to get the tea ready and tripped over on the old Iranian carpet from Isfahan. It was ragged at the end. As she got up, she clenched her fist, more out of embarrassment than pain. Before she left the room, she heard her mother say to Carys, 'You've only known my daughter for a few months. I have known her since birth. Don't think that gives you the right to criticise me.' Dahlia crept to the door and listened to Carys' response.

'Of course. I understand! Dahlia and I have only been going out with each other for a few months. But I listen to what she has to say without leaving out bits I feel uncomfortable with.'

Dahlia, worn out by the kidnapping, didn't want to hear the rest of the argument. After preparing the tea in the small, frugal kitchen, she was about to step back into the living room when she heard Carys say, 'Your daughter may suffer from what I think is called the Stockholm Syndrome. It may also be post traumatic syndrome. I'm not sure. A psychotherapist would know.'

Dahlia froze and waited. She heard Carys explain that the Stockholm syndrome was a situation where hostages became sympathetic to their captors in order to survive. Dahlia felt her anger bubbling inside her. She was not mentally disturbed! She felt as invisible as a lifeless ghost. Gritting her teeth, she entered the room and heard her mother tell Carys that the BBC wanted to interview her the following day.

Carys smiled at her as she came in. 'It's too early for an interview.' She added, 'CNN and Al Jazeera are trying to get an interview with you darling.'

Her mother's shoulders sagged a little further. 'Dahlia, you must not speak on television or participate in any interview yet. It would be a disaster. The BBC would sack you instantly. Not only that of course. You would be vilified in the press as being a sympathiser.'

Dahlia stared at Carys and her mother. She didn't know whom to trust now. Carys thought she had become irrational. *No one has the right to own me,* she thought. She staggered out of the room. Her head was spinning. She longed for the soft, sorrowful sounds of the Shimshal, a flute-like instrument that was played at funerals.

30

Hannah was relieved to be back in the British Museum in London. The flight back from Amman had taken about five hours. She watched Jonathan run his fingers through his hair while he was talking to an official on the bridge to the café. Tufts of his brown hair stuck out in all directions. His eyelids were still puffy from the long journey back home from Iraq. They had had no time to enjoy the Dead Sea in Amman and had opted to fly straight home to London.

Hannah watched a bead of sweat trickle down past his aquiline nose reaching a corner of his soft mouth. His lips were cracked at the edges. Jonathan moistened them with his tongue slowly. *He's so calm, not like Dahlia,* she thought.

Suddenly, Jonathan turned to look at Hannah across the room. She smiled at him. He stopped talking to the official and came towards her.

'Sorry about the long time this is taking, Hannah.'

'Don't worry, Jonathan. They have had to do without you for a few weeks and all because of my troubles.'

'The Museum executives would like me to write a report on our findings in Iraq.'

Hannah frowned and nodded. He would need energy for that. His weight had plummeted in Iraq. She had lost weight too. Anxiety and insomnia had plagued them both.

She took Jonathan's hands timidly and said, 'Thank you for arranging Dahlia's rescue.'

Jonathan was surprised. He lifted an eyebrow. 'What makes you think I had anything to do with it?'

'Well, you see, Dahlia told me that the British Museum was mentioned during the kidnapping.'

Jonathan raised his other eyebrow and said, 'I'm confined to silence.' He put his finger in front of his lips as if to seal them.

Hannah had not forgotten the bulge in Jonathan's bag when they were leaving the Museum in Iraq… what had he hidden, and where was it now? She would wait and see if he explained his action in the next few days. The rescue mission to free Dahlia and Carys and the reunion with them had seemed surreal. They had experienced enough commotion to last a lifetime.

'You do sound dramatic, Jonathan.'

He narrowed his eyes and replied, 'I'm trying to keep up with your family.'

Hannah laughed for the first time in days and said, 'Middle-Eastern people are passionate.'

Jonathan stepped closer to her and said, 'I'll take you up on that.'

He kissed her right cheek. Then he stood back and chuckled.

'Oh, I forgot. You kiss three times back home.'

He kissed her on the left cheek, perilously close to the corner of her lip. Her skin tingled as she felt the soft pressure of his lips. His hands held her closer to him. She sighed as he stroked her hair lightly. Then he stepped back. Hannah's eyelids felt heavy. *How far would she be willing to go with him*, she thought, eying his gentle hands. Maybe Dahlia was braver than herself.

'The three kisses are for relatives and family friends,' she said. She felt light, like floating somewhere in outer space. Maybe it would be easier in space, no conventions to adhere to and no society to judge you. She sensed the sadness that had overcome her. Jonathan squeezed her hand. 'I'm much more than a family friend now,' he said. Hannah nodded her head. 'You survived Iraq Jonathan.'

He took a deep breath. 'Our family survived this time.' Hannah liked the way he stressed the word *our.*

'Hannah, I don't know when and if ever, Iraq will be peaceful. I'm ashamed of what happened in Abu Ghraib prison. I saw the images on television. Not only men but also women tortured the Iraqi prisoners and posed for photos with their thumbs up.'

Hannah remembered seeing these images on TV. 'Jonathan, you can't begin to imagine what ISIS did to the Yazidi and Peshmerga. No wonder Dahlia's behaviour isn't normal.'

Jonathan almost groaned as he shook Hannah's shoulders lightly. 'Hannah, have you ever thought that the way Dahlia is leading her life with Carys may not only have to do with her time as a Peshmerga?

Hannah averted her gaze momentarily and when she looked back at Jonathan she said, 'You mean she may have been born that way?'

Jonathan looked thoughtful as he replied, 'You need to talk to her. Find out what her true self feels.'

Hannah sighed. Hadn't Carys mentioned that too when Dahlia had gone to wash the teacups in her aunt's house?

'Jonathan, I think we both need to let our children open up to us.'

Jonathan with his hunched shoulders and with her conditioning... both of them dreading the contradictions they were facing. It would be much easier to talk about the book Jonathan was writing than to entertain possibilities that Dahlia was not heterosexual or talk about Daniel's lack of manliness.

31

Jonathan had left the top button of his shirt open as Dahlia and he were strolling along the South Bank. There was still a bite in the air, the last residue of winter, such a contrast to the sweltering heat in Baghdad.

'Who would've thought we'd travel half-way across the world before we had actually met anywhere outside of the British Museum in London,' Jonathan chuckled.

'Now that we've been to Iraq together, we might as well try something new, have an adventure here in London,' Dahlia said, 'and we shouldn't forget your book, Jonathan.'

Dahlia couldn't help thinking of the frame of Carys' shoulders and her incredible posture. She always sat up straight with an air of pride, as if she was posing to be painted. She pictured leading Carys to her bedroom, t*hat model pose resting on her bed, and succumbing to her caresses.*

'My book?' Jonathan looked momentarily gripped by fear. Dahlia was jolted out of her reverie. 'Yes. The Gilgamesh Epic!'

'Ah yes,' he said with relief. 'Indeed, my book. Let's go to the Poetry Library. We can have a coffee. I have to say, it was an adventure for me when I first came to the Poetry Library as a student, to explore poems from the ancient world. They hold great discussion groups.'

'So, you got to know the Poetry Library so well?' Dahlia asked.

'Yes. I had a job here as a student and worked as a waiter during the summer months.'

Dahlia raised her eyebrows and said, 'Back home, academics never worked as waiters, not even during summer breaks.'

'Oh, I learnt a lot from my waiter friends. One of them, Harry, joked that I would marry a Middle Eastern lady someday due to my interest in Middle Eastern archaeology.'

Dahlia watched him push aside strands of his hair which fell across his eyes. Would he one day propose to her mother? She loved his honesty and couldn't imagine being disappointed in him.

'You'll like the Royal Festival Hall, it was officially opened in 1951. I used to bring Daniel here as a child during his half-term holidays. He used to dance in the foyer. Odd for a boy. He should have been more interested in rugby or football.'

Dahlia said, 'My problem with Mum was that I *was* interested in playing football when I could have been dancing with my friends.'

They both laughed. 'The view from out here at night is stunning,' Jonathan said, 'I always love the reflection of the lights on the Thames. The ripples wink back at you.' Dahlia smiled. They entered the Royal Festival Hall and chose a table in a quieter corner, away from the bustle of gallery-goers who were shuffling in and out of a photography exhibition.

Jonathan ordered a cappuccino for himself and the usual latte for herself. 'Dahlia, do you know about Rawlinson and the Behistun Inscription?'She looked at him blankly.

'Sir Henry Rawlinson was an English army officer who served in India in the early nineteenth century. While he was there, he acquired a knowledge of Arabic, Persian and

Hindustani. In Persia he became an advisor to the governor of your Kurdistan.'

Dahlia pulled her chair closer to Jonathan. 'What about him?'

'Rawlinson recognised the importance of some writing on a rock in Behistun in Western Iran. The rock was situated a hundred metres from the ground. He used ladders to climb up and copy the inscription. A Kurdish boy managed to squeeze himself up a cleft and help him.' He smiled.

'It took ten years for the entire inscription to be copied but, when translated, it led to the decipherment of cuneiform clay tablets. This monument was the cuneiform version of the trilingual Rosetta Stone that proved to be the key to cracking Egyptian hieroglyphics! Rawlinson was famed for his work.'

Jonathan waved his arms excitedly as if he had just come to a conclusion. 'I would love to be revered just as Rawlinson was.' His eyes shone.

'If I were to make a find, I could foresee the possibility of publication in established archaeological journals. I would become famous and move up the ranks in the British Museum!'

Dahlia frowned at the expression on his face. It almost looked callous. She brushed a doubt that had been encroaching on her aside and asked, 'Would it take that long to decipher a clay tablet if we found one?'

'It would take a few months. When the first objects from Mesopotamia arrived at the British Museum, Rawlinson and a fellow enthusiast, George Smith, worked on the clay tablets. Smith realised that he was reading the story of the Flood and he got so excited that he ran around throwing off his clothes! Imagine, Dahlia, if I found at least one clay tablet!' Dahlia blushed.

He opened his rucksack carefully, eyeing her cautiously. Out came a towel, a simple brown towel but when Jonathan unfolded it, there lay a small clay tablet, dark orange-brown and cracked in a few places. Jonathan started to whisper although there were no people around them.

'I found this in Iraq outside the museum, behind the statue of the lion. Some looters must have dropped it.'

Dahlia gasped and Jonathan looked at her with a worried expression. 'My plan has always been to hand it over to the British Museum. It would be safer there than in Iraq while it is still embroiled in civil war.' Dahlia tried to protest.

'No Dahlia, I believe it's the best protection for the tablet to be kept in Britain. And… I didn't want to tell you this, but the tablet has helped you already.' He watched her puzzled face.

'The British Embassy worked to free you and Carys from the kidnappers because they knew of my connection, my status, in the British Museum. The tablet would only be destroyed by ISIS if they resurged. '

Dahlia felt herself stiffen.

'Dahlia, I am an archaeologist at heart. I love preserving cultural artefacts. But besides that, I love your country Dahlia. This is part of your heritage and always will be. The clay tablet will be safe here and so will you. We are one.'

He let go of her hand and started feeling the clay tablet cautiously. He appeared engrossed by his findings and slowly formed the words, 'He who says everything, eleventh tablet…'

Jonathan grasped Dahlia's hand again and almost shouted, 'The Flood Tablet!' He quickly added, 'Dahlia, we can decide what to do with the clay tablet after deciphering it a bit.'

He noticed her putting her hands in front of her face. She had the right to be furious. He seemed at a loss how to smooth over the awkwardness of their situation.

'Are you crazy, trying to veer away from the gravity of your deed?' Dahlia had taken her hands away from her face. She was trembling. Was this the honest man she had been admiring all these months?

Jonathan took her hands and kissed them, frowning. 'Sweetheart, I'm proud of your heritage. Most of the twelve chapters of Gilgamesh were found in the last century at Nineveh. I want the clay tablets to be safe.'

'Safe from whom?' Dahlia whispered as she took her hands away.

'Protected from common robbers and ISIS.' He watched her eyes glance past him as if contemplating her next words.

'Jonathan, you must give the clay tablet back.' She screamed, then said quietly, 'I can't stay friends with a thief!'

Jonathan flinched. 'Of-course, as soon as possible. How could you doubt it?'

He ventured forward. 'One day, the Gilgamesh Epic will be complete, just like the Iliad and Odyssey. At the beginning of this century, Bruno Meissner purchased a big fragment of the Epic from a dealer in your country. In it, there are many parallels to Noah's Ark!'

Jonathan picked up his drink and sipped it while it was still hot. 'The Gods decided to impose a great flood on mankind.'

She looked at him, horrified. 'But don't worry, Dahlia. In the end, Ut-napishtim and his wife are given a great boat and a 'secret of the gods', a plant of rejuvenation.'

'I'm not shocked by the great flood, Jonathan!'

She struggled to compose herself, 'When are you going to give back the clay tablet you stole from the museum in Iraq?'

Jonathan reached out to touch her hand. She snatched it away.

'Dahlia, I think we should continue to decipher the clay tablet at my flat. I have kept some valuable utensils there to help us. We can share the credit later on.'

She flung her serviette at him. 'Are you deaf? I want nothing to do with stolen goods.'

She looked at him in disbelief and ran towards the exit of the library. The only man she had admired, had revealed himself to be a man with no noble values.

32

Carys was relieved that Dahlia had agreed to go back to London with her. She wondered whether she would ever join the *Médecins sans Frontières* after her ordeal with the kidnappers in Iraq! The damaging symptoms of Dahlia's post traumatic syndrome were persistent but were not the result of a Stockholm Syndrome, according to Carys' psychiatrist friend. Dahlia had not formed an affectionate bond with her captors! Carys felt reassured about that. They had taken a plane from Baghdad to London Heathrow. Carys felt her pulse quicken. She was going to visit Dahlia in her flat for the first time since their relationship began.

The East End had changed a lot since Carys' last visit. The Westfield shopping centre had expanded, and high-rise buildings had shot up. Carys made her way to Dahlia's flat and knocked on the door. Dahlia opened the door cautiously and then took the chain off as soon as she recognised Carys standing outside.

'You made it!' Carys took a step forward and closed the door behind her. 'I'd love to feel the softness of your hair.'

Dahlia's face broke into a smile. A shaft of light lit up a beauty spot on Dahlia's cheek. 'You smell good,' she said in a husky voice. 'You should use that perfume more often. Very seductive.'

Carys was glad she had sprayed on some Jo Malone perfume, albeit a present from her husband two years before. Dahlia's lips moved towards her cheeks and she kissed her lightly. Carys kissed the soft lips slowly at first, then faster as she felt Dahlia responding. They were locked in a tight embrace. Carys felt their bodies adjust to each other to fit perfectly. She felt Dahlia yielding and pressing herself nearer like tidal waves, Carys the shore. Here they were at last, both finding safe haven from anguish of the past and present. She slowly put her hand up through Dahlia's white blouse, felt for her breast and easily found the hardened nipple. She rubbed it between her thumb and forefinger. Dahlia's embrace became desperate. Carys felt her stiffen and sigh. 'Carys, don't stop!'

They went to Dahlia's bedroom and fell onto her futon bed, taking off each other's clothes quickly. Carys held Dahlia's hands above her head and started kissing her soft, small breasts, giving them equal attention. She drew circles on Dahlia's thighs, slowly, then quicker. She kissed her around the belly button, watching Dahlia breathe faster. She felt her hand move towards Dahlia's parted legs, where she knew a soft spot was awaiting her, like an oyster in a shell. She quickened her movements and after only a few seconds, she heard Dahlia's primal cry. Pleasure and pain intertwined.

Carys held Dahlia close. She felt she was helping to fulfil Dahlia's aching desire and was proud of it. She had always wondered how it would feel to make a woman yield to her touch and to make the woman that she loved happy.

Dahlia asked shyly, 'What about you?'

'Your pleasure is mine too. We are one. Next time.'

Simone de Beauvoir had written that sexuality was more of a transformative act than the quenching of thirst. *Hadn't she just proved that?* She had undergone a metamorphosis of her previous self by making love to a woman. She felt less self-conscious than making love to a man, even though there was a ten-year age difference!

Much later, after tea and Turkish Delights from a plate next to the futon bed, the two of them lay on Dahlia's bed.

'You know,' Carys began, 'it's a bit miserable of me to say this to you but, in a way, I was helped towards understanding the shock and hurt of your experiences because, well because… do you remember that terrible bombing on July 7th in 2005?'

'Oh, yes, I was so glad I wasn't anywhere near that part of London,' Dahlia said thankfully.

'I'm glad that you weren't there,' Carys said vehemently. 'I haven't told anyone… I mean I haven't wanted to talk about… but I feel that I can share it with you… I was there.'

She felt Dahlia tense.

'I wasn't in the underground, thank God, but I was at the BMA House by Tavistock Square. Jeez! It was a scorcher of a day, and the city was so happy because London had just won the bid for the 2012 Olympics!'

She smiled briefly. 'I was there to interview an Iraqi female doctor about the medical repercussions of the Iraq war, would you believe it, when there was a massive explosion.'

Carys frowned. 'I ran outside to see what had happened and I'll never forget… the sirens, Dahlia, the police cars, the ambulances and the fire brigade… the thick smell of gun-powder and this plume of smoke reaching up to the sky…'

Dahlia lay immobile. *How could I have bottled up this awful experience?* Carys thought. *At least I have someone to share it with now.*

'The explosion had propelled the roof of a bus into the

street. The metal framework of the bus was in pieces, fused into a distorted shape. Firemen were trying to get the passengers out of the bus. Some people were jumping off the top deck of the bus…'

Carys began to sob. 'We opened up the courtyard of the BMA to treat the injured passengers… I did what I could, Dahlia but thirteen people were killed just there, in front of me, and I couldn't do anything to help them.'

She let herself go into Dahlia's arms and wept away some of the horror that had haunted her in the years in between.

33

Elias gazed at his reflection in the mirror of his small bedroom. His beard was getting longer and wiry, silver strands had started to emerge. A pair of unapologetic eyes burnt back into him. He had all the right to be furious. After all, he lived in this shithole, had lost his job and, worst of all, feared his sister was whoring with that woman.

He picked up the pamphlets that were strewn on the table. His window overlooked the Westfield shopping centre. The pamphlets written in Arabic were artistic and beautiful. The English pamphlets looked bland by comparison. '*Join us against* capitalism *and greed.*' Just like their food. Tasteless and faithless.

His eyes traced the curves of the calligraphic Arabic; he was regretful that he couldn't read it very well. But that didn't matter; he could communicate with his brothers on the dark web in English. His brothers kept reminding him of the hopeful times he had spent in the Caliphate. Abu Fouad for one had kept the black flag flying, if not in the Caliphate, then at least in cyberspace. Elias would harness this cyberspace. He would remind people that the dream of equality for all men would not die so easily.

He picked up his cup of coffee and gulped it down whilst it was still too hot. He liked to do that. It was the little things, like taking no notice when the roof of his mouth was burning, that made him feel powerful. The infidels would feel the fury of his soul when he fulfilled his Project. That's what he would call his deed, the *Project*.

No one would know about it except his brothers. They had offered him a project in the Philippines, in Madrid or Nigeria. Elias smiled. *It had to be in London.* His gaze wandered to the Christmas lights and decorations outside the mall and he felt rage again. How could the Christians be happy when his brothers in Iraq and Syria were suffering from poisonous gas and lack of food? This was not a time for celebrations. He would see to that.

But first, he needed to shave and go to the barber. He looked too conspicuous in his current state. Whenever he used the Central Line to go into town, strangers would look at him subtly and watch his movements. He enjoyed their fear of him but not their disdain. Hah! At least they would remember spotting him after his Project had been fulfilled. First of all, he would need to go shopping. The items he needed to accomplish his deed were readily available.

His brothers would be proud of him. A better life in the other world awaited him. Virgins in abundance. But he would not go alone. He would take someone from his family with him. Elias felt calm for the first time since coming out of Iraq. It was necessary to be tranquil when planning such an important project.

The Westerners were more afraid of life than the Jihadis were of death. Elias had seen their soft faces in death after their deeds. He went to his mobile phone which lay on the only shelf in his flat and dialled his mother's number.

'Hello.'

His mother's voice sounded wary and lower in pitch. What

had this country done to her? She used to be confident. Now she sounded more confused.

'Daya, I miss you.'

There was a slight pause at the other end.

'I miss you too Elias. How are you?'

Elias told her that he was jobless but that he kept himself busy reading. He did not tell her about the content of his pamphlets. He did however tell her that he felt alienated from most people in London. He heard her sigh and wasn't happy that her tone sounded irritable instead of caring.

'Daya, this country is abominable,' he said. 'The people hold Pride Parades for the gays but not for the straight people on the right path. They pay for gender- reassignments defying Allah and his will. No funding is given to Muslims to integrate them into the country.' He paused to give his mother a chance to answer him.

'Elias, do you want to be integrated?'

He was taken aback by this question. 'No, I don't. I won't be part of a community which denigrates the glory of our Iraqi civilization. Nineveh, Gilgamesh and all our ancient relics.'

He loved the story of Gilgamesh, the ancient, Mesopotamian King, strong as a lion on his quest for eternal life. He smiled. Everlasting love would be in Paradise. The beguiling virgins would be dancing and beckoning him to join them. No more complicated women who wanted men to use condoms and refused to succumb to the sexual positions he preferred. Men would lead the way and women would follow.

'Elias, what did you phone me for?'

He scowled. His mother was just another woman confused by her role in life. How dare she go out with Jonathan and pretend that Jonathan knew more about Gilgamesh than himself?

'Daya, I know you're unhappy with me...'

He paused to see whether she would contradict this. There ensued a damning silence.

'I thought we could meet up with Dahlia and strengthen our blood bond.'

He smiled at the thought. Dahlia and he had cut their forearms as children in order to press them together and forge their blood-alliance. No, it was more than that, it was to flagship their love. He felt his blood boil when he remembered seeing a thin cut on Dahlia's arm two weeks ago. *She was betraying him with Carys.* How could she mingle her blood with an Infidel? Carys only had water to offer, not blood. The bond with her brother, Elias, was surely stronger? He would see to that.

His mother sounded reluctant when she agreed to meet him and Dahlia outside the Christmas market on South Bank. Elias smiled. It was just the right time to make a move, Christmas when the Infidels would feel relaxed. Once upon a time, he had felt at ease. Now all he could do was clench his fists and think of death. It was time for a role reversal for 'Master and Servant.' He smiled as he thought of uniting his family in the one way he thought possible.

34

Elias had texted to say that he wanted to meet up at the Christmas market on the South Bank near the Royal Festival Hall. Dahlia wondered why. He had never shown any interest in the market before. He couldn't drink the mulled wine or eat the German Bratwurst from the stalls because of his Muslim faith.

She walked towards a bench opposite London Bridge and sat down. She made sure that her white blouse was tucked into her tight black jeans. A loose blouse did not mean a loose woman, but Elias wouldn't appreciate it. The thought of constantly moulding herself to his expectations irritated her.

But it was hard to tell the difference between care and control. Perhaps he wanted to know her whereabouts all the time because he sincerely cared about her? Whatever it was, it was more bearable than the stringent captivity she had suffered recently under the Shia insurgents. She wondered whether Elias would ever acknowledge the damage ISIS had done to them both. Dahlia buttoned up her duffle coat. The December chill was biting.

A hand grabbed hold of Dahlia's right shoulder from behind. She jumped up and pushed the hand away. Elias stood behind the bench grinning.

'Why are you so frightened, Dahlia? Would you have

pushed away Carys like that?'

Dahlia looked into Elias' eyes which were full of taunting menace. She ignored his question.

'Why did you come from behind me?'

'I wanted to feel your joy from behind,' Elias mocked.

Dahlia was disturbed by the glazed look that had entered Elias' eyes. His childhood innocence had been taken by ISIS, just as hers had been destroyed.

He smiled at Dahlia and said, 'Where is *Um'* Elias?'

His mother was *Um' Elias*. Mother of Elias. It was the honourable Arabic way in which to identify a woman as the mother of her oldest son. Since when had he referred to their mother in that way? She had always been *Daya* to them.

'You mean *Daya*?'

Elias stamped his foot. 'It's for me to decide how to address our mother!' He had raised his voice. Dahlia shuddered. He was trying to change their mother's name and her whole identity. She cocked her head to the side as if to observe Elias from a different angle.

'Raise your words, not your voice. It's rain that grows flowers, not thunder,' she said pleasantly.

'Says who?' Elias said indignantly.

'It's one of Rumi's quotes, a fourteenth century poet from the Middle East.'

'What good is poetry? I listen to my brothers, the ones living here and now, not some wandering dervish who might as well have been gay with all his lack of masculinity. If you are born a man, then you must *be* one.'

Dahlia gasped. Elias continued to rant. He flitted from subject to subject with no pause. He seemed to be on a mission but to what exactly, Dahlia didn't know. It wasn't just the December cold that made her feel frightened.

'What about the Sykes-Picot Agreement during the First World War? The West broke their promises to us. You know how they carved up the Middle Eastern lands and feasted on them. Treachery!'

Elias was oblivious to the passers-by who were warily observing him. She could feel their eyes on her, watching her reaction. She took a step closer to her brother and said, 'Elias, you've got to stop reading those articles on Facebook. We know all that about Sykes-Picot. It just fuels the fire. And besides, you know about how exploited Facebook is. Remember how they showed a slave market for Yazidi women on there? Cattle are treated better than that.'

Elias sniffed the cold air. He seemed to be calculating something. There was silence for a few seconds, then he smoothed the creases of his coat. He traced down his torso, which looked bulky. Had he put on that much weight since she'd last seen him a few months ago? It wasn't likely; his face looked less full, more ashen than usual.

'Let's walk towards the bridge, Dahlia,' he said. 'Reconnect our family on it.'

His voice sounded softer. Dahlia looked at the bridge. She wondered if there was any hope of crossing the turbulent waters of their traumas. She led the way. They had after all told their mother that they would meet her there. As they stepped onto the bridge, Dahlia noticed that new barriers had been installed between the bridge's pavement and road; that would be because of the terrorist attack two years previously. Three pedestrians killed and multiple stabbings at Borough Market.

ISIS seemed to have infiltrated people's minds, even here in London. She looked sideways at her brother. Was he following ISIS ideology on twitter? What could she do to win him back?

Elias nudged her gently further along the bridge. She hesitated and he pushed her more forcefully. She tensed at his touch but kept moving. Tourists were constantly passing her by, speaking in the usual variety of languages and accents inherent to London's culture. It was the usual pre-Christmas hustle and bustle of visitors from surrounding cities and foreigners alike.

Dahlia knew an instant of pleasure. How good it felt to be far away from Raqqa and Sinjar. She was safe here and would never need to meet tormentors from the past. They were most probably hiding in other countries, just like the Nazis had fled to South America. A lot of the ISIS soldiers had been caught by Kurdish Peshmerga and were held in camps for an indefinite period of time.

The European ISIS soldiers had been stripped off their citizenships and their black uniforms had been replaced by orange jumpsuits. Dahlia sneaked a look at Elias. How had no one noticed that he had belonged to ISIS? The British intelligence were probably watching him closely.

She pulled the lapels of her coat closer together. Elias was looking at her suspiciously, as if he could read her thoughts. Her mind naturally flew to Carys when she got stressed. Carys would be angry with her for meeting her brother again. She didn't trust Elias. And yet, Dahlia had brought him up as a child long before ISIS had appeared in Sinjar. She remembered how he had shown her his first fallen tooth, proud that he had pulled it out himself. Now he looked up to ISIS, his fallen heroes. It always filled her with sadness to remember the innocent boy he had once been.

Would any of this have happened if their father were still alive? Would her mother notice how cruel Elias had become towards her and if she did, would she sweep it under the carpet, too afraid to accept the anger boiling away within her own son?

Elias started rubbing his sleeves with his hands, agitated. His eyes were flitting towards the dim London skyline.

Dahlia didn't want to stay on the bridge for long. She had forgotten her gloves. 'Elias, can we leave now? We can text *Daya* to meet us nearby. It's cold here.'

Elias didn't respond. Then she realised that this whole time, he had been deeply focused on the Shard. He said, 'Let a shard of glass cut through the heart of non-believers.'

'What?' Dahlia stepped back, almost bumping into a passer-by. Elias was starting to make her feel sick. She began to walk away, but he grabbed her arm and yanked her back. She tried to wriggle herself free, but his grip was firm. There again, plastered onto his face, was that wide, evil grin.

'Are you afraid of me, Dahlia?'

Suddenly she felt very unsafe. He was the stronger one.

35

Elias kept his hand on his sister's arm and scrutinised her face. The love he had seen in these eyes when they were children had disappeared. Instead he smelt fear, like a lamb just before being slaughtered. He bit his lip. *If I can't have love, then I'll take fear.* He grinned.

'Dahlia, don't you want to be in a place where you are respected?'

She blinked a few times as if unsure how to answer him.

'We're respected here.'

Elias shook his head. 'Do you know what I was called today, in a queue for that shard, a *fucking Paki.*'

She looked deadpan. He showed her the fist he had formed. Dahlia usually ran away when she was afraid, not like himself. He had joined ISIS because he was a brave man. He had faced death to make the world a better place. He had not received any rewards, any medals. Just a mobile phone and the promise of a wife that had been bought for him. What a useless wife she had been. The baby had died at birth, leaving him childless and lonely. He had sold his wife on.

'I'll throw a shard of glass through their hearts,' he repeated.

Dahlia grimaced and was quiet. He felt he was in charge, even if only for a few moments.

'Don't you want to go to a better place? Where there is no difference between a black and a white man, a rich man and a pauper?'

'You only talk of men, Elias.'

Elias clenched his left fist as he replied, 'What do you want, virgins? Carys isn't a virgin, is she?' Elias felt sick at the thought. Was no man good enough for his sister?

Dahlia's gaze was fixed on the dark ripples of the Thames. Elias remembered her obsession with water. As a child he had often been sent to the next village to get water from a well because their own had dried up. On his return, Dahlia always sprinkled some on her arms. He used to wonder why she would do this even when the weather was mild.

He would not let her wipe him away. They belonged together, like conjoined twins. She was part of his body, part of his soul, in life and in death.

He would show Dahlia the extent of his masculinity. He grinned and opened his duffle coat. Her eyes widened in horror and she gulped before she tried to drag her eyes away. He patted the suicide belt lightly, watching her breath quicken. Elias savoured her discomfort. He reached out to pull a string at the side of his suicide belt. If his sister wanted to share the virgins with him, he would let her. He was willing to share anything with his beautiful sister, even death.

'Stay away!' Dahlia's loud voice barked a command to the people nearby. 'This is a terrorist! He's wearing a suicide belt.'

His sister's voice sounded firm, not fearful anymore. She was stronger than he had thought. At last!

He watched with a smile as a woman pushing a pram and two men in suits looked terrified and ran away.

'You see, Dahlia? They are cowards.'

From the corner of his eye, he could see an older woman

in a familiar dark trench coat running towards him. He drew a knife from his interior pocket. It was his self-obsessed mother. This ungrateful woman had been cold and disloyal to his father since his death. He stared at her, realising that she had recently cut her hair.

She needed other parts of her body cut off! Stupid woman! Didn't she have other matters to worry about besides her outward appearance? He was sick of her research in the British Museum, fed up with the fact that she was always tending to her own needs. She never asked him how he felt, whether he had enough money or what his plans for the future were.

'Elias! What are you doing? What has got into you?'

He looked at his mother scornfully as he replied, 'I'm taking my sister and myself to a better place. Something you never managed.'

His mother's mouth gaped open in disbelief. Her eyes closed for a second. Then she opened them and looked Elias straight in the eyes. *She's provoking me*, he thought disgusted.

Dahlia looked at her mother imploringly. Elias saw the appeal and was furious. Dahlia should be locking eyes with him, not their mother.

A woman screamed and a sturdy man ran towards Elias and Dahlia and deftly kicked the knife out of his hand; they both fell backwards towards the railing of the bridge. The man knocked his head and lay stunned on the pavement. Elias didn't let go of his sister's arm. It felt limp, soft, typical for her!

His mother was screaming now. How good it was to see some emotions in her. He grabbed the edge of the railing and looked into his sister's eyes. Her pupils were dilated with fear. Elias loved this reaction. This was the time to say goodbye to pain, torment and sorrow. Elias pushed them both closer towards the railing and climbed over the parapet. Soon, there would be no more problems with their mother. His sister loved water. She had told him she felt like a ripple joining other ripples waiting to join the ocean of freedom. *We can do that together,* he thought.

Someone grabbed hold of Dahlia. His sister was pulled away from him. He had a second to see who was hauling her away from the railings. It was his mother! He snarled at her. Dahlia belonged to him, not his mother. The defiance in his mother's eyes was astonishing. She wasn't as weak as he had thought. Maybe women were stronger than he had anticipated. He let go of Dahlia, overbalanced and lost his footing on the parapet.

The fall into the Thames was sweeter than he thought it would be. His mother had sacrificed her son for her daughter. At last, Dahlia was getting the love she deserved. He didn't feel angry anymore, just at peace. With his sister, his mother and more importantly, with himself. He barely felt the cold water as he plunged and sank into it. His loosened suicide belt floated up to the surface and bobbed about on the water.

36

It had been a few months since the fateful accident on London Bridge. Hannah preferred to think of her son's death that way. She stood at the railings, looking onto the Thames and felt a void she had not encountered before, not even when her husband had died.

The grey river had enveloped and taken her son. He hadn't stood a chance in the cold water. She couldn't remember how or why she had stumbled and hung on to Dahlia instead of her son. Anyhow, nothing could be changed now. She would never see his youthful face and shining eyes again, never hold him close to reassure him that he would feel better one day. She wiped away her tears.

The Met police who had come to her house after the incident had told her that they had found bottles and tomato-juice cans in Elias' house. She had looked puzzled as one of the surly-looking policemen searched her face. Later she realised that he was looking for some sign of recognition, to see if she understood the significance of what he was saying. Then the officers had mentioned that there was a wire threaded through holes in the cans. This would mean that Elias had been planning a terrorist attack in various ways!

Hannah had frozen at that moment. Her son, a terrorist?! How could they believe that? He was just experimenting with his ideas of justice. He had never meant to harm innocent bystanders. It was the altercation with Dahlia that had driven him to his unstable state that day on the bridge.

He was just a boy disappointed with his life in London. Elias didn't have a wife to console him when he had been depressed and Dahlia had been no help. She had refused to leave that woman, Carys. Dahlia knew no boundaries. Her relationship with Carys was more important to her than her brother and her mother. *Where was her loyalty,* she thought. *Blood was thicker than water.* Now, all that was left for Hannah was a rebellious daughter who put her own interests before her family.

Hannah felt as if a limb had been cut off. She yearned to meet up with Jonathan. She owed him that much. He had been questioned by the police after the London Bridge incident. She was relieved that he had backed her version of events even though he had not been on London bridge with them. He had told the police that Elias had not been violent up till that moment on the bridge.

She longed to meet up with Jonathan soon but realised that a meeting with her daughter was more urgent. She arranged to meet Dahlia the following day for lunch in a café on South Bank. Dahlia had become vegetarian after her kidnapping in Iraq, explaining that she refused to have more toxins released in her body. Apparently, meat from animals was full of hormones to make them fatter.

Hannah frowned. All this talk about toxicity was irritating to her. She quickened her pace and entered the café. Dahlia was already sitting near the window furthest away from the entrance. Hannah approached her carefully. Her daughter reminded her of a volcano about to erupt.

'Hi Mum. I'm glad you made it.' Hannah was relieved to

hear that Dahlia's voice was civil. For the time being.

Dahlia stood up quickly. She had been studying the menu. Hannah looked into her eyes hoping to find some remorse about the incident on London Bridge. She couldn't detect the expression she was looking for. Dahlia looked more upbeat than usual. No wonder: she had survived the incident and Elias was out of her life.

Hannah sat down opposite her daughter. A waitress came over to them, eying Dahlia curiously. Hannah hoped she had not recognised her from the newspaper articles about the incident on the bridge. The waitress took their orders: Dahlia's a mint tea with Caprese salad and Hannah's a cheeseburger. The waitress ambled away as if she detected some difficult conversation coming up between mother and daughter.

'Mum. We need to talk about what happened to Elias. It will help us understand each other better.'

Hannah felt her blood boil. Hannah didn't want to understand Dahlia better. What she saw was more than enough. Why analyse and stir unpleasant feelings? Carys had put her up to this.

'Dahlia, what happened to Elias was an accident. You were arguing with him.'

'Stop right there, Mum. He was arguing with me. I was listening.'

'It takes two to start an argument just as it takes two to clasp hands.'

Dahlia leaned in towards her mother. 'You must have seen him grabbing hold of my arm.'

Hannah couldn't remember this. All she thought of was that her son was dead after a confrontation with Dahlia. She asked fiercely, 'What more do you want? I held onto you as you were about to fall into the Thames. You would be dead if

I hadn't done that.'

Dahlia pushed back her chair noisily. 'Would you have preferred me to die and Elias to survive?'

Hannah shifted in her chair. 'I could have released you.'

Dahlia grabbed hold of her mother's hand. 'Why didn't you?'

Hannah stared at Dahlia. Had her daughter wanted to die? More importantly, what would Hannah have felt, if she had drowned instead of Elias? Dahlia had a habit of creating difficult questions and scenarios.

It was tormenting enough to think of Elias' body in the Thames. The police had taken two days to find him. Hannah had vomited when she was summoned to the morgue to identify her son. She didn't know how to answer Dahlia. She thought it might be easier to ask a question. 'What do you mean, why didn't I release you?'

She watched Dahlia weigh up her next words as her eyes wandered to the waitress who was approaching them with their meals.

'I didn't mean release me from the railing.' Dahlia looked her mother straight in the eye. 'I meant, release me from your constant criticism of my behaviour and attacks on my lifestyle.'

Hannah was about to stand up when the waitress arrived and put the meals on the table, still watching Dahlia cautiously. Hannah kept quiet. For all she knew, the waitress might have called MI5 already. They could even have been followed to the café. The waitress strolled away, too slowly for Hannah's liking.

Dahlia had a defiant look in her eyes. Hannah put her plate aside and wondered whether she should leave the café and her quarrelsome daughter. However, she had no other children and was unlikely to have any further ones. This battle would have to be fought. Dahlia had never shown much resistance to her ideas till now. She had willingly gone to the psychotherapy sessions in Germany, had held down her job in the BBC and let her hair grow a bit longer, all at Hannah's suggestion.

Hannah reached out to touch her daughter's hand, but Dahlia had formed a fist. Hannah tapped her hand gently. She had done this when Dahlia had not wanted to go to sleep as a child. It had always worked. She had slept soundly afterwards.

'Dahlia, why would I want to criticise you? The BBC is happy about your work. You are a good-looking young woman…'

Dahlia pushed her own plate in front of her mother. 'Eat it now.'

Hannah looked at her daughter disbelievingly. 'Dahlia, it's your meal, not mine.'

Dahlia glared at her mother. 'Exactly. You don't like what I desire.'

Hannah pushed her daughter's plate back to her side of the table. She was acting like a child. Of course they had different tastes. Dahlia was a vegetarian and Hannah preferred lamb and chicken. *Was Dahlia trying to make a vegetarian out of her?* She was not going to sacrifice her preferences for her daughter. Dahlia must be out of her mind to expect it.

Hannah looked around her. The café was full of customers. Their waitress was watching them. Of all people she could be observing, her attention was focussed on Dahlia. Hannah noticed the waitress hold up a newspaper and nod at Dahlia whilst talking to her colleague.

Hannah pushed the plate of salad back to her daughter and

looked at her own one. She didn't feel like eating what was on either plate. She glanced at Dahlia whose eyes looked full of disdain. Hannah stared back. She would not be defeated by her own daughter. Dahlia pushed her plate back in front of her mother.

'Stop it Dahlia. What has gone into you? This isn't a game.'

'Exactly. It's my life. My soul.'

Hannah felt irritated. Dahlia was making a big deal out of a simple meal, which was meant to be a chance to get closer together. She was complicating a natural event, having dinner together. She pushed the plate back to her daughter as they glared at each other. Dahlia shoved it back to her mother. She knocked her glass of water whilst pulling her hand back. As Hannah tried to wipe the tablecloth, the waitress came over to them.

'I'm afraid I have to ask you to leave.'

She looked uneasy and glanced at an elderly man with balding hair who was standing near the till.

Hannah swallowed hard as she followed her gaze. The elderly man and his partner turned away when Hannah glanced at them.

'Why do you want us to leave?'

'A customer has complained about the noise and aggression at your table,' the waitress replied.

Dahlia pushed her plate of salad away. 'What the hell are you on about?'

Dahlia's mouth was contorted. Hannah had never heard her swear before. No doubt Carys had influenced her as usual.

'Hush, Dahlia!' She said.

Dahlia stood up and strode towards the door but not before she turned towards the shivering waitress.

'I'm not the aggressor. I'm the victim,' she spat out.

Hannah closed her eyes briefly. She neither wanted to look at her daughter leaving, nor did she want to admit embarrassment to the couple near the till. Most probably, they were the ones who had complained. She wondered whether they had recognised Dahlia from the newspaper articles. She heard the waitress ask her if she was okay. Hannah opened her eyes. The waitress was offering her a glass of water. Hannah declined.

'I'm sorry if we upset your customer. We're not coming here again.'

The waitress bit her lip. She looked the same age as Dahlia. Hannah decided not to ask for the manager. He or she most probably already knew about the problem. She looked at the meals on her table and asked for the bill. The waitress had tears in her eyes. Hannah sighed. She was just doing her job, most probably for the minimum wage.

'Don't worry. Just get me the bill.'

The waitress went back to the till and reappeared with a gleam in her eyes.

'Madame, you don't need to pay.'

Hannah didn't know why she was supposed to be happy about this. It seemed that the manager wanted to get rid of Dahlia and herself, at any cost. Neither Dahlia nor she was a terrorist and Elias had just been a disturbed young man. Hannah got up and left silently. She avoided London Bridge. She never wanted to set foot on it again.

37

Hannah phoned Jonathan at the British Museum. He had sounded distressed and it most probably wasn't only because he hadn't given back the clay tablet to the British Museum yet. He told her that MI5 officials had visited him!

She sat at the usual museum's cafe on the top floor and looked around her cautiously, tapping her feet impatiently. It had been shocking to see a photo of herself on the front page of a tabloid with the heading 'Mother of a terrorist.' She had decided to wear a blue blouse and black trousers. The colours were darker than usual. *Was she trying to camouflage herself?* She turned around to face Jonathan.

'I'm so sorry about the interrogation by the Met Police, Jonathan. I don't know how they found out about my contacts.'

He looked ashen, 'Never in my life did I expect to be involved with a terrorist family!' He frowned and conceded that it wasn't the whole family that was terrorist. It was just Hannah's son Elias and he had disappeared into the Thames.

Hannah had been on the verge of a nervous breakdown but still refused to spend a night with him. *What's holding me back,* she thought. She was a widow and he was alone. Were their cultural differences so vast that she could not free herself from them? Patience was not Jonathan's virtue. There were other women he could date. His hair had been thinning at the sides but most men his age were already half bald.

'Hannah, escaped ISIS soldiers from the Middle East can melt away into crowds in Europe, just as Elias sneaked back into Britain. All my principles and pride in being British have been turned upside down by my liaison with you. MI5 are watching my moves. The Cambridge graduate who had interrogated me was polite but firm about possible complications for my job that may have arisen by affiliation with an ISIS sympathiser, such as your son, Elias.'

She touched his shoulder gently, indicating that he should stay sitting. He looked crestfallen, but also apologetic.

'It's okay, Hannah. They soon noticed I had nothing to hide. My boss has been supportive but is keeping the whole story low key in the museum. No one else knows about my liaison with you. Not yet anyhow.'

Hannah winced at his choice of words. A 'liaison' was an understatement for their relationship. At least Jonathan still had a son, even though their relationship was fraught with misunderstandings. He tried to smile at her but all she could offer him were moist eyes. .

'You can help me with my translations of Gilgamesh. It may get you closer to Dahlia and her love of the Epic.'

Hannah wiped away a tear. 'Whatever I do for her, it's never enough.'

Jonathan patted her hand. 'Maybe she wants you to help her reconnect to herself.'

Hannah's look was reproachful. 'Why don't you accept your son's efforts to reconnect?'

Jonathan took a deep breath. 'You have a point there.' He sighed. 'My son reminds me of my deceased wife. They have the same mannerisms. They would both reach out for me, their palms held upwards as if waiting to be rescued. It never failed to irritate me. Thank goodness you're not that clingy. I need space for my clay tablets and my thoughts.'

He offered to take her to the storeroom he was working in, adding that he had a clay tablet to inspect. Hannah nodded her head. Where else could she go? Her son was dead and her daughter unavailable.

When they entered the storeroom, Jonathan locked the door to make sure no one disturbed them. His wrinkles deepened as he fingered the clay tablet in awe and concentration. Finally, he cleared his throat and said, 'Clay tablets were easily available in Mesopotamia and could be modelled into any desirable shape.'

Jonathan was lost in thought as he paused to press the tablet gently. 'The scribe used a stylus cut from a reed or from ivory or metal. Our scribe in this case used the front flat side of the clay tablet but didn't continue on the other side as some scribes did.'

He turned to look at her and asked, 'Do you know how this clay tablet survived?'

'You took it from the Iraqi Museum without telling anyone.' She folded her arms and glared at him.

He kept silent for a few seconds. Then he looked at Hannah imploringly, 'This is the earliest form of writing, of stories, of literature. You know, I will give it back to the Museum.'

Hannah nodded warily as Jonathan said,'The clay tablet I brought back with me from Iraq contains some lines of the Flood tablet. I have deciphered them already.' He pointed at a conglomeration of wedge-shaped signs triumphantly and said, 'Do you know what that means?'

He knew she would shake her head. 'The Great Flood took

place in the city of Kish near Babylon. Hannah, this means the Flood was a *historical* event, not a myth. '

He waited for her to digest this information, then continued. 'In the late 1920s, Langdon found traces of the Flood itself. His team penetrated the layer of earth from 3000 BC and found underneath it a sudden break in the pottery deposits, together with an unpierced layer of sand or clay with contained remains of aquatic life!'

Jonathan squeezed Hannah's hand strongly. 'Left by a Great Flood! Don't you see? The author of Gilgamesh mentions where the Flood took place, and this corresponds to the archaeological findings at Ur. The Flood of Sumerian history, the Flood on which is based the Story of Noah. It actually did take place.'

Hannah snatched her hand from his clasp. 'The clay tablet can also be a curse and we have had enough tragedies to last us a lifetime. I can't continue my relationship with you if you don't give it back.'

Jonathan planted his elbows on the table and peered at the tablet. He kept quiet.

'You must tell them as soon as possible.' Hannah roared.

Jonathan continued unperturbed, 'We're a team, Hannah. Don't be so hysterical.'

She gasped as he continued explaining that Lalish, fifty kilometres north of Mosul in Iraq, was where Noah's Ark came to rest. He took her warm hand again. 'As a child I was fascinated by this story. I tried to build a toy ark.'

Hannah jumped back. Jonathan continued untroubled, explaining that fragments of the Flood story had been found on tablets that dated back to 2000 BC, so before the dating of Genesis. He added, 'It is likely that the Flood story itself originated much before that, since the Sumerian cuneiform writing has been estimated to go as far back as 3.300 B.C.E. So, we have the Flood story in various cultures.'

He added quickly, 'In Genesis, the aftermath of the Flood is that God promises not to destroy humanity by Flood again and Noah and his family are told to multiply and repopulate the earth. In Gilgamesh, Utnapishtim and his wife are granted immortality and the Gods create fourteen human beings to help repopulate the earth.'

Hannah felt nauseous. She screamed, 'What consolation is this? My only son is dead and you are merely a post-colonial thief!' She felt her heart beating quickly and ran to the locked door. There was only so much grief she could tolerate!

38

Dahlia had deliberately asked Carys to visit her in her flat in Stratford. She had not met Carys' ex-husband and had no intention of meeting the philandering man. From the descriptions Carys had given her, he seemed arrogant and sarcastic. Carys deserved more than him. The only place Dahlia could meet Carys was in her flat.

She wondered whether Carys would be willing to take further risks with her. The journey to Baghdad and the kidnapping had been harrowing for both of them. She had planned to cook a Kurdish meal. Her mother had taught her how to cook as a teenager.

When the bell rang, Dahlia ran to open the door. Carys stood outside with a bunch of pink roses. She wore black corduroy trousers and a green blouse with a black necktie which hung loosely on her. Her slender neck was adorned with a pearl necklace. The matching earrings swayed as Carys tilted her head in order to view the meal on the dinner table. She wore some blush but no lipstick.

Dahlia smiled. She had also opted not to wear any lipstick. Her own black jeans and blue pullover appeared very simple compared to Carys' freshly ironed clothes. She looked radiant. Dahlia looked into her blue-green eyes which appeared darker than usual. She could get lost in their depth.

After a brief hug, Carys said, 'Well, aren't you going to let me in? I can't wait to taste your Kurdish food.'

Dahlia gulped. 'I'm sorry. Didn't sleep much last night.'

'Oh. Sorry about that. What were you worrying about?'

Dahlia let her in, saying that she would tell her after their meal. Carys went towards the small rectangular table with the red tablecloth. Two plates were laid out and a bottle of red wine. Dahlia motioned Carys to sit near the window and explained the dishes. The kibbeh, which was a mixture of bulgur wheat, minced onions, spices and ground meat, was put on one side of Carys' plate and some okra stew on the other.

Carys tasted it. 'Mm. This is delicious.'

The okra was slow cooked in a tomato sauce, lemon juice giving it an acidic undertone. Carys helped herself to a spoonful of biryani, which consisted of basmati rice, currants and nuts, on her plate. She reached out for the okra stew and Dahlia explained that she had also cooked Dolma, stuffed vine leaves and aubergines, filled with rice and minced meat.

'Dahlia, this food is a feast! It's going to make me tipsy.'

Dahlia laughed as she put some Dolma onto her own plate.

'Are you trying to seduce me, Dahlia?'

Dahlia blushed. She had never cooked this way for anyone. Dahlia told Carys to try some pink sherbet, a drink made from flower petals. Carys tried it gingerly, then guzzled it down as it was sweet.

Carys patted her slim waistline as she said, 'I can't eat any more.'

Dahlia asked her if she would like to try some gum tea made or dried lime tea. Carys opted for the latter as it sounded more familiar to her.

Dahlia went into the kitchen and returned with the dried

lime tea. She put it in front of Carys who took one sip. Her face lit up. Dahlia felt a pride she hadn't experienced in a long time. She laughed as she said, 'If we were men, we would be drinking black tea with cubes of sugar on the side and playing dominos.'

'I can think of more exciting games to play,' Carys said sensuously with a mischievous grin. Her voice had acquired a deep timbre.

Dahlia bit her lip as she met Carys' deep gaze. She trembled and felt irresistibly drawn to Carys. She thought of her every day, sometimes for a few minutes and at other times for hours. The longing and fear of disillusionment made her feel exhausted. Untold fantasies that overcame her at night were blissful and disappointing at the same time.

'I meant playing with hula hoops. What were you thinking of?' Carys smiled at Dahlia with mock reproof. Dahlia turned away from Carys' knowing eyes. A tingling feeling crossed her body slowly. She kept quiet.

'You're not competition for me, Carys. You're my… soulmate.' Dahlia exhaled a mini sigh. Carys leaned over her empty plate and said, 'Which reminds me, you promised me some of the soul music you love.'

Dahlia felt partly relieved at this sudden distraction, yet somewhat fearful. She had not felt this close to any other woman till now. Dahlia was afraid of ending up like Icarus who had flown too close to the sun. His wax wings had melted, and Icarus had fallen to his death. Icarus should have listened to his father's warnings. Maybe Dahlia should take more heed of her mother's warnings. She tried to sound jovial as she turned to look at Carys again.

'What do you want to listen to? Diana Ross, Marvin Gay or Aretha Franklin?'

'Aren't you a bit young for that genre?'

Dahlia smiled. She loved the intensity of feeling in soul music. It was something she yearned for in her life but had never experienced till now. She also identified with the vulnerability of African American singers, the suffering they had been through due to their ethnicity. Dahlia slowly walked towards the CD player and put on Diana Ross.

As she sat down again, she waited for her favourite song, 'Ain't no mountain high enough.' She watched Carys sip her lime tea slowly. Nothing she did was rushed or impatient like her mother's movements. Other than at work, Carys moved slowly. Dahlia felt not only accepted, but also cherished by her.

'Why do you like this song?' Carys had a coquettish look about her as she angled her head to mirror Dahlia's.

'I think it's because of the Mountain of Sinjar. My problems started there. Carys, I want to go back to it, to close the ring of despair.'

She watched Carys put her cup down as she collected her thoughts.

'Alone?'

'There's only one person I would like to go with.'

She hesitated and Carys waited for her to continue.

'You.'

Carys took a deep breath, thinking of the harrowing trip to Baghdad, the kidnapping, the aggression of Elias, his death with all its complications. Now, Dahlia was asking her to go a step further and accompany her to another dangerous zone where ISIS still lingered.

'I would understand if you declined,' Dahlia said gently.

'Why do you want to go back to your land of torture, Dahlia?'

Dahlia looked out of the window. The sun was going down. The skyline was an explosion of red and orange waves. The day was settling. Dahlia yearned to resolve her fear and anxiety. She wanted to go down, let go and close her eyes too, just like the sun.

'Let's just say, I'm tired of running away from myself all the time.'

Carys nodded her head. 'Okay. I may go with you if you play me one more song by Diana Ross.'

Dahlia looked confused. 'Which one?'

Cays looked at her intently and said, 'I'm coming out.'

Dahlia laughed nervously. There would be time for that at the Brighton Pride Parade next month. She would need to confront her mother one last time before travelling to Sinjar. What a contrast she mused. Brighton and Sinjar like the sun and the moon, the open day and the dark night.

'Why not a different one?'

'Hmm. 'You keep me Hangin' On."

Dahlia felt she was being teased but she enjoyed the insinuations. She wanted to play the game too.

'What about 'Stop! In the Name of Love.' Or 'You can't hurry love."

Carys looked impressed by Dahlia's choices.

'Someday, we'll be together.'

Dahlia blushed. Carys chuckled. She started singing 'Upside down you turn me…'.

Dahlia had never heard Carys sing before. Her voice was soft, and Dahlia felt a surge of heat overcome her. She got up and held out her arms for Carys to fall into. Carys stood up quickly and put her arms around her gently. Their embrace became more urgent when Dahlia felt herself pulling at Carys' waistline. She couldn't tell which one of them turned her mouth towards the other first.

Dahlia felt herself press her lips onto the warm edges of Carys' mouth. She felt impatient. She pressed herself onto Carys with more force as she gave in to the gentle teasing of her tongue. It intensified the moisture she felt down below. Dahlia gasped as she broke off the kiss. Her breasts felt sensitive, she felt herself dampen even more with the expectation of other sensitive areas of her body being stroked. Her whole body was aching. She needed release from this tortuous longing. There was no turning back.

Carys turned to look at the bedroom door which was half open.

'What's next? Diana's song 'Touch me in the morning?"

Dahlia moved closer. She felt breathless as Carys took her hand and led her into her bedroom. Dahlia felt self -conscious although the scars on her lower arms were barely visible. Since meeting Carys and her psychotherapy sessions, the desire to self-harm had diminished. It had been replaced by a different craving.

Dahlia felt elated but also impatient as she felt Carys hot breath near her ear. Carys kissed her slowly, running her hands over her flushed cheeks. *What intense and tender look in Carys' blue eyes.* Her skin awoke to the caresses like a rosebud opening up to the sun's rays. She felt the urge to grind herself into Carys' thigh.

Dahlia kissed the notch on her slender neck, relishing the sweetness of the beads of sweat trickling down towards Carys' breasts. She felt drawn to her like a bee seeking nectar from a lavender plant. Dahlia felt waves rolling over her. She didn't want to climax yet. She held back, savouring the love that some would say *dare not speak its name.*

Dahlia felt light-headed, somewhere between life, death

and self-oblivion, and was relieved when Carys pulled her jumper off. Carys pushed her gently onto her bed, trailing kisses across her naked navel and along her hips. Dahlia had never given herself so readily to anyone before. They weren't two separate beings, they were a union of one body, savouring the climax of each other. This felt right. *No need to label this,* she groaned.

39

Hannah had been relieved that Jonathan had finally agreed to give the clay tablet to the British Museum. She had been incandescent with rage, but she realised that she needed Jonathan. She would be able to reach her daughter through him. No need to be ashamed of that!

They had decided to go to Brighton to forget about the clay tablet for a while. They watched hundreds of people lining the streets, screaming as they viewed the Pride Parade go by. Dahlia had arranged a meeting here of all places. There had been no explanation as to what this seaside resort had to offer them. Dahlia most probably felt at ease with the variety of people here. Hannah frowned. London was multicultural. Surely, that would have been more appropriate for a meeting if Dahlia was intent on talking about going back to Sinjar.

It was the end of July. Hannah wiped the sweat off her forehead as she peered at three slender men dressed in tightly fitting pink costumes with the giant cardboard letters LOVE planted on their heads. Their hands were joined as they proudly marched past Brighton Pier.

She had read that almost a hundred thousand people were expected that day. Hannah felt irritated as she detected a man with a bright red frock. He had pink feathers in his hair. The man waved at the crowd, occasionally walking towards someone to blow them a kiss. She felt uneasy as she watched the floats go by. She turned to Jonathan who looked as if he was enjoying the crowds.

'That man has a pink nest on his head.'

Jonathan laughed, shaking his head. 'Hannah, he looks happy to me. Nest or no nest. Is it the colour that is disturbing you?'

Hannah looked at him reproachfully and asked, 'Where's Dahlia?'

Jonathan picked up a rose one of the men had thrown at him and said, 'Dahlia told me that we were to meet near the hotel at the Waterfront after the parade. She said we should watch the parade.'

'Why should we watch this parade? 'She shielded her eyes from the brightness of the sun.

'I don't know. She said it would be great.'

'Well if the parade is that great, why isn't she here?'

Jonathan was distracted by a cowboy who walked towards him and handed him a rainbow flag. 'Thank you,' he said and smiled at the man. 'I don't know. Maybe she's here somewhere.'

Hannah looked around her. It would be difficult to see Dahlia in the crowd. She shielded her eyes from the sun as she caught two women giving each other a fleeting kiss. *How unnatural*, Hannah flinched. The women were dressed up as stewardesses. Their red costumes and grey neckties stood out from the crowd of men dressed up as pilots cheering behind them. Jonathan nudged Hannah as he saw her cover her eyes,

'Do you want to borrow my sunglasses?'

'No. It's not the sun I'm shielding myself from. It's these…' She sighed, feeling her jaw muscles tense.

Jonathan moved his sunglasses to a more comfortable

position on the bridge of his nose and said, 'Dahlia mentioned it would be a fun parade. It's great, Hannah. Have you never been to such a carnival before?'

'I've been to carnivals before in the Rhineland. Rose Monday is the highlight of the German carnival and takes place on the Shrove Monday before Ash Wednesday, at the beginning of Lent.'

Jonathan peered at her amused, 'Darling, this has nothing to do with Lent.'

Hannah tightened her lips. She felt nauseous. Jonathan smiled as he spotted a man dressed up as a matron dancing with another similarly dressed-up man. Hannah decided to ask Jonathan about his son. He replied, 'Since he came back from Iraq, he's more pensive than before.'

Hannah took Jonathan's hand and squeezed it. The wrinkles around his eyes deepened as he spoke about his son. She loved the way his eyebrows almost touched each other when he felt agitated.

'I thought Daniel would be more mature after his work in Iraq, but he's come back sickened with himself. He was shot in the leg and there was no good hospital to treat wounded soldiers.'

Jonathan took a deep breath and continued in a low voice, 'He wasn't treated like a hero.' He shook his head. Suddenly, he looked up at Hannah expectantly and said, 'You should speak to Daniel. He bonded with you when you visited me at the Museum. Daniel needs a gentle approach which I evidently haven't got.'

Hannah gave him a kiss on the cheek and replied, 'You've got a tender touch. I know that now.'

She looked at him coyly as he pressed her towards his chest in an almost urgent manner. She could still smell the aftershave he had put on that morning. Hannah was surprised they got on well with each other's children, but not with their own. What a contradiction! Perhaps they needed to re-assess their own values?

She took a step back and looked at Jonathan, remembering why they had come to Brighton. 'Dahlia said she had something important to tell me.' She turned towards the next float. Her gaze fell upon a young woman dressed up as a mermaid in a blue bra with a blue and white tail which camouflaged her blue trainers. She was blowing kisses to the crowd, smiling as she pushed back some wisps of hair from her forehead. Hannah jostled the man in front of her as she leaned forward to take a better look at the woman. The aquiline shape of the nose, the melancholic eyes. She looked like… Hannah gasped and screamed,

'Dahlia, what are you doing in the Parade?'

The mermaid sauntered towards her. 'Are you enjoying it, Mum?'

'Why are you dressed up like this?'

'Let's just say, I'm proud to be a mermaid.'

Dahlia looked at her mother defiantly. Hannah meanwhile scanned the area with a worried expression. This was no time for jokes.

'What if someone from our family or our community sees you in this costume?'

'Tell them I'm having a party with my mermaid sisters. Tell them I feel nothing from the waist down. My fishy tail will stop me from shameful encounters.'

Hannah looked into Dahlia's angry eyes and said, 'I've my morals and principles. Don't you respect my conscience, my values?'

'They aren't more important than my happiness, Mum.'

Hannah grimaced as Dahlia continued, 'Remember when I was a teenager, you told me to be proud of who and what I was? Well, now I am.'

Hannah turned to Jonathan and said, 'She's confused. This abomination… it's a phase.'

Dahlia raised her voice and said, 'No Mum. I'm not confused. I don't feel guilty anymore. I have a right to live the way that makes me happy, just like you do.'

Hannah shifted her position. Her scrutiny drifted over to some youths dressed up as stone age men. She took a deep breath. *Am I a stone in my daughter's life?* She lowered her voice as she put her hand on Dahlia's arm.

'Listen, Dahlia. Don't you want to have children? I'd love to have grandchildren.'

'Maybe I'd like to have children. But that's something I'd discuss with my partner. We could undergo IVF treatment, or we could adopt a child.'

Hannah recoiled. She wanted a natural baby. She heard herself say, 'Your child would turn out abnormal.'

Dahlia looked at her mother aghast and said, 'You and dad weren't *abnormal,* and I turned out to be as I am.'

Jonathan put his arm around Hannah and said, 'Dahlia, I don't think you can switch your mother over that quickly. Maybe this isn't the right place or time.'

Dahlia turned to him and said, 'There's never a right place or time. Maybe I should swim back to the sea again, and be invisible.' She looked at him imploringly and said, 'you understand me, don't you?'

Hannah put her hand up to silence her daughter and said, 'Darling, parents want to keep harm and hurt away from their children.' She thought of her own parents who had arranged her marriage to her late husband. It had been devoid of passion, but it had felt secure.

Dahlia wiped a tear away from her eyes as she said, 'Mum, I know what hurts me most.'

She kicked her tail, took out a giant shell from her pocket and produced a white pearl. Smiling forcefully, she said, 'I'm like this pearl, Mum, and I'm coming out of my shell. I'm not going back in.'

'Dahlia, I know who put you up to all this. It was that woman you're hanging out with, Carys.'

Dahlia's look was defiant. She replied, 'No, it was my idea. I had to tell you how proud I am to be my true self somehow. You only respond to shock tactics.'

Hannah winced and looked around her as she asked, 'Where is Carys?'

'We were shipwrecked.' She looked at her mother mockingly. 'Carys is on the NHS float now.' Dahlia raised her voice. 'What would you do if your doctor were that way inclined, Mum? Would you run away? Think it was contagious?'

Hannah felt faint. *Were the other mermaids swimming away?* She rubbed her eyes, then opened them again and peered at the naked pearl in her daughter's hand. Dahlia tossed her head and skipped back towards the next float which consisted of some laughing belly dancers bouncing around each other. The shrill noise was unbearable.

Hannah buried her face in Jonathan's shirt. Why didn't the ground beneath her open up to swallow her? After a few seconds, she more-or-less demanded to leave the parade to see the Royal Pavilion, saying that it was a lovely mixture of Indian architecture and Chinese inspired interiors. Jonathan looked surprised about her sudden description of the building in such circumstances but gave in to her wishes.

They rushed through Brighton's Bohemian Lanes oblivious to their surroundings and barely speaking to each other. Only at one point did Hannah grunt a few words in Jonathan's direction. 'I don't know what's worse, this maze of alleyways or the labyrinth of Dahlia's life.' She stopped and grabbed Jonathan's hand.

'Maybe Dahlia should have had a more positive male influence.'

Jonathan shook his head, at a loss for words. Hannah realised that his son had had male influence and was still prone to confusion about his role as a man. She couldn't make out why more and more people were getting puzzled and perplexed about their gender roles. Animals couldn't change their sex, and neither should humans. It was as simple as that. Procreation was meant to be. Feelings were secondary and volatile. They only led to misery.

40

It had been almost half a year since Hannah had seen Dahlia. Her heart felt heavy. While ironing, she looked at Jonathan sideways. He was sitting on her sofa with his feet propped up on a small stool, reading a newspaper intently.

They had spent the last few nights in her flat. She had allowed herself to be intimate with him. Hannah felt irritated that she had not only had to be a dutiful wife but also a loyal widow. *Were there parallels to her daughter's situation*, she wondered, *both of them breaking away from their society's unwritten laws of obedience?* To kill someone was a crime. But why did loving someone unconditionally pose a crime?

She watched Jonathan turn the pages of the newspaper. Occasionally, he would shake his head and mutter disapproval at the content of some of the articles.

'Hannah, what do you think about the Americans leaving Iraq after the war?'

She put her ironing board next to the wall in the sitting room and replied, 'Saddam was an evil dictator. Thousands of innocent civilians were killed by his poisonous attacks and the Anfal campaign. Now he's been killed by his henchmen, the Americans have nothing more to do in Iraq.'

She watched Jonathan get up and carry the ironing board back to the kitchen. When he returned, she added, 'But, Iraq entered a civil war after the Americans left. ISIS spread like wildfire.'

She reached out her hand to hold on to something as she swayed slightly to one side. Jonathan dropped his newspaper on the floor and rushed to her side. He bumped a small table on his way. Hannah heard the cracking sound of broken pottery. A red vase had fallen to the floor. Hannah sat down on a nearby chair.

'Oh Jonathan! What happened to this vase?'

Jonathan tried to pick up the pieces of broken pottery.

'Darling, I'm sorry.'

'Oh no, don't worry, it's just that Dahlia made it for my birthday.'

She started to sob. A broken vase and a broken heart. Where was her daughter now?

Longing was worse than shame. She needed to see her again.

Jonathan ran to get Hannah some tissues and put his arm around her.

'Have you heard from Dahlia?'

Hannah shook her head. 'I can't carry on like this, Jonathan. I miss her. I feel as if a part of me is missing.'

Jonathan patted her shoulder. He put her head between his palms. His hands felt soft and reassuring. He said, 'Hannah, it's time the broken pieces of things were put together again.'

She waited a few seconds, sitting with a faraway expression on her face. Then she got up decisively, went to the telephone and dialled a number. She was about to put the phone down when there was a clear voice at the other end. It was Dahlia.

Heaving a sigh of relief, she told Dahlia how much she missed her and that she would like to invite her to a place she had never been to before. She had to do something! This difficulty with Dahlia was dragging her down and it was onerous for Jonathan to make up for the void in Hannah's life. Jonathan wasn't happy about Daniel. His son had not visited him for a few months.

If Hannah approached her daughter with more understanding, perhaps it would ease her relationship with Jonathan. 'Dahlia,' she said firmly, 'bring Carys.'

There was a long pause. Hannah said, 'I'm inviting you to the Gilgamesh restaurant in North London. Jonathan can tell you how he's getting on with decoding the missing clay tablet.'

She paused. 'It's the Newroz Festival on the twenty-first March, Dahlia. We can celebrate the Newroz Festival together.'

After Dahlia had accepted the invitation, Hannah said, 'Erm, you can come dressed as a mermaid if you want. Just put a shawl around your shoulders because it can be cool in the evenings.'

Jonathan heaved a sigh of relief when he heard Dahlia laugh through the phone. Then the receiver was put down. Hannah felt her cheeks heat up. They had taken on a faint rosy colour. Jonathan came over to embrace her and asked her to tell him a bit more about the Newroz Festival she had mentioned to her daughter.

'It means New Day in Kurdish and signifies the festival of the spring,' she was happy to tell him. 'It is celebrated across Iran, Pakistan, parts of India and even countries of Central Asia.'

She waved her arms around to convey all the countries which celebrated this spring festival. Hannah felt ready to embrace the whole world now that hope for a reconciliation with Dahlia beckoned.

'According to the Kurdish legends, the Newroz Festival celebrates the overthrow of Dehaq, a tyrant who had snakes growing out of his shoulders and who required human sacrifices to control his appetite. Mostly it was children that were sacrificed to him.'

Jonathan winced at the story. 'It sounds like the taming of the wild man Enkidu in the Epic of Gilgamesh.'

Hannah shook her head and continued explaining Newroz.

'Not quite, this is about a Kurdish blacksmith named Kawa who led a revolt against this tyrant and freed the people. He then lit a bonfire to tell all the people of Mesopotamia that they were free. Newroz means new day.'

Hannah smiled. She was in high spirits after her months of anguish. But how long would she stay that way?

41

Hannah and Jonathan were at the Gilgamesh restaurant in good time. Jonathan had invited Daniel too. Hannah had the impression that he was trying to form a big family from a diverse crew of people. She looked sideways at Daniel. He was wearing the usual blue and white striped Breton jersey, promoted by Jean-Paul Gaultier. His slender hands were placed on the table, palms upwards, as if he were beckoning for some offerings of the half divine Gilgamesh.

Hannah was restless and unsure whether Dahlia would come. She occupied the waiting moments by studying the wood carvings of epic battle scenes on the walls of the Gilgamesh restaurant. Images of frenzied creatures which were trying to kill each other stared back at her. Jonathan nudged her gently underneath the table. She tried not to look too eager about the reunion with her daughter. But her eyes betrayed her. They shone at the thought of this family get-together.

'Hey dad, when are my two older *sisters* coming?'

Jonathan looked at Hannah apologetically and turned to Daniel saying, 'Since when are they your buddies?'

Daniel laughed and said, 'They are intriguing. We may have a few things in common.' He winked at his father, adding 'fashion, make-up.' Jonathan looked at his son sternly.

Hannah stifled a giggle and then turned sharply towards the door as Dahlia entered followed by Carys. She wore a mauve skirt with a white shirt peeking underneath her black svelte jacket.

Dahlia looked younger than her actual age and more feminine when Carys was with her. Hannah wondered how Carys could make her daughter so happy when no one else had managed to do this. She sighed, realising that she was forced to rejoice because Dahlia was happy.

She stood up and moved towards her daughter, hungry to embrace her. As she pulled Dahlia's head towards her shoulder, she smelt the fragrance of a perfume which Hannah loved using herself. Dahlia had grown her hair longer. She looked more feminine than ever with red lipstick and faint green eyeshadow. Mascara made her eyelashes look longer.

'Where did you leave the mermaid?' Hannah asked as she disengaged herself from the tight embrace.

'I was afraid she would eat all the sushi.'

Hannah laughed and said, 'I was afraid you would come as a belly-dancer. It's quite cold at this time of the year.'

Dahlia took her mother's hands and turned towards Carys who was smiling behind her. Carys was wearing a tweed skirt and jacket, making her look at least twenty years older than Dahlia. Hannah realised she hardly knew anything about her daughter's companion. She frowned, wondering if that word was the right one to use for the woman at Dahlia's side.

Carys moved towards Hannah quickly and said, 'I decided to come dressed up as myself so as not to scare anyone here.'

Hannah had a faint smile on her face. She would need to get to know this woman better, but not just yet. She introduced Daniel to Carys, hoping she wouldn't detect his faint green eye shadow. Carys smiled at him, eying his sweater. She said levelly, '*Croeso.* Lovely to meet you. Your dad didn't tell us you were a sailor. Where's your white cap?'

Daniel chuckled and said, 'My obsession with Jean-Paul Gaultier is getting the better of me. *L'Hommage a l'homme.*' He took off an imaginary hat and bowed.

Dahlia laughed and said shyly, 'Mermaids like sailors.' Carys looked at her in mock-reproach and nudged her gently.

Daniel replied quickly, 'Sailors adore mermaids too.'

Hannah raised her eyebrow. The younger generation seemed to be toppling the traditional concepts of masculinity and femininity through eccentric creations such the ones Gautier had initiated. Men in skirts, conical bras. Whatever next? Men in high-heeled shoes?

She wanted to brush away these intrusive thoughts, elbowed Jonathan and said, 'What better place for us to have a party than here surrounded by bloodthirsty mythological creatures killing each other!'

She waved at the walls of the restaurant and Jonathan guffawed. They all looked at the copper friezes portraying soldiers armed with spears, riding on chariots. Hannah frowned when she saw that some of the soldiers wore skirts. She would like to have covered those up and was glad Jonathan diverted them to their table.

They took their seats, and after a short silence Hannah said, 'We are gathered today to celebrate the beginning of spring and to bring light and hope to our lives.'

She watched Dahlia close her eyes as if deep in thought. Hannah told her that Jonathan had prepared a speech for this special day. Drawing out a piece of paper, he cleared his throat and began to read.

'This is a passage from a poem of Ahmedi Xani, the author of *Mem û Zîn*, a Kurdish love story of a couple who meet during the Festival of Newroz. It's from the seventeenth century.'

They were quiet and eager to listen.

'Bartender, for the love of God, please
Pour some wine into the crystal glass
Let the glass and its wine show the world
Let there appear whatever it is that we wish
Let the events ahead of us come to light
Let us know if the future holds promise for us
Look! Our misfortunes have reached their zenith,
Have they started to decline now; do you think?
Or will they remain so,
Until comes upon us the end of time?
Is it possible, I wonder, that for us, too
A star will emerge out of the darkness?'

Everyone clapped their hands. Carys held her hand up in mock fear, 'Hopefully these mythological creatures on the wall will not scupper our reunion!'

Jonathan stroked his chin and replied, 'Mythology shows you stages of life. It teaches you to turn inward. The ancients teach us that there is a path to wisdom. The story of Gilgamesh is not only about a quest for immortality; it's an epic about the path to wisdom.'

It was a relief to Hannah that Jonathan was talking about the ancients, rather than about modern fashion designers like Gaultier who dressed men in seductive clothing. She was happy to see Dahlia smile and wish Jonathan good luck with his book on Gilgamesh. While she was talking to him, Carys turned to Hannah and looked at her closely as she said, 'Hannah, I'll support and love your daughter as well as I can, wherever we are and whenever she needs me.'

Hannah shifted her position in her chair but willed herself to listen. She took a deep breath and glanced at her daughter who was chatting to Jonathan and appeared relaxed. He was explaining the deciphering of clay tablets to her and how important it was to understand the Epic of Gilgamesh.

Hannah clinked the glass of water in front of her and said suddenly, 'I have a speech too.'

They all stopped talking and turned to face her.

'Dahlia, I realise now that there are different paths to happiness. There is unity in diversity, diversity of faith, diversity of preferences and diversity of race. If we don't understand that simple message, sitting here amidst our own small family, then how will we be able to deal with the hatred in the world?'

She looked around her to gauge the reaction from her small family. Dahlia's eyes had swelled up with tears. Carys and Jonathan looked relieved.

'Terrorist attacks may continue in our world, but sympathy and mercy will succeed in our family.'

Dahlia stood up to hug her mother and kissed her on both cheeks.

Hannah kissed her back and added, 'Newroz smells of a new beginning. It smells of ancient times and new times. I can smell Hope and I can smell Spring. Long live the New Day!'

Dahlia and the others stood up and repeated the words,

'Long live the New Day. Biji Newroz!'

Hannah beamed at her family. *United at last.* They sat down again. 'So, now Dahlia, have you made plans for the future? Are you going to continue working for the BBC?'

Dahlia glanced at Carys who nodded her head as if to prompt her to answer her mother.

'Mum. I'm so happy about this reconciliation. But there's still something I need to do.'

Hannah looked baffled and turned towards Carys. Silence ensued. Dahlia half opened her mouth. Then she closed it again. Finally, she took a deep breath and said,

'I need to go back to Sinjar. I need to look for Yasmine.'

Hannah felt her throat constricting and with a shaking hand, she grabbed her glass of water. After a few sips, she took her daughter's hand in hers. 'Why are you doing this to me, Dahlia?'

Dahlia looked bewildered and angry at the same time. She took her hand away and replied, 'I need to do this for *myself,* Mum. I have unresolved issues and I need to go back to the place where these problems originated, free myself of my fear.'

Hannah turned towards Jonathan for support. He kept quiet and waited to hear what Dahlia had to say.

'Every day whilst I was in Germany for counselling, I would dread coming face to face with one of Yasmine's ISIS captors! Imagine mum… one of my friends in Donaueschingen was threatened by her former captor!'

She turned to face Carys. 'You needn't worry, Mum. I have asked Carys to come with me.'

Hannah couldn't help grimacing in pain. A few moments ago, Carys had seemed like a friend. Now she was more like a traitor. Sinjar was still full of ISIS soldiers. This Newroz Festival was not a renewal of a suffering relationship. It had turned out to be a rupture.

Hannah stood up to leave, tears welling up in her eyes. Jonathan followed her out of the restaurant. She saw him mouth the word *sorry* as he glanced at Dahlia and Carys who remained sitting. Hannah was angry that Dahlia made no attempt to stand up and reassure her. Daughters should respect their mothers and include them in such important decisions. She wiped her eyes and ran out of the diner. Would their battle with each other never end? Jonathan followed her but Daniel stayed seated with Carys and held Dahlia's hand gently.

42

Carys watched Dahlia hanging up a self-portrait. The contours of her face in the portrait were dark, almost harsh with bold strokes. In the portrait, Dahlia was looking into the room, past Carys, as if she were on the lookout for someone else. Her eyes had a hint of resentment in them.

Carys felt uneasy. She knew Dahlia was waiting for her decision about going back to Sinjar, the place of Yasmine's torture. She had told Carys how she had watched a programme which depicted brave female fighters on a mission to bring ISIS soldiers to justice without killing them. Carys was dubious that such a mission would lead to impartiality.

She strolled to an unsteady chair near the window of Dahlia's small flat in Stratford and sat down, waiting for Dahlia to start the conversation. A beige-coloured rug lay at Dahlia's feet. She pushed it aside with her foot brusquely. Dahlia had picked up her carelessly strewn clothes from the rug so that it lay obliquely. This irritated Carys.

'How come you've never invited me home to your place, Carys?'

Carys frowned. Of all the questions, she wasn't expecting this one.

'You know my ex-husband still lives there.'

She took Dahlia's hands and put them close to her mouth.

She kissed both knuckles and looked into Dahlia's vulnerable, tearful eyes. 'Let's sit down and talk things through.'

Dahlia took her hands away and walked towards the table. She sat down and waited for Carys to speak again.

Carys sat down at the table and sighed. 'Dahlia, I know you want me to go to Sinjar with you. I can't just leave my job again so suddenly. Why do you want to go back?'

Dahlia frowned and said, 'I need to rescue at least one ISIS bride, maybe even find Yasmine. I don't want to kill anyone, just free myself from my memories.'

'What's my role, Dahlia?'

'You're a doctor. Your role is to help the injured. You don't need to fight.'

Dahlia looked out of the window. A soft drizzle was falling. At least, there was no pounding rain. Carys studied Dahlia's profile. Her aquiline nose looked more prominent when she was deep in thought. It contrasted with the soft roundness of her cheeks.

'Orlando,' Carys said suddenly.

Dahlia turned to look at Carys, puzzled. 'I'm Dahlia.'

Carys laughed. 'Haven't you read this book by Virginia Woolf?'

Dahlia shook her head.

'Orlando enters one chapter as a man and later on in the novel, turns into a woman. Male and female are not binary oppositions, but part of a fluid scale.'

Dahlia looked at Carys attentively. 'When did she write this book?'

Carys smiled at Dahlia's interest. 'In the 1920's, long before transgenderism was something tangible.'

'Why are you telling me this?'

'Orlando has an affair with Elizabeth the First and a

Russian princess. He then serves as ambassador in Constantinople and then as a woman, he lives with gypsies before returning to England.'

Dahlia tilted her head, trying to understand the significance of this story and how it related to her.

'Am I Elizabeth the First or the Russian princess?'

Carys raised an eyebrow. Dahlia hadn't included the gypsies. Carys chose her words carefully. 'You're the nomad.'

Dahlia looked as if she didn't know whether this was a good or a bad thing to be.

Carys took Dahlia's hands again and peered into her questioning eyes.

'What I'm trying to say is that if I go to Sinjar with you, I will miss the maze of underground tunnels in London. I had thought about searching for archaeological relics in the Thames,' she said in all seriousness and laughed at her own joke. 'However,…'

Dahlia stared at her expectantly.

'I have decided to come with you as I can inspect archaeological relics in Sinjar too.'

Dahlia got up quickly and her chair fell backwards. She hugged Carys who broke away from the embrace, surprised at the sudden display of emotion.

'St Thomas hospital will be undergoing a CQC inspection soon. So, I can't stay too long. I have to help fill in all the paperwork.'

Dahlia stepped towards Carys again and squeezed her hand, tears welling up.

'Hold me, Carys. This is so important for me.'

Carys cradled Dahlia as she replied, 'Important for *us*.'

Dahlia clung to Carys for a few seconds. Carys smelt her minty, freshly washed hair and rubbed her nose in it.

Dahlia stepped back to observe Carys. 'Does that mean you're coming with me to look for some more clay tablets?' She hesitated before continuing, 'Like Jonathan.'

Carys laughed. 'There's no need to doubt my intentions. I'm not an Assyriologist like Jonathan.'

Her eyes slid over Dahlia's slender body which leant over like a silver birch, ready to bend or snap depending on the pressure exerted on her.

Carys compared her to Enkidu, shaped out of clay and transformed by quests and undertakings with a man, a woman and a monster.

'In the Gilgamesh myth, the monster that Enkidu and Gilgamesh intended to slay was named Humbaba.'

'Darling, I'm not coming to dance the rumba with Humbaba or even slay him...'

Carys noticed Dahlia's stern look and changed tack. 'I mean that I'm coming with you to support you in any way I can. Also, I may be useful as...' She folded her arms. 'A doctor, but not for ISIS soldiers or their wives.'

Dahlia shuddered at the thought. Carys unfolded her arms and took a step towards Dahlia again. She wished Dahlia hadn't been wearing a turtleneck pullover. She folded down the turtleneck and felt the collarbone of Dahlia's white neck. It was like an alcove waiting to be discovered each time they got together.

'Dahlia, Enkidu and Gilgamesh go on their treacherous trip to the Cedar Mountains, crossing seven mountains...'

Dahlia gave her a puzzled look.

'We must be wary of the possibility of death... In the Sinjar mountains and surroundings.'

Dahlia frowned. She turned to look at her lonely self-portrait. 'I can go alone if you're scared.'

Carys followed her gaze and asked, 'Have you ever read 'The Well of Loneliness' by Radclyffe Hall?'

Dahlia shook her head.

'Her novel written in 1928 shows how loneliness and alienation can lead to mental illness and stress just by belonging to a minority.'

Dahlia listened attentively.

'I won't let you go to Sinjar alone. We belong together.'

Dahlia placed a hand over her heart and looked at her longingly.

Carys felt her pulse quicken as she grabbed hold of Dahlia's shoulders and pulled her closer. She kissed her soft earlobe and asked how much time they had left.

Dahlia smiled for the first time since Carys had entered her flat. Carys had to acknowledge that Dahlia's psychotherapist in Germany had advised the trip to Sinjar even though it was dangerous. There was no turning back now, even if she was about to make a fateful choice! *Life is so absurd,* she thought.

She shivered, hoping it wouldn't end in one of them dying, the same as in the Gilgamesh Epic. She tried to remember who had died in the Epic, Enkidu or Gilgamesh? She would stand by Dahlia's side, whatever the outcome and no matter how unsafe the trip to Sinjar. She had already given her life to Dahlia.

43

A day after landing in Arbil, Dahlia and Carys hired a driver called Kake Raouf to take them to a village near Sinjar in North-Western Iraq. On the way there, Dahlia watched many oil fields gushing with oil in the distance. *Was this the main attraction for Western countries?* She frowned.

Carys had agreed to stay in a Peshmerga stronghold for a few weeks. They were to receive training to overcome the remaining ISIS soldiers, bring them to justice and rescue brides of the soldiers.

Carys was to deal with any casualties. Dahlia wondered if all this would be possible within a few weeks and without killing anyone. She sat cross-legged on the bright red Isfahan carpet in a slightly dilapidated village schoolroom near Sinjar. She had let her hair grow and braided it like most of the other ladies in her Battalion. Dahlia had also tattooed her eyebrows before coming to Sinjar. If she died, she wanted to look like most of the other fighters. She was careful to cover her forearms with long sleeves. The scars were still slightly visible.

Dahlia felt excited, alive as never before. Since watching a documentary of the Battalion on TV in London, she had felt restless, waiting to pounce on ISIS soldiers wherever they were hiding. She trembled as she thought of herself as a possible fatality. How would Carys ever get over that? She wondered which one of her friends would help Carys if she didn't survive the fight.

Evin, one of the more opinionated fighters, had hardly looked in Carys' direction and barely spoke to her. Dahlia watched wearily as the other women tried to get Carys attention and ask her about their parents' ailments and possible cures.

It had been Evin's turn to cook for the fifteen warriors in their battalion. Evin had managed to heat up dolma, a mixture of stuffed aubergines and onions.

She laughed as she picked up some of the stuffed aubergines.

'ISIS fighters are scared of being killed by a woman because they worry they won't be rewarded with Seventy-Two virgins in heaven.' Evin smiled wryly, 'We'll stop them from getting into paradise.'

Dahlia turned towards Evin and asked, 'Why do they prohibit singing and music?'

Evin screwed her eyes as she answered, 'Ha. The bastards don't need that. They get their joy from sexual jihad.'

She picked up a paper cup and squeezed it, growling, 'The ISIS fighters had better watch out.'

Dahlia winced, got up briskly and almost tipped over her glass of water. She glanced at Evin's long silky hair which had been tied back.

Beside her, Asia, a twenty-three-year-old fighter, clapped her hands and smiled at Evin. Asia had endured ISIS captivity and had tried to commit suicide by drinking petrol.

The attempt failed and it was only when her family had managed to pay ransom that she had been freed to come back to Sinjar.

Dahlia wondered whether Evin would be capable of killing

an ISIS fighter. Dahlia told herself that she would just try and liberate an ISIS captive. It would feel like freeing herself, putting an end to her nightmares. *Redemption at last.*

She turned to Carys who had been allowed to accompany her due to the fact that she was a doctor and a photographer. Her presence embodied the hope of giving the fighters a voice outside the compound, in Europe and in the whole world.

Carys smiled, 'Dahlia, I feel so privileged here. I was the only one given a sturdy cotton mattress to sleep on.' She chuckled into her small water bottle.

Evin ignored her and turned to Dahlia, 'We're grateful to you for accompanying us on our journey… I was born in Kocho on the Nineveh plain and I went to school with Nadya Murad.'

Dahlia bowed her head in acknowledgement and understanding. She remembered how Nadya Murad had addressed the UN in New York. She had spoken of gang raping and other atrocities by ISIS fighters.

Dahlia nudged Carys and said, 'Remember, you heard Nadya's speech on TV when she won the Nobel Prize… It is liberating to have a voice.'

Carys smile was warm. Dahlia noticed that her own voice was not constantly resounding with pain since she had come to join the Battalion. It had become steadier and more assertiveness had crept in.

Evin leaned over the water bottles towards the naan while she spoke, '7000 Yazidi women were enslaved by ISIS. We don't want the world to forget.'

Asia added softly, 'Some Jihadi brides are attempting to return to Britain. Their families have turned to the British Home Secretary for help. One of them has had a baby boy in a refugee camp in Syria. The baby is innocent and should have the right to live in peace…'

'Ha!' Evin flung the naan at Asia. 'Has the English government forgotten the beheadings that the Caliphate ordered? The rapes of children? The anguish of their families?… Do the brides, some of whom willingly joined ISIS regret these brutalities?'

Dahlia watched as Carys lifted her hand in an attempt to stop the anger, saying,

'Some were groomed online… any extremist group may have caught their attention. Many ISIS brides were brainwashed into joining ISIS.'

Evin glared at Carys. 'The public in Europe need to be protected… Why didn't the British parents of these Jihadi wives take their parental duties more seriously?'

Carys said calmly, 'Some people say we may need the returning refugees as helpers for counter-terrorism…'

Evin's nostrils flared and she was just about to stand up when Carys turned towards her camera and said

'Angelina Jolie hasn't been in this war zone yet. I need to take some photos to entice her to come. She's a film director and there's plenty of movie material here… Evin shall we start with you?'

The female fighters started giggling as Evin rearranged her curly fringe. She stopped suddenly as she realised some of the girls had covered their mouths to suppress their laughter. She looked from Carys to Dahlia who were sitting a bit too close for her liking.

'How did you two meet?'

Dahlia shifted slightly as Carys responded, 'I was interviewed by her when she was working for the BBC.'

Evin raised her eyebrows, 'Is that all?'

Dahlia steadied her hands as she put her glass of water

down but Carys smiled coolly at Evin. 'I worked as a doctor and she interviewed me; you never know when I might need to patch you up, Evin…'

The two women stared at each other, not moving.

Asia broke the silence. 'Well, ladies. We need to get up early tomorrow. Our Commander wants us to attack one of the last enclaves of ISIS fighters at dawn.'

The ten women nodded their heads, glad to change the subject, and their chattering about their families resumed.

After their dinner, Carys walked towards Dahlia and sat on her mattress. Evin had gone out to get some sandbags to pile in front of the compound.

'Are you okay, Dahlia?'

'I didn't like Evin's questions.'

Carys frowned, 'Instead of talking about FGM or honour killings in these regions, she asks us how we bloody met…'

Dahlia flinched. She knew 'cut' girls were seen to be sexually pure after FGM and therefore protected the family's honour. Female sexuality was deemed to be shameful and something to be hidden. FGM aimed to control girls, make them submissive.

Even in more progressive cities such as Sulaymaniyah, this procedure was still being celebrated. Dahlia felt her rage rising. In the past, she had cut her arms but even this couldn't help inhibit her sexuality. After meeting Carys she had realised that this was an integral part of her identity. She took a few deep breaths to calm herself down.

Carys took her limp hands and shook them, 'The only problem now is whether you really want to go out to fight the ISIS compound tomorrow.'

Dahlia felt her inquisitive but caring look.

'Yes, Carys, I need to do this… it's my chance… .'

Carys nodded her head, 'I could say you're ill my dear and need to stay here…'

Dahlia shook her head vigorously, 'ISIS is crumbling, and we'll be fighting one of the last enclaves.'

Carys frowned, 'Let me have a look at your arms.'

Dahlia peered at Carys' weary eyelids. They were painted with faint green eye shadow and appeared as vast as the lush green garden Dahlia had watered in Kocho. *I could lose myself in those innocent blue-green eyes,* she thought. Dahlia hesitated a moment, then pulled up her sleeves.

The horizontal lines above her wrists were getting thinner and less marked than they had been in London.

Carys heaved a sigh of relief as she prodded a cushion at her side.

Dahlia quickly pulled down her sleeves as she said, 'Tomorrow could be my salvation, or it could be my ruin…'

She felt ready, not only for the fight but for some other eye-opener which she could not yet fathom.

The gravity of their situation was gnawing at her. She had to keep Carys safe. She would kill herself if anything happened to her. It would be her fault. She would not be able to live with the guilt.

The generator was humming in the background like a lawnmower cutting grass but without the thought of a bright summer day. The young fighters all got their mattresses ready for the final sleep before the fight. Dahlia jolted a few times in her sleep. She remembered her dream before it evaporated. Carys had been wandering in the Cedar Forest to slay the monster Humbaba. She had been killed at the fight. Dahlia woke up sweating and distraught.

44

Commander Ariyah strode into the barracks in Snuny, Nineveh, and eyed her 'Sisters of the Moon.' Carys didn't want to know how many would come back alive after the attack on one of the last strongholds of ISIS. This was all so surreal and far away from her monotonous life in London. Her colleagues and family must think she was mad following a journalist to her place of torture.

Carys felt that she was more of a prisoner, spellbound by Dahlia's quest for redemption. She wondered if she would ever need recovery herself. The fighters stamped their feet in military style as the Commander walked in. Ariyah's chin and cheeks were marked with tiny dark-blue tattoos, distinctive to the Yazidi region. Her broad lips jutted forward like those of the soldiers she was about to send to war.

'Daughters, you have been through weeks of target practice, learning how to encircle ISIS soldiers and how to dodge booby traps.'

The Commander looked around proudly at the fighters in their camouflaged green and brown khaki army costumes. They all wore red berets and the small Kurdish emblem was etched onto their sleeves.

Dahlia had told Carys that she enjoyed jumping through barbed wires and old tyres during training, and the cleaning of their Kalashnikovs. Dahlia had emailed the photos to the BBC in London. Hopefully, they would not be used as 'Poster Girls.'

The Commander cleared her throat, 'None of you will forget the Sinjar massacre in 2014 when thousands of Yazidi were abducted, killed and raped by ISIS. They either had to pay a levy or convert to Islam. In 2017 the city of Raqqa was liberated from the Islamic State and women helped fight on the front lines of Afrin.'

The young fighters stood in silence. Carys experienced a camaraderie she had never felt before. She was delighted that Dahlia's arms weren't sore anymore, that she had not felt the need to wound herself in the last few days. Carys suppressed a smile as she felt Dahlia's caring eyes watch her from afar like earth-brown soil embroidered with sumptuous green gardens of mint.

Did she see a part of herself in Dahlia? Her own vulnerability was a trait Carys felt they shared but she hid it behind her humour and trained self-possession. Carys looked at the Commander in wonder as she addressed her soldiers.

'Remember to keep an extra bullet in case you are caught by ISIS fighters. You must not allow yourselves to become part of the spoils of war.'

Commander Ariyah crossed her arms. Nobody flinched.

The image of Helen of Troy and the Trojan War flashed across Carys' mind. In Greek mythology, beautiful Helen was said to have been abducted by Prince Paris of Troy after the Goddess Aphrodite promised her to him. Had nothing changed for the fate of women?

Her heart was pounding as tried to block out thoughts of possible casualties and the cacophony of war.

The skin at the back of her neck crawled as if a ladybird was coming out to look for its prey.

45

The jeeps were kicking up dust like dervishes did when they were swirling in a trance.

Carys clutched her bullet proof vest and canvas bag of surgical instruments. She saw Dahlia's mouth set in an almost straight line. Her eyes were fixed on the horizon. The ISIS fighters had burned oilfields to cover their tracks when escaping villages.

The buildings in the ISIS village started to appear. Carys recognised the black and white flags adorned with Arabic writing. She had been told that the white banner at the top read, 'There is no God but Allah. Mohammad is the messenger of Allah.'

This declaration of faith was used across Islam and was known as the Shahada.

Carys wondered how these words had been hijacked by ISIS extremists. *ISIS hates moderate Muslims as much as they hate other religions,* she mused.

Underneath these words and with a white background, black writing read 'Mohammad is the messenger of God.' This was meant to resemble the Prophet's seal.

'What do the colours in the Kurdish flag represent?'

Dahlia looked at Carys bewildered, 'What a time to ask!'

Carys replied, 'What if you're not able to answer me after

the attack?'

Dahlia smiled. 'Okay. I'll tell you. The red at the top of the flag symbolises the blood of the martyrs and struggle for freedom and dignity. The green at the bottom expresses the beauty and landscapes of Kurdistan, life and vitality.'

Carys added in a husky voice, 'Also the natural beauty of Kurdish women.'

Dahlia giggled and almost blew her a kiss. She stopped herself when she felt Evin glance in their direction.

'We're not going to a wedding, Carys.

The white bit in the middle represents peace and equality.'

Carys wondered whether Evin was jealous about the relationship she had with Dahlia. The pending conflict with the ISIS soldiers and her desire for Dahlia made her feel excitable. She felt she was riding a wave that had to come down. Carys decided to tone down her exuberance

'I knew about the white bit. What about the sun in the middle?'

'The sun is an ancient symbol and represents the source of life and light of the people. It has Twenty-One sunbeams. They represent March Twenty-First, the Kurdish New Year.'

Evin raised her hand, motioning them to keep quiet. The jeeps stopped. The fighters turned towards the Commander, waiting for her orders. Their position was a few metres away from the village. Carys looked at her watch. It was nearly five a.m. The village was quiet.

The steady voice of the Commander said, 'Move in pairs. Get the Yazidi brides out of the houses and into the jeeps.'

The fighters looked at her for further orders, but she said no more. Carys realised that, how the women were to deal with the enemy, was left to them. The Commander had given no indication.

Evin jumped out of a truck and beckoned to Asia to accompany her. Asia turned towards Dahlia. Carys put her arm around Dahlia, prodding her to move with her, not with Asia. Her Kalashnikov felt heavy.

Soon, the fifteen female fighters were moving forwards stealthily like tigers coming out of a cage.

Carys watched Dahlia creep towards a dilapidated house. She followed close behind her. Dahlia stopped to peer through the window. It had no net curtains. A woman was sleeping on a mattress clutching a toddler in torn, striped pyjamas. The toddler looked dehydrated.

Dahlia walked towards the next dusty window which was sealed by tape to stop it from crumbling. Carys followed her cautiously. They both looked in the direction of a bearded, middle-aged man. He was sleeping in his black combat ISIS attire. Could he be Yasmine's previous captor? Carys shuddered.

She looked over Dahlia's shoulder and thought how all extremist groups were like the Ku Klux Clan, the IRA, al-Qaeda and Neo-Nazi groups. They chose their attire to look homogenous and individually inconspicuous. But they were all harbingers of terror.

She followed Dahlia as she walked back to the first window and knocked it lightly. The slight woman stirred slowly and eyed Dahlia with an expression of shock and puzzlement.

Carys caught her breath as Dahlia gasped and whispered slowly 'Yasmine.' *Shit!* Carys should have known Yasmine was possibly imprisoned somewhere here. Her throat felt dry as she eyed Dahlia, waiting for her next move. Dahlia stiffened, closed her eyes, then opened them again quickly, mouthing the word 'sorry,' as she faced her previous school friend, Yasmine.

Carys felt a charge running through her as she watched Dahla hold up the Kurdish emblem. She motioned Yasmine to leave through the backdoor. Yasmine hesitated a split second. Then she slowly picked up her sleeping toddler and moved towards the back door.

Her ISIS 'Master' leapt up at the sound of gunfire that had begun to cackle like the fireworks that herald the New Year in London. Only this was not a celebration. It was a war. Carys let out a scream. Yasmine stood frozen, her arms reaching out for her toddler and screamed 'Vian!' The child started crying. Carys watched Dahlia point her Kalashnikov at the bearded fighter. He growled as he jumped behind his bride. To him, Carys realised, his wife was merely a useless human being and could be used as a shield.

'Allah Akbar '', the fighter screamed. He came face to face with Dahlia at the window and spat on the blood-stained floor, shouting 'Amrika, Britanya.'

The fighter made swift signs of beheadings. His eyes were glazed with hatred and contempt towards the female fighter standing in front of him. His hands moved towards his trouser pocket. The knife glinted like a fish flung into a dry bucket. Carys held her breath. Dahlia would die in this village. She felt a surge of hatred towards the bearded, middle-aged soldier. Carys could smell his musky tang. Dahlia stood frozen facing the soldier, unable or not willing to kill him, even when facing death herself.

Carys bit her lips and closed her eyes for a split second. She should have known that Dahlia would not be able to take revenge or even protect herself from being killed. Carys remembered the Hippocratic Oath to uphold ethical standards and to do no harm. A single gunshot reverberated loudly. The ISIS fighter screamed as he turned around to face the person who had fired the shot, Yasmine. She dropped her Kalashnikov, ran towards her daughter and started rocking her. Dahlia raced towards them and hugged them both, wiping away Yasmine's tears with her sleeve.

Carys couldn't feel any remorse or pain. In fact, she was incapable of feeling anything at all. She opened her eyes. The fighter lay on the old blood-stained floor. Old and new blood mixed like the vibrant colours of sunset when heralding the night. Carys felt a wave of disgust overcome her, revulsion for the fighter and for herself. The fighter's skin appeared tight; his muscles relaxed. Soon his skin would turn purple and his eyes would sink into his face. She remembered all the bodies she had certified as dead in A&E – the purpling of the skin and pooling of blood until, after a few hours, the body would stiffen, and rigor mortis would set in. The sobbing of Yasmine, mingled with the screams of her daughter brought Carys back to the present time, where life and death certificates meant nothing. The Iraqi government would never forget that Vian was born to an ISIS father! She would most probably not be issued with an identification card unless another male relative would be registered as her father.

She stood in the doorway, dazed by the killing and shook her head in disbelief as Dahlia staggered towards her. Dahlia squeezed her gently and kissed her hot cheeks again and again, as if to banish the reality in which they found themselves.

Carys felt herself slump down next to the body. The bullet had gone straight through the ribs and into the heart. The blood was still dripping through the soldier's tunic. He lay motionless on the dusty ground. She felt his carotid pulse. It had already ceased. There was no movement anywhere; she couldn't feel the wind, the sky took on a dark shade and she wished the ground underneath her would swallow the corpse and herself. Soon the stench of death would set in and the jackals would seek their nourishment!

'What have we done?' Carys shook her head as she pushed the Kalashnikov away.

'I came here as a doctor… Now, I've witnessed a killing. How can I ever work as a doctor again?'

She thought of the Gilgamesh Epic; *the lovely young women-in their prime, death comes and drags them away. She couldn't have let that happen to Dahlia.* But it had been Yasmine who had saved Dahlia with just one bullet. Dahlia let go of Yasmine and her daughter and reached out to kiss Carys' burning slender neck, now ashen with dust.

'I'm so sorry, Carys. I shouldn't have brought you here.'

They were both sobbing and clinging to each other. Carys looked up at Dahlia. Her eyes shone like oysters liberated from their shells. They were worth shielding. As at the beginning of their relationship, the image of ethics forced itself upon her. The standards of Good and Bad melted into a quagmire of uncertainty. She took a deep breath. A tear fell onto the filthy earth, stained by the dirty murder.

Out of the corner of her eye, Carys could see Evin approaching them from the next derelict house. She wiped her eyes, stepped backwards and turned towards Yasmine and her daughter who were still standing in the same position. A father had been killed. The killer, Yasmine, was cradling her daughter; she looked up at Carys with swollen eyes, her face a mixture of pain and relief.

Carys beckoned her to come over and embraced her tightly, not knowing if the death of the ISIS soldier would release her from her anguish or perpetuate it. She shuddered as she looked into Dahlia's horrified eyes. Would she have been able to kill the ISIS soldier herself? There would have been no time.

Suddenly, Carys heard footsteps. Evin stumbled into their house saying, 'We can leave now. The bastard fighters have escaped through a secret tunnel. We dare not go down there. I don't know what ammunition they have collected.'

Carys nodded wearily and heard herself say, 'At least we freed some of the women.' She watched Dahlia place her arms around Yasmine whilst patting the head of her daughter. How long Dahlia had waited for this moment, to be reunited with her childhood friend!

Evin didn't seem to realise that an ISIS soldier had been killed and lay bleeding in the room next to them. Carys was relieved. Evin stood in the doorway looking in the direction of the jeeps. 'Commander Ariyah says we should all go back to the jeeps and return to our base.'

Carys stumbled as Dahlia helped her and Yasmine move towards the jeep. They scuttled past a Madrassa school near a mosque. Carys' was stunned to see another teenage ISIS bride lying on the ground. She was full of puncture wounds from chips of bricks and charcoal. The clothing was stuck to the skin. Carys felt this would be a chance for restoration of her sins.

She turned towards Dahlia and said, 'We need to take her back with us, put some antiseptic over her wounds and do a dressing.'

She helped the groaning lady up into the Jeep and added, 'She needs an intravenous infusion. We don't want her suffering from sepsis. I will slip in a cannula back at base.'

Carys blocked out the thought of the dead ISIS soldier. She covered her face with her sooty hands and frowned as she remembered the ethical promises she had made when she joined the medical profession – *first do no harm, do good, the importance of justice (ensuring people were treated fairly and equally).* She had always made sure she adhered to patient confidentiality, stating conflicts of interest, checked consent forms of patients and their capacity.

Her ethics were worthless now! From this day onwards, she would be sceptical of moral absolutes. She had always admired the German philosopher Kant. He had stated in his '*categorical imperative*' that you should never treat people as a means to an end, but always as an end in themselves i.e. never subject a human being to anything that is not right, even if by doing that, many more people would benefit.

Killing the ISIS soldier may have benefited or saved hundreds of other women, but surely,it was against ethics! Had her love for Dahlia swept away her morals and beliefs? Carys felt a streak of lightning run through her worn-out body. What a dilemma, what an inferno!

46

She had yearned for atonement ever since Yasmine had been abducted from her village whilst Dahlia was perched on the mountain with wavering loyalties, back in 2014. Should she have disregarded her Commander and run down the mountain to shield Yasmine? There would have been no opportunity for that as the ISIS soldiers outnumbered her.

But this was her chance now. She smiled. She would travel to the holy temple in Lalish which was about sixty kilometres north of Mosul. She explained to Carys that the temple was a part of Sumerian and other ancient Mesopotamian civilisations. At least once in their lifetime, Yazidis were expected to make a pilgrimage to Lalish. Yasmine would be washed of her sins there!

Dahlia sighed. At first, it had only been she who needed cleansing, now Carys had been exhibiting signs of distress after their fight in the ISIS stronghold. She had been muttering unintelligible words whilst sleeping. Dahlia had to wake her up frequently to stop her from shaking and attracting Evin's attention. They slept near Evin. And Yasmine felt terrible about killing the ISIS soldier, her hated husband.

However, Dahlia felt that Yasmine's culpability was drenched with her own personal relief. She had hoodwinked death. Liberation from her past made her feel reborn, an innocent baby again. She brushed this fleeting thought aside. *Freedom through death?* Casualty should not at any time lead to relief. It was easy to convince Yasmine to travel to Lalish with her and Carys.

To get to Lalish, they had to drive through the parched hills of Northern Iraq. Dahlia felt her lips needed water just as much as the acrid land they were passing. Carys seemed to lighten up when she saw the conical roofs of a Shrine and tomb of Sheikh Adi. She parked a distance away from the holy place. They walked barefoot towards a small cave. Carys exclaimed, 'A mulberry tree… here in Lalish'. Dahlia grinned, 'Surprising reminder of London, isn't it?'

Dahlia smiled as she watched some women leaving the cave with wet, white headscarves. They were laughing. Dahlia held hands with Yasmine and her daughter Vian. A little girl ran up to Yasmine and took her hand to lead her into the cave. The entrance to the cave was so low that Carys had to bend down to get inside. They finally reached the venerated holy white spring.

An old woman with a rough, tanned face and lots of wrinkles took Yasmine's hand. The child skipped back out of the cave. The old woman revealed a toothless smile. Dahlia couldn't understand everything she said but she realised that the woman's name was Iman. She told Yasmine to kneel on the soil.

Yasmine stopped before Iman and was sprinkled with water, cool and soothing water. She took a deep breath, clasped the old woman's hands gratefully and dried herself with her sleeves. Like all women who had been enslaved by ISIS fighters, Yasmine was now showered with water in a ritual seen as washing her clean of her past in the eyes of her community. Dahlia felt tears trickling down her cheeks.

'At last, we are released from our past, Dahlia.' Yasmine peered at Dahlia shyly.

Dahlia looked at her reflection in the water. Her image was clear now, not hazy and splintered as it had appeared to her in the Thames in London when she had been on her way to interview Carys. At last. Water was transformative, not divisive, just like Love.

She stood up and turned towards Carys, 'Thanks for coming with me. You have no idea how liberating this ritual is to Yasmine and me.'

Dahlia slowly spread the water droplets on her arms. The death of the ISIS soldier had filled her with dread. She didn't want to think of it as retribution. Only pure water could lead to liberation from her past anguish. She watched Carys dry herself with a tissue.

'This ceremony must feel strange to you.'

Carys shook her head, 'Not really. Catholics dip their fingers into the holy water and make the sign of the cross when entering a church. Hindus and Muslims proceed to their prayers only after they have cleansed themselves with water.'

She moved towards the spring and splashed some water on her face, 'Hey, I need more of that!'

Dahlia observed Carys, relieved that she was beginning to take on a more jovial tenor since they had arrived in Lalish.

'You're not the only one who needs cleansing, Dahlia.' Carys moved towards the spring and Iman cackled as she repeated the ritual cleansing on her.

'Now, we're both wet, what are we going to do?' Dahlia looked at Carys hopefully. Maybe, she would overcome her heavy-heartedness here. It had been weeks since they had kissed passionately. The ordeal they had been through had weakened her dreadfully.

'Let's get out of here, Carys.'

'What are those symbols carved onto the walls of Lalish?'

Dahlia turned to look at the figures.

'I don't know. They look like the Sumerian representations that my mother and Jonathan are trying to translate. Isn't it exciting that we're witnessing a step back in time?'

Yasmine peered at her bare feet and said, 'They feel cleansed, not dirty like when I was with the ISIS soldiers and had to walk barefoot.'

Near the entrance to the cave, Carys watched a woman tying knots in a bright coloured material. 'Why is she doing that?' Dahlia was relieved to hear Carys asking questions.

'I assume that, if she ties knots here, elsewhere they will be loosened.'

Yasmine looked at Carys hopefully.

Carys prodded Dahlia gently, 'Enough questions now. It's time to unravel our future.'

Dahlia's voice took on a more serious tone as she said,

'You who have walked beside me,

steadfast through so many dangers, remember me.

Never forget what I have endured.'

'Isn't that from your Gilgamesh Epic?' Carys asked.

Dahlia looked at her gleefully. So, Carys had been listening to her tales of the Epic.

'Yes. I'm like the wild man Enkidu and you are King Gilgamesh who adores me.'

Carys raised her eyebrow in mock irony, 'Now, let's get this straight. I'm not half man and half God. And you're not a wild one, most of the time!'

Dahlia giggled and pulled Carys towards her in a quick

embrace. But she glanced at Yasmine and let her go.

Yasmine turned to look at Dahlia and said, 'Yazidis celebrate the New Year in Lalish by lighting 365 lanterns to usher it in with light. This New Year fell on the first Wednesday of April, which we called Red Wednesday. People put red flowers on their doors. It looks glorious.'

Carys appeared to be fascinated by the description.

'Dahlia, we could celebrate all these traditions. I like to dance at every party!'

Dahlia chortled, remembering some of her variable dance moves. For a moment, she had forgotten their experiences with the Battalion of fighters. But her thoughts soon returned to the horror. She looked at Carys fearfully and asked,

'Do you think we're safe from ISIS now that Abu Bakr al-Baghdadi has been killed?'

They had heard on the radio that Ibrahim Awad had detonated his suicide belt during a raid by Americans. Awad's nom de guerre was Abu Bakr, the same as the first caliph after Muhammad's death; Baghdad was the Abbasids' capital in Iraq.

In 2014 Awad had broken away from al-Qaeda and rejected orders to stay in Iraq. He had used Baathists and Saddam's former officers in Iraq to seize control of Syria. He considered raping women a spiritual exercise. Dahlia shuddered and studied the expression on Carys' face. It was a mixture of thoughtfulness and wariness.

Carys looked up towards the darkening sky and said, 'Even If ISIS are defeated, their ideology will live on. In sleeper cells and mixing with innocent bystanders. I can't see that Europe will be immune from danger. Shall we head for London?'

'I'm worried about staying here,' Dahlia said, 'The Kurdish Peshmergas are guarding the ISIS captives in Syria and those soldiers will escape if the American Kurdish allies have to leave the area. I'm anxious about the stability in the region. Kurds have been betrayed by other countries before and are said to have *no friends but the mountains.*'

Carys listened carefully and said, 'I'm your friend, and family!'

Dahlia cupped her face and said, 'I know, what would I do without you?' She eyed Yasmine who was talking to Vian at the other end of the cave.

'With all the shifting alliances in the area, Yasmine wouldn't survive another attack by ISIS soldiers. We need to ask for asylum in Britain as soon as possible.'

A foreboding overcame her, and a dark cloud appeared just above the cavernous cave they had walked out of. She didn't trust anyone but Carys. They joined Yasmine and walked towards the green hill they had passed on their way to the cave. No genocide or ethnic cleansing could exterminate a nation. She turned to look at Carys whose eyes were searching the horizon.

When Carys spoke, her voice was low. 'Genocide is a recurring theme throughout history. Think of the Armenian genocide, the Jewish genocide, the Bosnian genocide perpetrated by Serbs and the Rwandan genocide.' Then she asked, 'What could we or anyone do to stop the extermination of people?'

Dahlia smiled suddenly and replied, 'We could have a baby. We could call her Amal.'

Carys' eyes gleamed as she remembered the English translation for the name. 'Why not just call her 'Hope'?

Dahlia chuckled, recognising the redeeming power of a baby. 'Would you want her to become a Human Rights lawyer?'

Carys smiled at her weakly. 'We can all be Human Rights advocates.'

She wiped some water droplets off her forehead. 'Do you know that the Corona virus may return to London? Remember I told you about the first epidemic when we met in the hospital a year ago?'

Dahlia frowned. 'I've been getting emails from my colleagues at the BBC. COVID-19 appears to have transgressed species and countries and is leaving bodies in its wake in China. It seems that every few years, a new virus appears. We'll have to book flights immediately before it reaches Sinjar, although healthcare is getting better here.'

How nurturing it would be to parent a baby, give it a chance to thrive without the dangers she had faced in Iraq! 'Which one of us would stay at home with the baby, if we had one?'

Carys laughed and said, 'I'm thinking of leaving the GMC and becoming a full-time mum.'

Dahlia looked at her in disbelief, 'We'll fight over our parental rights later on. Let's get me pregnant first!'

She would ask for a water birth, far away in London. Dahlia chuckled at her obsession with water. At last, the water at Lalish had put out the fire in her soul.

47

Dahlia had asked her mother to meet her at the place where Elias had plunged into his death a year ago. It was his 'anniversary'. She wiped away a tear that had begun to roll down her left cheek. When other tears followed, she felt like collecting them and throwing them into the Thames.

Elias had been swallowed by the water. Dahlia's salty tears would mingle with salty ripples. Ashes to ashes. Dust to dust. Water to water, salty or not. The media had at first described Elias' death as an 'incident' unravelling on London Bridge. What a euphemism. She had not gotten accustomed to English understatements. In her own language, people would say 'their liver was on fire'. Jonathan was not that theatrical, even when in pain. The beat of her sad heart slowed down as she thought of him, unrepentant. She sighed. Hadn't she suffered enough?

She tightened her checked cashmere scarf and stayed well away from the railing. People strolling past her would have no idea about the conflicts of a sister who was torn between her disgust for Elias and her anguished mother. Perpetrator and victim, both members of one family, her own. Was she also both perpetrator and victim? Dahlia turned towards the banks of the Thames. In death, people were all the same, inanimate and identical. Peace at last. She took a step closer to the railing.

'Mum. It's been such a long time.'

Her mother turned around slowly. Dahlia's beige coat was a pleasant contrast to her previous dark coloured duffle coats. Her cheeks had turned rosy with the cold London air. She looked anxious but seemed also energised at the same time.

'Dahlia, I'm so relieved to see you. I was so worried when you went back to Sinjar. I thought I would lose you.'

Dahlia put down her outstretched hand. Relief swept over her face.

'Mum, I would have been lost if I hadn't been able to rescue Yasmine by going back to Sinjar. Sometimes redemption lies in walking towards danger rather than safety.' Hannah looked at her puzzled.

'Yasmine saved my life when her ISIS husband tried to shoot me.'

Her mother gasped. Dahlia had read in the papers that ISIS prisoners were escaping from the crowded prisons because the Kurdish Peshmerga who were guarding them were retreating. But she felt enlightened from the unspoken burdens she had been carrying for many years. There was a glistening shard of hope. Dahlia held out her arms for an embrace. Her mother leaned in. It was the first time Dahlia had initiated the hug. She smiled.

'Dahlia, I'm very glad that you and Carys are safely back. In a way, I need to rid myself of the shadows that have darkened my past. My marriage to your father was a semi-arranged affair with little affection. No stars were sparkling in the sky like, I have to say,' she said shyly, 'there are when I'm with Jonathan.'

Dahlia put her gloves on and said, 'Like fluttering colours of a butterfly. I know how that feels, Mum.'

Dahlia watched her mother scan the Thames and its ripples. No doubt she too was thinking of Elias. He was like a shadow, sometimes an overpowering memory and at other times, sinking back to oblivion.

'Oh, Dahlia, we can't rewrite our culture,' she said with a sigh, 'our obstacles and the atrocities that have been inflicted upon us. But we can oversee our future.'

Dahlia turned towards her mother. Her eyes welled up as she said,

'And it doesn't have to be a conventional future. We can have more than one identity.'

Her mother hesitated, then smiled and said, 'Hmm, no, alright, I have to admit that it doesn't need to be conformist.'

Dahlia gave her another hug. 'Now, tell me, Mum. How far are you and Jonathan with putting the pieces of the Epic of Gilgamesh together?'

Her mother closed her eyes for a second before she answered, 'You'll be pleased to hear that Jonathan has given the Flood clay tablet to the British museum, the one he took from Iraq. The curators have decided to decipher the tablet and then return it to the museum in Iraq. Thank goodness, the Iraqi officials have agreed to this. And fortunately, Jonathan will suffer no punishment. I can't tell you what I felt that day, when I heard how he had stowed the tablet away in his bag. The curators have already started the process of deciphering the clay Flood tablet.'

Dahlia was relieved. She asked, 'How is Daniel getting on with Jonathan now?'

Her mother looked past her and replied, 'Much better since Jonathan bought him a sailor hat!' They both laughed and her mother added, 'Daniel can't wait to meet up with Carys and you again.' Dahlia replied that they had already arranged to meet up at her flat the following week in order to celebrate the Gaultier stripes in fashion.

Her mother laughed. Dahlia noticed that, since coming back from Lalish, a calm seemed to have descended on her. She smiled to herself. Water was not only a threat as in the Great Flood. It was restorative too, the water of Lalish being the liberator.

Dahlia took her mother's hand and squeezed it. 'Let's go to the Shakespeare Globe Theatre as we're near. No plays for King Gilgamesh there though! Great in depth though he grew to be, in the end, he had to accept his own mortality.' She laughed.

'Not as well-known as Shakespeare, but as with Shakespeare, his story is universal and will surpass time. Dahlia, we'll let the land of stories be our *wattan*, our motherland, our solace and spiritual home.'

Dahlia clasped her mother's hand as they both looked towards the Globe. Her mother had always admired the English oak timber-framed building.

'Mum, do you know that the Globe has the only thatched roof permitted in London since it was destroyed in the Great Fire of the seventeenth century? What about building a toy ark if we could get hold of some straw and reed for the roof. Would Jonathan like it?'

Hannah let out a laugh. 'He built one as a child.' Dahlia followed her mother off the bridge, a bridge that had so recently become a bridge of terror. The Thames was primordial and had flowed on as tragedies such as the Fire of London and the Plague, raged on its banks. Waves undulated in different directions but found common ground on its shores.

Her thoughts turned to Jonathan and her mother; their togetherness was so complete since she had felt able to respond to his loving affection. There was the problem of the strict code of conduct for relationships between mixed religions but somehow, if thousands of other couples ignored the structures then so could they! They would build a new community without disrespecting the old one.

'Dahlia, it's time to meet up with Carys and Jonathan now. They said they would be waiting for us at the front of the theatre.' Dahlia took her mother's hand and felt her squeeze it with a vigour she had not felt a few months before. 'Jonathan told me briefly on the phone that Carys mentioned a baby in the family. What on earth did he mean by that? Does she have a sister?'

Dahlia smiled mysteriously and said, 'Let's wait till we meet up with them.' She patted her belly carefully. She already knew who the sperm-donor was, a gentle soul whose interest in fashion would benefit them all. She chuckled but didn't elaborate on this to her mother.

Dahlia stepped off London Bridge and looked at the Globe Theatre. She couldn't wait to embrace Jonathan again. He had told her how he wanted to find a final resting place for Gilgamesh next to the Globe. Shakespeare's plays and the Babylonian stories were immortal in his eyes and never failed to excite him. Her mother's gaze fell upon a middle-aged woman passing by with a golden bird cage in her hand. There was no bird in it. Her mother glanced at her. 'How could a bird sing in such a small cage?'

Dahlia squeezed her hand. 'It can't, Mum. The canary sings best when it has been set free.' Rebellion had been locked up in the cage of obedience for too long. The young canary had flown out of the enclosure and found its voice.

Acknowledgements

Heartfelt thanks to my daughter Lana, who carried out meticulous readings of my first drafts.

Thank you also to Elizabeth J. Lister who corrected the manuscript page by page and has been a loyal friend.

Thank you to Kathryn Bell and Ellie Lister for proof reading.

Thank you, Tanya Byrne and James Essinger for editorial advice and encouragement.

The following books have been particularly helpful during the writing of this novel: *The Terrorist Factory* by Father Patrick Desbois and Costel Nastasie, *Revolution Day* by Rageh Omaar and *Gilgamesh* by Stephen Mitchell.

Thank you, Juliette, for your support throughout the years.